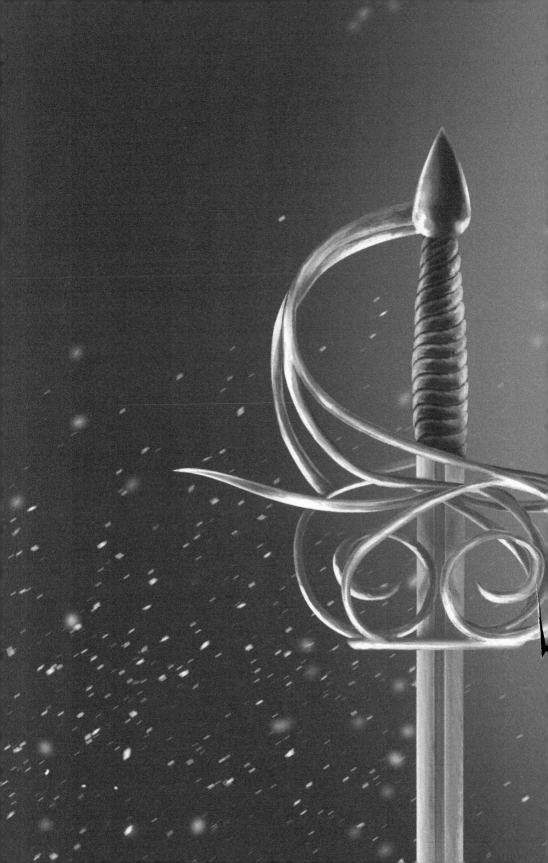

THE WENDY

ERIN MICHELLE SKY
& STEVEN BROWN

TRASH DOGS MEDIA, LLC

Copyright © 2017 by Erin Michelle Sky & Steven Brown
All rights reserved. No part of this book may be reproduced in any form without written permission from the publisher.

Library of Congress Preassigned Control Number: 2017917721

ISBN: 978-1-946137-05-0

Printed in the United States of America

Cover art by Benjamin P. Roque
Layout & design by Jordan D. Gum
Edited by Lourdes Venard

Trash Dogs Media, LLC
1265 Franklin Parkway
Franklin, GA 30217
trashdogs.com

10 9 8 7 6 5 4 3 2 1

For everyone
who has ever suffered judgment
just for being who they are

CHAPTER

1

By the year 1780, London was bursting at the seams. Almost a million people had been stuffed into every nook and cranny, and a good number of these had no idea where they had come from. Nestled in baskets and swaddled in rags, they had appeared overnight on the doorsteps of almshouses all over the city. Babies. Staring wide-eyed at mystified caretakers, demanding explanations.

But there were none to be had.

This was why Wendy Darling believed in magic. It was the only thing that made sense.

Opinions, however, were divided on the subject.

"Babies don't come from *magic*. They come from *mothers*."

Mortimer Black was seven and thought he knew everything. He was different from the other children because he had arrived with a note. The note gave his name, penned in a woman's delicate hand, and he lorded it over the rest of them every chance he got. Mortimer *knew* he had a mother.

"Just because *some* babies come from mothers doesn't mean they *all* do," Wendy would argue. She was also seven, but she was very logical.

"Yes, they *do* all," he would counter. "You're just jealous 'cause you don't have a real name."

"You take that back! Wendy Darling *is* my real name!"

But she had her doubts.

Mrs. Healey, the caretaker, was fond of the name Wendy and thought her a darling child. *Wendy, darling, fetch me the pitcher, please,* she would say. Or, *Wendy, darling, where has little Charlie run off to?*

Wendy secretly thought Mortimer might have a point.

"You're *nobody*," he would tell her, laughing and poking her with a cruel finger. "You're just a *foundling*!"

Fortunately, Wendy had an excellent right jab. That usually ended the matter, at least until she was ten. Ten was the year Wendy's whole life ended before it had even begun.

The disaster struck at Bartholomew Fair, in September of 1783.

The almshouse barely took in enough money to *feed* everyone, let alone send the children off to fairs. But there was a particular lord in London who loved fairs more than anything, and Bartholomew Fair most of all, with its acrobatics and its puppet shows and its exotic beasts smelling of faraway places. Of desert spices and fever dreams.

Unfortunately, a lot of drinking went on there too, and he was a public figure. He had to keep up appearances.

So this lord, whose name we won't mention so as not to rat him out, came up with the scheme of funding a trip for the alms-house every year. "For the poor foundling children," he explained, addressing the querulous, upturned noses of high society, "who have no mothers to take them on outings or to buy them sausages or gingerbreads or hot pies or puddings."

He was especially fond of puddings.

He would arrive at dawn on the appointed day in September with a handful of carriages, each drawn by two fine horses, and the children would all line up behind Mrs. Healey—arranged alphabetically so she could keep proper track of them.

"Adam, Agnes, Arthur, Bartholomew," Mrs. Healey would bark, ticking the children off on her fingers. "No, Bartholomew, the fair was not named after you. Bridget, Cecilia, Charles," and so on.

As each name was pronounced, she would tap the correspond-ing child lightly on the head, and he or she would be off like a shot, tumbling into a carriage. They laughed and screamed and piled on top of each other to fit in. All but Wendy, who was always last in line, terrified that *this* time they would run out of room after Valentine and she would be left behind.

"Wendy," Mrs. Healey finally pronounced.

Wendy raced to the first carriage, but Mortimer Black stuck his head out the window before she even got to the door.

"No room!" he yelled. "Go to the back of the line!" Wendy could see for herself there was plenty of room, but she heard Mortimer's friends laughing and carrying on. "Back of the line!" they echoed. "Back of the line, Wendy!"

Wendy looked despairingly down the line at the rest of the carriages, all stuffed to the gills, with little heads and arms poking out the windows. But then Charlie, to whom one of those heads

belonged, called out to her from the fourth carriage. "We have room, Wendy. If we squeeze a little more."

Wendy trotted toward him, but only as far as the horses—a lovely pair of matching brown mares, with black manes and tails and wide, strong hooves.

"Excuse me," she said to them both. "Do you think you could pull one more? I hate to ask it. I can see you have a full load already. But I would very much like to go to the fair too, if you think you could manage it."

"What's this, then?" the driver grumbled. "You don't have to *ask* them, for heaven's sake. They're just animals."

"All right," she said, to appease him. But then she whispered to the horses anyway, "Could you?"

The mares looked at each other, and they looked back at Wendy. They puffed out their chests and held their heads high, each nodding just once against the bit.

"Thank you," Wendy whispered. Only then did she run to the door and clamber on top of the pile.

It was a beautiful day for a fair, and London had come out in droves. The children wanted to see everything at once. "The high wire! No, the fire-eater! No, the rhinoceroses!" Rules were set, compromises were made, motions were passed, and a schedule was confirmed.

First, puddings. Acrobatics from 9:00 until 10:00. Then meat pies. The strong man and other amazing feats from 10:30 to 11:30. Then gingerbreads. Exotic beasts at noon (they were always

Wendy's favorite). And so on. Unfortunately, the world ended before exotic beasts, at 10:48 on the dot.

The foundling congress was mobilizing from the strong man to the fire-eater when it encountered a small contingent of officers in the Royal Navy. The men were tall and fit, handsome and proud, resplendent in their blue long-tailed coats and fine gold buttons. The sea of children parted around them, but not Wendy. Wendy stopped dead in her tracks and stared.

Ever since she had read *The Life and Strange Surprising Adventures of Robinson Crusoe*, on loan from Mrs. Healey, she had longed to sail the seas, embarking upon fantastical escapades and witnessing all the strange and magical wonders of the world. When one of the sailors noticed her attention, he tipped his hat and smiled, and all the yearnings of her heart welled up in her small chest, bursting out of her at once.

"When I grow up, I'm going to be an officer, just like you!" she declared.

"Are you?" he asked with a chuckle.

"Yes, I am," she insisted, but his laughter confused her, and she looked less certain than before.

"What's this?" asked one of his companions.

"She says she's going to be an officer," he repeated. "I'd watch your back if I were you, William. She'll be after your job soon." And now they both laughed.

"What's so funny?" Wendy wanted to know, but the cold grip of dread had already wrapped its icy fist around her heart.

Before they could reply, Mortimer Black, who had heard everything, hollered out, "*Girls* can't be in the navy! Girls take care of *babies*! You're so stupid, you don't know *anything*!" He looked around with a cruel gleam in his eye, shouting even more loudly. "Did you hear that? Wendy thinks she's going to be in the navy!"

Everywhere she turned, children laughed and pointed.

She whirled to face him, but the crowd kept on spinning. Spinning and spinning. Like the carousel. Faster and faster. The sky closed in around her. Gray fog and then smoke and then starless night. And Mortimer's pale face swam up through its depths, his eyes pitch black. Black as his name, black as his heart, piercing her soul. Over and over, around and around. And she thought she heard him singing.

If women ever sail the sea,
They'll scrub the decks for men like me!
They'll marry none but Davy Jones,
And for their children, only bones!

She closed her eyes and fell to her knees.

It isn't true. It isn't real.

The thought steadied her, and the ground snapped back into place. Solid beneath her knees. Beneath her fingers splayed out for balance across the cobblestones.

She launched herself to her feet and ran.

CHAPTER

2

She ran away. That was all she knew. Away from the laughter. Away from Mortimer Black. Away from the darkness that clung like cobwebs and from the song that trailed behind.

But as she darted madly through the crowd, ducking savage elbows and hurdling violent parasols, the sun worked its quiet magic, burning it all away like a dream. Ladies and gentlemen strolled under the bright blue sky, smiling at each other and marveling over the fair's attractions, and there were no pitch-black eyes or dead pirate demons or mysterious fogs to be scared of.

So Wendy stopped running.

And then instead of being frightened, she was furious. How dare that awful Mortimer Black make fun of her in front of everyone!

But beneath the anger, she was also sad. Because she thought what he had said might be true—that when she grew up she would have no hope of becoming a sea captain. She would have to become a mother and take care of babies and never see the world.

And *then* she thought she might prefer to marry Davy Jones after all. Because at least that would be *interesting*. Which was the exact moment in which she met Olaudah Equiano. (Although he was known as Gustavus Vassa at the time.)

Wendy was tired of running. She needed a place to rest and think. And to brood a little, because she was feeling sullen. But the fair was crowded. The only place to sit was upon a small two-seater bench, which was already one-half occupied by a dark-skinned man in a dated, but well-pressed, white linen shirt, green frock coat, and black breeches.

She sat down next to him, crossed her arms over her chest, tucked in her chin, and harrumphed. (At the age of ten, Wendy was already a highly accomplished harrumpher.)

"Goodness!" exclaimed Olaudah Equiano (or Gustavus Vassa). He was the man sitting next to her, as you had probably guessed. "What could have produced such a grand harrumph on such a fine day?"

"I was just thinking," Wendy admitted, "that I would rather marry Davy Jones than grow up and take care of babies."

"Oh, you must never think such a thing!" he cried. "Never, never, never!"

"Why not?" Wendy uncrossed her arms and looked up. The man was so adamant that she became immediately curious, and she forgot all about being sullen.

"I know too many men who have ended up at the bottom of the sea. Many, many men, God rest their souls. To invoke that name is very bad luck. *Terrible* luck. Do not attract his attention. In the middle of a starless night, he will send a wave crashing over the deck of your ship, pulling you into his arms forever."

"Oh," Wendy said, slumping her shoulders and dropping her

head to stare at the ground. "It doesn't matter, then. I'll never be a sailor. I'm just a girl."

"Just a girl? What does that mean?"

"It means I can't ever be a sea captain," Wendy said. A tear started to form in her left eye, but she swiped it away furiously.

Mr. Equiano (or Mr. Vassa) regarded her for a long moment before speaking again.

"Believe me, Miss...?"

"Darling," Wendy said, sniffling. "Wendy Darling."

"Miss Darling. My name is Gustavus Vassa. I am pleased to make your acquaintance." He bowed in her direction without standing up. "Forgive me, Miss Darling, when I say you are far too young to know what you will or will not become."

Wendy glanced back up at him, clearly hoping he would go on.

"Take me, for instance," he continued, happy to oblige her. "I was born in Africa with the name Olaudah Equiano. When I was only a boy, even younger than you, I was captured and sold into slavery. I thought surely I would die. And I almost did. Many times. But I ended up sailing all over the world.

"I have seen the Mediterranean and the Americas and the islands of the Caribbean. I have seen fish that fly and men whose lives were saved by their dreams. I have seen poisoners found out by magic, by the men who carried their victims' coffins, and I have seen women who could tell you both your past and your future without ever having met you before.

"I have been a free boy named Olaudah Equiano and a slave named Gustavus Vassa, and now I am free once again. I have been a plantation manager and a barber and a scientist and even a sea captain for a time."

"You were a captain?" Wendy exclaimed, interrupting.

9

"Yes. As I said, for a time. I have learned how to make fresh water from the sea, and I have used that knowledge to save my life in a land where the sun never sets and where entire ships are trapped in ice forever. I have done all this, but when I was a boy I thought I would spend my whole life in my mother's village. So you cannot say today what you might or might not do tomorrow. That much is certain."

"Yes, but you're a man though," Wendy pointed out. "Women are different."

"People would say the same about a slave, I think," Mr. Vassa (or Mr. Equiano) suggested gently. "But women are not as different everywhere as they are here in England. In the village where I was born, we did not have sailing ships. But we did have weapons— swords and bows and even firearms. Both men and women were trained to fight, to protect the village. When I was a boy, I once climbed a tree and watched my mother charge into battle carrying a broadsword. I was terrified for her life, but she was glorious."

"Did she live?" Wendy blurted out. *A woman! Wielding a sword!* Her limbs trembled at the thought of it.

"She did," he affirmed. "She fought fiercely that day, and she survived. She protected our village. I was very proud of her. My sister and I were only captured while she was away. If she had been home, no one could have taken us. My mother was too strong, and too brave."

"*Cowards,*" Wendy snarled under her breath.

Mr. Equiano—Wendy's mind had just now settled on this name for him, in honor of his mother—raised an eyebrow and shot her an appraising glance. He grunted his agreement in the back of his throat but said nothing more, and they fell into a companionable silence. A harbor, smooth as glass, amidst the fair that stormed around them, all raucous laughter and affected screams.

"What happened to your sister?" Wendy finally asked.

"I don't know," Mr. Equiano replied sadly. "It is my greatest regret. If I knew where she was, I would buy her freedom. If I knew where my mother was, I would try to see her again. But I was taken too young."

"I don't know how to find *my* mother, either," Wendy admitted softly. "I don't even know who she is. Or if I have one at all."

"Then where do you live?" he asked in surprise.

"At the almshouse."

Wendy shrugged. There wasn't much else to say about that.

"I see." He watched her for a long moment, clearly mulling something over, and then he slapped his hands decisively upon his knees and burst to his feet. "Right! I shall help you find your way back, of course. But I have just returned from Wales, and I shall be in London all winter. If you would like to learn how to make fresh water from the sea, I would be happy to teach you."

"You *would*? Oh, yes, please!"

"Good," he said, nodding. "It is something every sea captain should know. That, and how to navigate by the stars. And how to fashion a mast from a tree trunk, in case of emergency. And how to repair a sail. And how to fire a musket, as well as the cannons, of course ..."

The world, which had ended at precisely 10:48, started back up again. And Wendy's heart, like winter's ripe cocoon upon the first kiss of the sun, burst into a thousand rainbow wings, heralding its joy to the sky.

Mr. Equiano cleared his throat.

"Perhaps," he suggested, "I should make a list."

11

CHAPTER

3

That was how Wendy came to study with Olaudah Equiano. Whenever he was in London, he would teach her navigation and shipbuilding and marksmanship and how to handle a sword. And when he went to sea, he would leave her with a list of books to read while he was away. (Fortunately, the lord benefactor of the almshouse had an excellent library.)

Wendy begged him to take her along, of course, but he always refused.

"If it were my own ship, Miss Darling," he would tell her, "I would hire you without hesitation. You have a keen intellect and a persevering nature. But I am not the captain. I could not protect you if the men decided upon some nefarious purpose."

"But if you won't take me with you, why teach me anything at all?" Wendy would complain.

"Because I saw a spirit in you the day we met," he would reply.

"I believe you will eventually find your way onto a ship, one way or another, and I want you to be prepared."

And then he would finish with, "Just not today," which Wendy would say right along with him, bobbing her chin in time with his and rolling her eyes.

Despite this frustration, life at the almshouse was much better after Wendy began her studies. The other children still snickered when she talked about the navy. Or when she stood out in the cold, studying the stars. But Wendy didn't mind. Her life had a purpose, and no one could take that away from her.

When she went to visit her mentor, only Charlie bothered to ask where she was going. And when she read in the parlor, Charlie would plop himself down at her feet and ask about the book. Eventually, he even stood next to her through the cold, winter nights, staring up at the stars.

"Do you see that one?" Wendy asked him one night, as they were doing just that.

"Which?" Charlie asked.

"Look. There's a first star, there. And then a second, to the right a bit. And if you draw a line between them and keep right on going, there's another one they almost point to, off by itself and not quite as bright. Do you see it now?"

"I see it!" Charlie shouted.

"That's the North Star," she told him. "All the other stars spin around that one all night long, but that one doesn't move. That's how you can tell where north is, even without a compass. So you can never truly be lost."

"Never?" Charlie asked.

"Well, not in the northern hemisphere, at least. They have different stars on the other side of the world."

"The northern what?"

They stared at each other for a moment in silence, shivering.

"Come with me," Wendy finally said. "I need to show you on a globe. It's easier."

"All right," Charlie agreed.

"Now, you know," Wendy warned him, "if I start showing you things, the other children will laugh at you, too. So you'd best be prepared."

"I don't mind," Charlie promised. "They laugh at me anyway. But you never laugh at me. I'd rather be friends with you."

Wendy smiled. "All right," she said. "That's what we'll do, then."

And that's exactly what they did.

So, Wendy had a tutor and a friend and as many books as she could read. That would have been all she ever needed if she could have remained a child forever, but all children grow up. And grown-ups need to earn a living.

The way they managed this in London in 1787 was to place children in apprenticeships. The children would learn blacksmithing from a blacksmith, for example, or tailoring from a tailor. And then, after seven years, they would become blacksmiths or tailors themselves. These apprenticeships could begin any time after the age of fourteen. In an almshouse, as you might imagine, fourteen-year-old children were practically shoved out the door.

Children didn't feed themselves.

Wendy wanted Mr. Equiano to take her on as an apprentice,

but he refused on the grounds that he could not take her with him to sea and also that he did not practice a proper trade in which he could certify her.

"And what will I tell a ship's captain in seven years' time?" he asked her. "That I have taught you to be a sailor? When you have never once set foot upon a ship?"

"Then take me with you!" she argued.

But, of course, he would not.

And Wendy was running out of time.

"You must accept an apprenticeship," Mrs. Healey declared on Wendy's fifteenth birthday. "There is a dressmaker who inquired just yesterday."

Another dressmaker. Wendy shuddered. No one wanted to apprentice the girls. Dressmakers, weavers, housemaids. Perhaps the occasional milliner. Only boys became blacksmiths. Or shipbuilders. Let alone sea captains.

Dresses? Undergarments? The very thought filled Wendy with dread. She would rather face an entire fleet of pirates than spend one day sewing whalebone into ladies' corsets.

"Send Bridget," Wendy begged. "Please, Mrs. Healey? Bridget loves dresses."

Mrs. Healey pursed her lips and rubbed the fingers of her right hand together for several long moments.

"Very well," she agreed finally. "But you must choose *something*, Wendy. You cannot delay forever, or I shall decide for you."

After that, Wendy made herself as scarce as possible. She

begged Mr. Equiano for chores that she and Charlie could perform for a farthing, or perhaps even two, and when he was away at sea, they ran odd errands for their lord benefactor. They scraped together just enough to pay for meager suppers of stale bread and hard cheese, so they wouldn't have to eat at the orphanage.

While the other children were slowly divvied out among London's poorest tradesmen, Wendy and Charlie stayed out of sight. They climbed into the dormitory windows late at night, just to sleep, and they snuck back out before daylight. It was during this time that Mortimer Black was apprenticed to a shipwright, of all things. A shipwright! Wendy thought she might vomit, it was so unfair.

"I can't believe it!" she lamented. "Mortimer gets to be a shipwright, while Charlie and I have to sneak around after dark like a couple of thieves!"

"There are worse ways to live, Miss Darling," her tutor admonished her. "This life is of your own choosing. You could make dresses or hats if you desired. There is a price to changing one's destiny."

But not one of them at the time—not Mr. Equiano or Wendy or Charlie—knew just how true those words would prove to be.

CHAPTER
4

Ⅰn the autumn of 1789, when Wendy was sixteen years old, a note arrived one afternoon at the home of Olaudah Equiano, addressed to "Miss Wendy Darling."

"For me?" Wendy asked.

"So it would appear." Mr. Equiano handed it over with a frown of concern.

Wendy opened it with no small trepidation herself, and in but a moment, all their fears were confirmed.

"What does it say?" Charlie asked, so Wendy read it aloud.

Miss Darling,

Do not believe for one moment that I have forgotten about you and Charlie. I know how many of the beds in my charge are occupied. I have chosen to overlook your behavior until now, but the nursery is full. Your beds are needed. Select an

apprenticeship by January, or I shall send you both off with the first house servants who come asking.

Euphemia Healey,
Almshouse Caretaker

"I'm so sorry, children," Mr. Equiano said. "This is sad news, indeed."

"But, Mr. Equiano, sir!" Wendy protested. "You could take us both on! Please!"

"There is no such thing as a sailor's apprenticeship, Miss Darling, as I have explained many times. One merely signs up for naval service, and I have no ship of my own. You would have to find a captain who would accept you into his crew."

He looked so pained that Wendy couldn't bring herself to beg him again. She knew there was nothing he could do.

"But no captain wants a woman for a sailor," she whispered, as though saying it too loudly might make it even more true. Her face fell, and Charlie rushed to place a comforting arm around her shoulder. He was only fifteen, but he was already taller than she.

"You should sign up, Charlie," she said sadly. "They'll take *you* at least. You shouldn't have to be stuck here just because I am."

"Not without you. *Never* without you." He said it firmly, without any hesitation, and his loyalty made Wendy smile. At least a little.

"It will be all right," Charlie promised. "Perhaps we can both serve in the same household. At least we'll still have each other." If he looked almost hopeful about the prospect, Wendy clearly didn't feel the same way.

"But ... *house servants!*" she wailed. "It isn't *right!* We've worked so hard! And for so long!"

"What the heart desires most in all the world," Mr. Equiano

reminded her gently, "does not always come to us when we wish it. Such yearnings cannot be rushed. We must work for them. And we must *continue* to work for them. Even when all seems lost. So that we will be ready, should the heavens find a way to deliver us."

"Yes, sir," Wendy replied, but she didn't sound happy about it.

She spent the rest of the afternoon trying to focus on her studies, but her eyes kept glancing toward the window. Toward the wide world beyond. Toward a freedom she felt slipping away.

By December, there was still no hope in sight, and Wendy was feeling more desperate by the day. She imagined wild schemes, sharing them with Charlie in whispers as they walked back to the orphanage through winter-darkened streets.

"We could run away together," she murmured.

"And go where?" Charlie wanted to know. Not that he was against it. He just liked to have a plan.

"Anywhere!" Wendy said, her eyes twinkling in the light of a streetlamp as they passed through the edge of its lonely halo. "The Mediterranean! The Caribbean! I don't care. Just ... *somewhere!*"

"It's always the sea with you," Charlie commented, but he said it with a fond grin.

He blew on his hands, trying to warm them, his breath curling visibly into the night. Suddenly, Wendy grabbed his elbow, and Charlie stopped in his tracks. He stared at her hand, his arm perfectly still, as though a wild sparrow had landed upon it and he was scared that even the tiniest movement might frighten it away.

"Charlie," she breathed. "Look!"

He followed the line of her other arm, which was pointing at a stray newspaper page, lying on the ground at their feet. Just then, a wind picked up, and the paper lifted off into the air.

"No!" Wendy tore away from him and leaped forward, snatching it before it could get away.

"Wendy?" Charlie asked, clearly bewildered. "What is it?"

Wendy held the page in trembling hands, tears welling in her eyes. She didn't say a word, handing the paper to Charlie and swiping one rough, woolen coat sleeve across her face.

Charlie scanned the notices until he found the box that had drawn her attention. He hadn't known what he was looking for, but when he found it, he recognized it immediately. It was an unassuming rectangle in the bottom right corner of the page.

The Home Office seeks men and women of apprenticeship age to serve the Kingdom of Britain, it said. *Applicants must be of strong mind and body, able to read and write.* The ad was followed by a London address, where British citizens might apply in person.

"This is it, Charlie!" Wendy exclaimed, gripping his arm again, this time with both hands. "It's our way in!"

"But ... how did you even see that?" Charlie demanded, his voice filled with wonder. "In the dark ... that tiny notice ..."

"I was *meant* to see it!" Her eyes flashed with a power that almost made him want to take a step back. (Almost, but not quite.) "Men *and women*, Charlie! To work for the Home Office!"

"That won't get you overseas," Charlie pointed out, his voice hesitant. He didn't want to disappoint her, but it was the truth. "It's the Foreign Office that travels the world. The Home Office, well ... it's called the Home Office for a reason."

"But it opens the door! Who knows where we can go from there! It's our *chance!*" And then she added, more quietly, "It has to be."

Charlie looked into her eyes. For a long time, he didn't say

anything. But then he nodded. "All right," he agreed. "If this is what you want, we'll go tomorrow."

Wendy threw her arms around his neck and hugged him with all her might. "Everything's going to be all right, Charlie. I just know it is."

If Charlie didn't feel quite as certain as she did, he kept it to himself.

"Miss ... Darling, is it?"

"Yes, that's right." Wendy smiled her most friendly smile at the elderly gentleman who sat behind the desk. He was thin, almost frail, but he had a sharp edge to his glance that made Wendy nervous.

"And why do you want to join the Home Office, Miss Darling?"

"To serve His Royal Majesty, of course," she said immediately. "And the Kingdom of Britain."

He pierced her with a terrible stare and raised one eyebrow, catching his right cheek between his teeth and working his jaw back and forth. He was clearly judging her. Sizing her up. But what he was looking for, Wendy had no idea. She held his gaze all the while, still smiling, her hands folded neatly in her lap.

"You'd have no control over your post," he warned her, tilting his head slightly to prompt a reply.

"I understand," she agreed.

"And you'd have to be able to keep a secret." His lips pressed themselves together and shot toward the left corner of his mouth, broadcasting his skepticism. He obviously didn't believe for a second that any woman could withstand the temptation to gossip.

"I can keep a secret," Wendy assured him.

The man snorted. "Can you prove it?"

"Can *you*?" she replied evenly. "If you were to divulge a secret to me, right now, just to prove that you can keep one, well then, you would only be proving that you cannot. I, of course, suffer the same logic. The fact that I will *not* attempt to prove it is at least some evidence of my trustworthiness. But, I admit, it is not *proof*. I don't see how I *could* prove it. I don't see how anyone could."

"Hmm ..." he replied, still noncommittal.

They held each other's gaze. Wendy remained silent, using the time to study him. Never had she seen a man more accustomed to holding authority. His raised eyebrow. His tight-pressed lips. The fingers of his right hand, drumming steadily upon the desk. Pinky, ring finger, middle, index. All in rapid succession. One–two–three–four. One–two–three–four. One–two–three–four.

Everything about him commanded respect. She could use that where she was going.

Where she hoped she was going.

She waited him out.

Not speaking.

Not moving.

"All right," he said finally. "We'll see how you do. Come back tomorrow for your induction. Then I'm sending you to Dover. But remember, Miss Darling, the Home Office requires your discretion. You'll tell no one that you're joining us, or what we're hiring you to do."

He paused a moment and then added one final comment, muttering more to himself than to her.

"Not that anyone would believe you anyway."

CHAPTER
5

Admittedly, things could have been better.

Charlie had been assigned to a ship, and Wendy had not.

Charlie's knowledge of mathematics and science and a thousand shipboard skills had catapulted him to the rank of officer, despite his low beginnings. A feat all but unheard of in the British Navy.

Wendy's exact same (if not *slightly* superior) skills had been ignored altogether, and she had been assigned to Dover Castle. Destined every day to stare out at the sea, without ever once embarking upon it.

She missed her friend, to be sure, and she thought her treatment unfair. But still, she was lucky to have a post at all. Or so she told herself. She had known from the beginning what she was up against. And even the post in Dover was so much more than she could have hoped.

Well, more than she might have ended up with, at any rate.

At least she wasn't a milliner.

"A dire threat to the Kingdom of Britain," they had said. "You will know it when it comes. Watch, and wait. Be ready. Protect the realm."

So she had watched. And she had waited. She had continued her training with the men of Dover in firearms and in swordsmanship. She had gently and humbly shared her own knowledge of mathematics and science and a thousand shipboard skills. She had earned their respect. Over the course of a year.

An entire *year* ... and nothing.

She was not one step closer to sailing the world.

She tried to keep her mind occupied. To prepare herself. To learn what she could about the enemy. But all she had uncovered so far were lies. And foolishness. And the bitter sting of disappointment.

Like *this* ridiculous thing: *Dissertazione sopra i vampiri.*

A Dissertation on Vampires.

Wendy stared at the book reproachfully, but it merely lay on the table in silent rebuttal, entirely nonplussed. The text had been penned for the Vatican by Archbishop Giuseppe Davanzati in 1744. But the title was a lie.

It should have been called *A Refutation of Vampires.* Or better yet, *A Regurgitation of Popular Opinion on the Subject of Vampires, which Wendy Darling Will Read in the Year of Our Lord 1790, Only to Be Profoundly Disappointed.*

She shoved this most recent offense onto a tall stack of equally useless volumes and began drumming her fingers on the table. Both John Abbot and Michael Bennet knew what that meant. So did Nana, for that matter. But it wasn't so much the action that gave her away. It was the cadence.

Wendy had spent a significant portion of the past year refining

24

a finger-drumming repertoire to match her every mood. Happy drumming, for example, demanded a frenetic staccato between her thumb and ring finger—a snare drum of enthusiasm that heralded shouts of joy and gleeful dancing about the room. That one was Michael's favorite.

Mournful drumming, on the other hand, required an agonizingly slow succession of unadorned thumps, meted out by her third and fourth fingers together. Thump ... thump ... thump .... It was heartbreakingly soulful despite its simplicity, like the funeral tolling of a church bell, and it always brought a tear to John's eye. Not that he would ever let you see it.

This particular drumming, however, was a quiet, tense cadence that went like this: one, one–two–three, one ... one, one–two–three, one. This was the rhythm of extreme frustration. The one that John and Michael both called the March of the Executioner, although never where Wendy might overhear them.

The two men looked at each other now, sharing a meaningful glance from one desk to another across the thick carpet of John's private office in Dover Castle, and the glance said this: "Do you think we can sneak away before she notices?"

But this particular glance was so eloquent as to come dangerously close to conversation, and everyone knows it is impolite to enter into conversation without first performing the proper introductions all around. So let us pause for a moment to do just that.

Wendy Darling is now seventeen years old, having matured into an uncommonly beautiful young woman. She has honey-brown eyes and long ringlets of thick brown hair. In direct sunlight her locks appear reddish, or at times almost blond, while at night they appear quite dark indeed, so that you might imagine her with any color of hair you wish, and you would not be entirely wrong. She has a fetching smile (with a secret kiss in the far corner) and a

charitable disposition, especially when it comes to orphans and foundlings.

She is attached to the Fourteenth Platoon of the Nineteenth Light Dragoons, a British regiment that no longer exists, having been disbanded seven years prior in June of 1783. (Or rather, it clearly *does* exist, its Fourteenth Platoon still prowling about Dover Castle on matters of domestic security, but the Home Office isn't admitting it.) She is paid as a nurse, which suits her quite well—even though her true purpose in the regiment has nothing to do with nursing—because it provides her with a convenient excuse to borrow numerous scientific texts from the local gentry.

John Abbot is a second lieutenant and the Fourteenth Platoon's ranking officer. He is Wendy's brother-in-arms, but he is in no way related to her, despite what you might have heard. He is tall and lean, with unmistakably dark hair. He is profoundly responsible. So much so, that you could follow him about for an entire fortnight and never once catch him indulging in a lighthearted moment. At twenty-two years of age, he has yet to grow out of the proud and stoic silence of his youth, and Wendy has begun to suspect that he never will.

Michael Bennet, on the other hand, is fair-haired and broad-shouldered, with a devilish gleam of fiery red that permeates both his locks and his character. He is John's platoon sergeant, another brother-in-arms. He is dashing and charismatic, known to woo and abandon the fairer sex as quickly as Wendy can devour a book, which is saying something. Wendy is often the subject of his affections, but she cannot take them at all seriously, given that he casts them so broadly about and in such an offhand manner.

Each of these men would have thrown himself at Wendy Darling with complete and eternal devotion had she ever given him so much as a *hint* that she wished for him to do so.

Much to their respective disappointment, she had not.

As for Nana, she is a shaggy, dark Newfoundland monster of a dog who follows Wendy's every move without exception. According to her official papers, her name is "Sheba," but Wendy calls her "Nana," so that is how the dog has come to think of herself. She has chosen Wendy above the others because it is abundantly clear to her who is *really* in charge and who is *really* looking after whom, despite what John seems sometimes to believe.

Dogs *always* know.

So there you are, the most basic of introductions complete, the rest to be discovered as time goes on (which is how we get to know everyone when it comes right down to it), and we are back at the part where John and Michael were sharing a glance that said, "Do you think we can sneak away before she notices?"

This also happens to be the part where Nana comes in.

Wendy's drumming had roused Nana from her nap just in time to catch John and Michael sharing their conspiratorial glance. Understanding them perfectly, Nana stood up from her self-appointed spot at Wendy's feet, stretched languorously, walked to the doorway, and plopped herself down across it, blocking any hope of exit for either one. She looked pointedly at Michael with a satisfied tilt of her left ear and fell promptly back asleep.

As quickly as that, the conspiracy was broken. Now the two men glared back and forth at one another, silently demanding, "Say something; no, *you* say something," until John finally gave Michael a new look altogether that said, "I outrank you; that's an order."

Michael grimaced and cleared his throat.

"Any luck?" he asked, although he already knew the answer.

"No," she said, her voice sharp with annoyance. "There is no such thing as science anywhere to be had when it comes to the

everlost. First, popular opinion followed the church; now, the church follows popular opinion. Either way, there's no truth to any of it. This last volume attributes every eyewitness account to mass hysteria. Every single one. Can you imagine?"

"Fools," John grumbled, quick to match her mood. Truth be told, John had been in something of a foul mood since autumn, when the Home Office had begun paying him as a pastry chef. It was just a cover of course, but still, it rankled. His tenure in clandestine service was not living up to his expectations. (This was just one of many issues upon which he and Wendy thoroughly agreed.)

"Seems to me that's good news," Michael protested. "At least we won't be facing widespread panic. Let the Vatican denounce the everlost as figments of the collective imagination. All the better. And pray the Royal Society continues to believe its own 'enlightened' skepticism."

"You're right, of course," Wendy demurred, pursing her lips into a reluctant frown. "Belief would be worse than ridicule. But it leaves so little in the way of scientific inquiry. How are we supposed to learn anything about the threat—or how to counter it—if science doesn't believe in it in the first place?"

"I don't see why it matters," John countered. "We've been stationed so far from London we don't have a chance of running across them anyway. The everlost aren't going to attack Dover. We're in a lot more danger from the French out here."

"Not from them either," Michael commented. "The French have their own problems."

"At least the trouble in France has been keeping them on their own side of the straits," John agreed. "Not that I'd mind a bit of a skirmish now and then. It's a depressingly boring post, isn't it?"

"Be careful what you wish for," Michael retorted.

But of course, Wendy agreed with John. Not that she was about to admit it out loud. *If the French* were *to attack,* she couldn't help thinking, *at least that would be* interesting.

She shoved her chair backward and rose to her feet, prompting both men to stand as well. "I could use some fresh air to clear my head," she announced. "It's just about time for Nana's walk, if either of you would care to join us."

And because Michael did not want Wendy to go walking alone with John, and because John did not want Wendy to go walking alone with Michael, they both agreed to join her.

If we're lucky, Wendy thought, *perhaps someone will try to rob us. There's no harm in* wishing, *after all.*

Which should tell you, despite all her years of believing in magic, searching every library she could find for even the tiniest scrap of reliable information, just how little she had managed to discover.

CHAPTER

6

B y the time they returned to the castle—depressingly un-
scathed, the lot of them—thunderclouds had rolled in over
the Straits of Dover, blocking out the stars. A wind had picked up,
and the afternoon, which had already been chilly, was giving way
to a positively bitter evening.

An ill wind blows through Dover, Wendy thought, although it
surprised her the very instant she thought it. It felt as though the
idea had arrived on the wind itself, caressing the back of her neck
with icy talons. She was glad to return to John's private office and
the small writing table she had come to think of as her own.

Positioned nearest the hearth, it was by far the warmest spot in
the office through the long winter months, and the two men had left
it for her by silent agreement. Wendy scanned the dwindling stack
of unread books in her borrowed library and sighed. She would
need to make the rounds of the local gentry again soon, although
the pickings were growing slimmer with every passing month.

Between the fire and a hot cup of tea, the chill of the walk was easing away, especially with Nana's thick winter coat curled protectively around her feet. Wendy was about to select one of the older tomes, hoping some ancient legend might be able to fill in the gaps that modern science refused to acknowledge, when a vague sense of unease brought her up short. Her hand paused in midair, hesitating, and then retreated, her thumb running distractedly along her fingers as she tried to figure out what it was that had disturbed her.

A sense of nervousness (or was it exhilaration?) began to twist in the pit of her stomach, reminding her oddly of fireflies and stolen summer nights beneath a ripening moon. And then her very skin began to prickle, as though a lightning strike were somehow imminent, despite the fact that she was safely indoors.

She had never felt so alert in all her life.

"Do you smell that?" she asked of no one in particular.

There was an odd scent in the air, wafting in from the night, and she breathed it in slowly, letting it fill her awareness. It was a bit like the first hint of winter, she decided—that sense you have when you wake up one morning and somehow you know that the last warmth of the year has well and truly gone, even though it isn't especially cold yet and the first snows have not yet fallen. It was subtle and rich and somewhat frightening.

Winter, then summer, then winter again, she thought. *How strange the mind can be, playing tricks upon us in the dark.*

She felt herself drawn to the narrow opening that served as a window, so she stood and wandered toward it, her head tilted slightly to one side as though she were listening for something she couldn't quite hear, until she finally stood directly before it, staring restlessly out into the night. But she could hardly see anything beyond the edge of the ancient stone.

"All I smell is that godforsaken dog," John grumbled. "Why you insist on taking her for long walks under threat of rain is beyond me. It's not even rightfully spring yet. You'll both catch your death."

"Well, then we shall be out of your hair for good, which will be a great relief to you, I'm quite certain," she snapped, a bit put out by his criticism. After all, no one had forced him to go with them. "Besides, she's a strong animal. She doesn't need to be cooped up inside all day. She needs her exercise."

"So do I," Michael interjected with a wink and a grin, "but I don't see you doing anything special for me."

"Hush," Wendy said, still sniffing at the air. "By all that's holy, what *is* that?"

Nana padded across the room and pushed her head briefly into Wendy's palm. Then she reared up onto her hind legs, placing her front paws on the window ledge and growling into the unfathomable darkness below.

"What's what?" Michael wanted to know, his flirtatious efforts already forgotten, which was perfectly typical of him.

"It smells like ..." She trailed off, her eyebrows knitting a delicate crease above the bridge of her nose. "Heavens, I don't know! That's precisely why it's so bothersome! If I knew what it was, I suspect that I'd forget all about it right away, but I can't quite put my finger on it. Even though it seems familiar. Or at least, it seems as though it *should* be familiar, even though it isn't. Does that make sense?"

"Not in the slightest," John muttered, his eyes never straying from the papers on his desk.

Michael's grin broadened as he watched her. His cheeks dimpled, and his eyebrows shot up as though he were right on the cusp of laughing. But he managed not to, if only just.

"There's a hint of ... cool water," she continued, "in the back of a cave on a hot spring day ... And a taste of pickles—"

"A *taste* of pickles? In the *scent*?" Michael's right eyebrow rose even higher than his left, and he finally did chuckle a little, but not much, to his credit. It was a puzzled sort of chuckle that held not even a hint of scorn. (Michael was rarely scornful of any-one, and certainly *never* of Wendy.)

"Yes, pickles. Now *hush*," Wendy repeated, swatting at his shoulder for interrupting her. "Let me concentrate. As I was saying ... water ... cave ... taste of pickles ... Oh, yes, that's it. Green. Definitely green. It smells more like the color green than anything I've ever known in my life. Green and ... Oh! Oh, no!"

At her exclamation, even John looked up from his accounts, suddenly alarmed.

"What is it?" he demanded, rising at once and reaching for his coat.

Nana's growl rose in volume until the dog was snarling vicious-ly at the air coming in from the window.

"Magic!" Wendy cried. "It smells like magic!"

Her eyes flew wide as she turned to meet John's gaze. Not even Michael was smiling now.

"The everlost," she whispered. "They're here!"

CHAPTER

7

"The everlost?" John scoffed, already lowering his coat. "Why, that's—"

Quicker than the beat of a hummingbird's wing, Wendy's eyes narrowed dangerously, and she raised a single eyebrow that managed to be both elegant and defiant at once. If eyebrows could speak, this one would have said, "I'd be very careful what you are about to say, John Abbot, for the sharpness of your tongue in this next moment may be visited back upon you a thousandfold."

As it could not speak, it was forced instead to poise itself gracefully above Wendy's left eye, saying nothing. But the implied threat was clear enough.

In fact, John had been *about* to say that the very idea of the everlost appearing here, in Dover, was patently ridiculous, implying in turn that Wendy *herself* was being patently ridiculous, but the eyebrow had stopped him just in time.

"Why, that's highly unexpected," he finished instead, his tone cautiously respectful. "Are you absolutely certain?"

"I'm quite certain. Yes." She looked down and slightly to the left for just a moment, as though reconsidering the entire question, but then she returned her gaze to John's and locked onto it with unwavering conviction.

"Yes, I am," she repeated, and John couldn't help but notice that she seemed rather more pleased than frightened by the prospect.

Wendy didn't know how she *could* be certain of it, having never been in the presence of the everlost before. In truth, up until this very moment, she had been more than a little concerned that she might never be certain of it at all. That was her duty, you see, within the Nineteenth Light Dragoons: to sense the presence of magic and warn her platoon of any impending attack. It was just that she had never before had occasion to do it.

Her induction into the ranks of the Home Office had been full of surprises, to say the least. It had gone something like this ...

England faced a most terrible threat.

A threat! How exciting! At last, a chance for real adventure!

Magic, as it turned out, was real.

Of course it was! She had known it all along!

This magical threat was terrorizing England's poor, and the orphans of London in particular. Stealing children away in the middle of the night.

No! Not the orphans! How dare they?

The creatures were known as the everlost. With preternatural strength and speed. There were reports of flying. And drinking human blood. So little was known for certain. Only women and dogs seemed able to sense their presence.

England needed her! She would protect the men of her platoon! And,

of course, the children! But how would she know when the everlost were near?

It was a woman's intuition, they had assured her, and she would recognize it when the time came.

So she had read everything she could find on the subject, and she had trained twice as hard as the men in both swordsmanship and marksmanship, just to prove her dedication. But there was no training to be had in the one task for which her feminine presence was tolerated. To have discovered at long last that she could serve her designated purpose with precision and confidence ... well, it came with tremendous relief, as you might imagine.

She looked from John to Michael and back again, a gleam of excitement in her eye, waiting to see what might happen next.

John stared at Wendy a moment longer and then glanced down at Nana, who was now barking and snapping so furiously at the open window that he would have feared for the dog's safety had she not been far too large to fit through it.

Finally, he turned to Michael.

"Gather the men, and meet me seaward of Saint Mary. Swords and muskets, both. May she have mercy on our souls."

Michael snapped to attention with a proper salute, racing off as soon as he was dismissed. This was the first time Wendy had ever seen such military formality pass between the two of them, and the very sight of it sent a quick thrill of fear racing down her spine.

As though reading her thoughts, John turned his attention back to Wendy.

"You are to stay here," he said, and he swung the heavy wooden shutters across the window, barring them securely. "Do not leave this room, and do *not* open this window. Under no circumstances

are you to set even one foot outside of these walls before sunrise. Have I made myself clear?"

"But—"

"You have done your duty, Miss Darling. Now let us do ours. You are a part of this regiment, and I expect you to follow my orders."

Wendy thrust her chin forward and glared at him defiantly. Her eyebrow was threatening to have its own say on the subject when John took an uncharacteristic step toward her and caught her hand in his own.

"Please, Wendy," he said, sounding much more like himself and at the same time nothing like himself at all. "I couldn't bear it if anything happened to you."

He looked into her eyes until she finally gave him a small nod in reply, too surprised to speak.

"Pray for us," he said, and with that he strode briskly away, his posture irreproachably straight, his shoulders squared in determination.

Wendy watched his long, lean back until he was out of sight.

"Well, now. That was quite unexpected, wasn't it, Nana?"

The dog, who had ceased her snarling as soon as John had barred the window, now stared at the door without comment.

"Oh, I agree," Wendy assured her. "Of course we have to follow him."

Nana glanced up, her eyes uncertain. She had been hoping only that John might come back, not that her mistress might charge headlong into the night after him. Especially not with such strange and disturbing smells lingering in the darkness.

"Don't look at me like that," Wendy scolded her gently. "We're only *attached* to the regiment, Nana. We don't report to

John directly. He can't just order us about. Besides, how are they to know where the danger is coming from without our noses to guide them? It's our duty."

Nana sat a little straighter and turned back to the door, growling this time. She was, after all, an exceedingly honorable dog. Nothing tugged more directly at her heartstrings than the call of faithful responsibility.

"That's my girl! Come on, then. But be quiet now. They mustn't hear us unless we need them to."

Nana fell silent at once and padded stealthily behind her mistress, following her through the barracks and out into the night.

CHAPTER
8

It is a strange feeling indeed to hide not only from one's enemies (which is a perfectly natural thing to do from time to time), but from one's own friends and comrades as well. It makes the entire world seem that much larger and more frightening than it already is, and it makes one feel very small and alone within it. Nevertheless, that was precisely what Wendy knew she had to do.

If John and the others had caught sight of her, they would have felt it their moral obligation, out of unbridled chivalry, to squirrel her back away inside the castle for safekeeping. But no one in the history of the world has ever proven their mettle without taking a risk or two along the way, and Wendy was no exception. Her platoon needed her, whether they realized it or not, and so she would come to their rescue. Whether they wanted her to or not.

At least she had Nana, who held no prejudgments whatsoever about her gender, and who was as grateful to have Wendy by her side as Wendy was to have Nana—it being the very nature of a

dog to possess a profound understanding of friendship and cama-
raderie.

Now, the church of Saint Mary in Castro (which is just a fancy
way of saying "Saint Mary in the Castle") stood ironically a good
bit away from the castle proper, next to the old lighthouse, afford-
ing Wendy and Nana very little opportunity to hide while dashing
between the two. John had mustered the men there because reports
from London indicated that the everlost had begun raiding supply
houses, and the church was being used as a storage facility after
having fallen into disrepair.

What the blood drinkers could possibly want with flour and
sugar and salt and turnips was anyone's guess, but they weren't
going to get England's turnips without a fight, by heaven, or so
the Home Office had boldly proclaimed. (They weren't going to
get England's blood either, if anyone could help it, but that much
seemed to go without saying.)

Blood drinkers. Wendy shuddered. She waited until she and Nana
were utterly alone before racing across the grass, carefully skirting
the graveyard—with another shudder for that—and trotting around
the far corner of the church. Opposite the direction the men had
gone, just to be on the safe side. She finally poked her head around
the front and caught a glimpse of John and Michael and the rest,
twelve of them in all, standing in a line, muskets at the ready, their
eyes fixed on the storm-blackened skies.

Wendy felt oddly relieved to see them there, as though a part
of her had been afraid they might be spirited away by magic in the
dead of night without a trace. But even the everlost couldn't do
that, could they?

Wendy followed John's gaze to see a strange sort of movement
in the clouds, as though the storm itself were growing tendrils and
dispatching them toward the earth, seeking fertile soil in which

to take root. First one and then another and then yet another writhing funnel materialized in the air, until the thunderhead had produced more than a dozen twisting extensions full of dark gray mist, all plummeting toward the walls of Saint Mary.

"Demons!" a man shouted. Wendy thought this might have been Reginald, an exceptionally pious man from Yorkshire who had always been polite to her, but she could not be certain.

"Hold your ground!" That was John—she would know his voice anywhere—and his men did as he commanded, holding their ranks, their muskets tracing the progress of their enemies as they descended from the skies.

Between the darkness and the swirling mist, the rippling coils were almost impenetrable, but it seemed to Wendy as though there were a hint of a figure cloaked within each narrow vortex. More than a dozen men falling to earth like stones, their arms crossed blithely across their chests. But then, when they were no more than a hundred yards up, the twisters dissipated all at once, the mist flying suddenly away, as tremendous wings burst outward, extending from each man's shoulders to catch his fall.

They slowed as one, pausing no more than fifty yards above the ground to hover impossibly in the air, and it was all Wendy could do not to gasp in wonder. They were men, young men to be sure, but men as truly as any she had ever seen, clad in an array of green and brown leathers, with swords dangling from their hips and wings extending from their backs.

"Fire!" John shouted, and the night exploded with a dozen gunshots. But not one of the flying men fell.

Wendy began to wonder if they were demons after all, even though their pinions were feathered like a hawk's wings, rather than solid like a bat's, and their faces appeared utterly human—nothing like any demons she had ever seen in all the texts of supernatural

phenomena she had studied. The nearest of the creatures dropped twenty yards closer as the men on the ground struggled to reload, and Wendy finally got a clear look at him.

He was brown-haired and blue-eyed, and his features were the finest Wendy had ever seen. Like a statue, she thought, sculpted by the hands of angels. For a moment, she felt inexorably drawn to him, as a compass is drawn toward the north, and she had the strangest notion, quite without meaning to, that as long as he was near, she could never be lost, no matter where she might find herself.

But then he smiled. His teeth gleamed in the darkness, with canines that looked more like a wolf's than a man's, and his eyes possessed a hardness that shattered any illusion she might have been under. These were the everlost, and he was her enemy.

"You want to play?" he growled. "Excellent. Let's play!"

With that, his brethren howled with glee, and the winged horde fell upon the humans before the men could fire another round.

Wendy almost expected the strange creatures to grow claws to match their teeth, but they drew their swords instead, some of them dropping to the earth and fighting on two legs, while others flew in and out of reach, striking from above. They swung at their adversaries with wild abandon, like swashbuckling pirates scattered improbably about the manicured lawn, but the Nineteenth Light Dragoons fought back with well-trained discipline, parrying and striking with purpose.

Without another thought, Wendy and Nana raced to join them.

In the heat of battle, no one was likely to notice one more person in the mix, but a dress was a different matter altogether. The Nineteenth Light Dragoons no longer existed, officially speaking, so they did not wear the proud red uniforms of the British army.

Instead, they wore civilian clothing in various shades of blues and browns, their government-issued weapons the only common element among them. Not one of them, however, wore a chemise dress.

Fortunately, Wendy had considered this problem ahead of time. At the very edge of the battle, she sloughed off her riding coat, and then her dress as well, beneath which she wore a man's dark blue breeches, brown leather boots, and a simple white shirt. Utterly certain that no one would recognize her now (expectations in 1790 being rather intractable regarding one's attire), she threw herself into the fray, stabbing the nearest of the winged men in his side while Nana sank her teeth triumphantly into his ankle.

Wendy had expected, rather reasonably, that the creature would fall to his knees at the very least, having been mortally wounded. She was already withdrawing her weapon from his body when she realized, quite all of a sudden, that he wasn't falling down at all. Instead, he allowed her to remove the sword from his flank and then twisted casually in her direction, raised his own weapon for a decapitating blow ... and then halted mid-swing when he caught sight of her face.

It was the angel-wrought statue of brown hair and blue eyes, and Wendy would never be certain, for all the rest of her days, which of them was more surprised in that moment: she, to see him utterly nonchalant after having been skewered through the right lung, or he, to be staring into the eyes of a woman.

CHAPTER

9

Of the two, it was Wendy who recovered first, and she thrust her sword at the belly of the everlost, intending to gut him like a fish.

This time, however, he saw it coming.

In the blink of an eye, he flipped his saber upside down. Catching her blade with his own, he pushed hers off to the side with the metallic screech of steel sliding along steel and then leaped back, his wings bursting outward to catch the air in a rippling explosion of feathers.

He fell to earth lightly, landing easily on the balls of his feet, and began to circle her, watching her with interest, as though she were some sort of exotic creature, the likes of which he had never seen before.

He moved more like a panther than a man, Wendy thought. His reflexes in defending himself had been fast and fierce, but now

he moved slowly, his steps graceful and calculated, his eyes fixed indelibly upon her, stalking his prey.

Nana, having fallen back when their initial attack failed, now rushed toward him again in earnest. But a dog's teeth were no match for the sword of an everlost, and Wendy feared for her life.

"Off, Nana! Off!" she hissed, not wanting the men of the platoon to hear her voice and realize she had left the keep to join them in battle.

Wendy urged the animal behind her, very much against Nana's better instincts, who did not like the idea of Wendy fighting without her. Not one bit. She backed up reluctantly, growling all the while, hoping for some opportunity to arise in which she might be permitted to rip out the man's throat.

"What?" Wendy demanded, for the everlost was now staring at her with a mocking sort of smile that tugged at the left corner of his mouth.

"I find it interesting that you would order your guard dog not to protect you," he replied. "It seems ... counterintuitive. What's the point of the dog then, I wonder?" (Which, as it happens, was precisely what Nana was thinking.)

He looked at her so smugly that Wendy was sorely tempted to tell him her plan—which was to wait until she had distracted him sufficiently and then order the dog to attack while his guard was down—but telling him so would have made the plan far less clever, of course.

She also wanted to tell him that she and Nana were both a proud part of the Nineteenth Light Dragoons of the British Home Office, thank you very much, and who was he to question their methods? But that was the trouble with impressive covert missions: you weren't allowed to use them to impress anybody.

"Perhaps I promised her fresh meat for dinner, and she's here to collect when I'm through with you," Wendy shot back instead, which she regretted almost immediately, as it was rather a gruesome thought. But it only made his smile grow wider.

"Well, then. We'd best get to it, I suppose," he said. "I wouldn't want her to go hungry." His face grew solemn when he said it, but Wendy had the feeling he was still only playacting, enjoying a private game of his own design to which no one else had been invited. She raised her sword before her, acknowledging her enemy with a nod, but her eyes never left his.

"Good form," he said, nodding back, and all of a sudden he was grinning wickedly again, his canines obvious even in the dark.

With a thunderous clap, his wings disappeared from his back, and Wendy couldn't help but gasp in surprise. The everlost pounced forward in the blink of an eye and touched the flat of his blade lightly to her left shoulder, moving back out of range as quickly as he had attacked, clearly toying with her.

"Never let your guard down," he advised. "In battle, surprise is either your best friend or your worst enemy. You don't want it to be the latter."

Wendy's eyes narrowed. *You're not the only one who can play games,* she thought. *Just keep thinking I'm a foolish little girl. It will be the last mistake you ever make.*

Seeing that he was not trying to kill her, or at least not yet anyway, she slowed her attacks, careful to seem hesitant and even a bit clumsy, letting him believe in the untested woman he clearly expected. But all the while, she watched him, studying his moves. When she thrust like *this*, he would counter with a parry to the left. If she swung in just *so*, he would spin away to the right.

After all her painstaking hours of training—six years with Olaudah Equiano and another year with the men of the Fourteenth

Platoon—mishandling her sword and trying to appear off-balance was more of a challenge than she would have thought. It even proved to be somewhat humiliating, much to Wendy's annoyance. When she pretended to misstep to her right, overextending a thrust that sailed past his left side, he swatted her rump with the flat of his blade for her trouble and danced away gleefully.

Wendy merely gritted her teeth against the indecency and kept up the charade, biding her time.

"So tell me," he asked, clearly enjoying the diversion, "when did the army finally decide to allow women to join its ranks?"

"Why would you think me a soldier?" she retorted, chopping clumsily at his left shoulder without any chance of actually hitting him.

"Forgive me," he responded smoothly, dodging the blow and watching her stumble (or at least pretend to stumble) as her blade passed through the empty air. "I only assumed, due to your considerable skill. You have been highly trained, that much is obvious." He said it with a straight face, but Wendy knew better.

Liar, she thought to herself. *No British soldier worth their weight would ever fight this badly, male or female.* Clearly, he was trying to flatter her, but to what end, she couldn't guess.

"Perhaps I am but a lowly serving girl with a patriotic heart," she replied, to which he laughed out loud.

"Perhaps. But I believe there is more to you than meets the eye, Miss …?" He bowed deeply in mock introduction, ducking beneath a poorly aimed thrust to his chest.

"If you wish to learn my name, you'll have to earn it," she replied, pretending to work harder than was truly necessary not to stumble into him.

"As you wish," he said, reaching out his free hand to steady her, but she only glared at him for his trouble.

She pretended to be even weaker on the left than on the right, slowly moving their encounter away from the rest of the fray, all the while knowing she was doing her part just by keeping one of them occupied. But she couldn't wait much longer. The false nature of her skirmish allowed her to see what the others could not, each of them too caught up in the deadly fight before him to grasp a sense of the battle as a whole.

The everlost were gaining the advantage.

They were faster and stronger than the human men; that much was clear. Even with their brazenly piratical style, using twice as much energy with every swing and thrust as the well-disciplined Nineteenth Light Dragoons, they exhibited the same level of enthusiasm now as they had from the beginning. They danced about the lawn and darted through the sky, hooting and shouting into the night like wild children, while the human men were beginning to falter.

Here and there across the field a voice rang out in pain when a man was wounded. The Fourteenth Platoon was already outnumbered. If the wounded began to fall, the tide would turn quickly. Whatever Wendy was going to do, she had to do it now.

With a burst of determination, she fell upon her enemy with everything she had.

Her first deliberate thrust pierced the everlost through the left thigh all the way to the bone, and the shock that registered upon his face in that moment satisfied her more deeply than any other thing in all her days.

His surreptitiously mocking grin—whether he had intended it or not—had reflected a thousand equally condescending smiles, each of which had been inflicted upon her throughout all of her seventeen years for no better reason than that she belonged to "the weaker sex." To see that grin wiped away by the work of her own hand was such a triumph as to feel almost intoxicating.

He winced in pain as she withdrew her weapon from his leg, but he barely evidenced so much as a limp once it was free of his body. Nonetheless, this time she was prepared, pressing her attack without hesitation.

She feinted at him twice, once toward the chest and once in a half-swing toward his left side. When he spun away from the latter, having realized by now that she was in earnest, he discovered too late that her sword was waiting for him. He came to a brutal halt at the end of the turn when her blade pierced his gut, cutting deep into his abdomen and slicing through several inches of entrails.

It was a blow that would have left a human man on the ground in agony, dying in a bloody pile of his own innards.

But what the everlost man did instead was this: He grimaced at the initial pain and then slowly grinned at her once again, his lips parting into a wicked smile as he gripped her blade with both hands and removed it forcefully from his belly.

Wendy shivered, and these words passed through her mind: *the soulless, the undead, the everlost. They're going to kill us all.*

"I applaud you, my lady. I truly do," he told her, each word piercing her heart, another nail in her coffin. "You are an excellent actress. Worthy of the royal stage, I dare say! It was my own folly to think you would join such a fight unprepared, and I have paid a worthy price for it. Surprise was my enemy, after all. But it is not quite so easy as that to kill my kind, I'm afraid."

An ear-piercing cry split the night, only to be silenced mid-scream, and Wendy knew without question that the first of the men had fallen.

"No," she whispered. *John! Michael!*

She turned to try to see who it was, but there was no way to tell. Another voice cried out in agony, and then a third.

"Fall back! To Saint Mary! Fall back!" That was John. He was alive, at least. Wendy waited for Michael to pick up the order and start shouting directions, but the seconds ticked by with no other sounds beyond the clash of steel, more groans of pain, and the creaking of the old church door.

"All in! Bar the entrance!" John's voice was the last human sound Wendy heard before the door creaked shut, a bar slammed down across it from the inside, and the night fell still.

She was alone with the everlost.

She whirled back to face her adversary only to find that he had moved up behind her while she was distracted. There was hardly a hand's breadth between them now, and the unmistakable scent of magic permeated the air as he gazed down upon her, a look of cold, merciless appraisal in his ice-blue eyes.

CHAPTER
10

When confronted by the imminent possibility of one's own death, the important thing is not to panic. That is what everyone says, and they say it because it is true. Remaining calm will not *always* save you, which is precisely what makes it such a difficult thing to do, but panicking *never* will, which is why it is absolutely, positively never the best choice.

Still, it is one thing to say that we must remain calm, and it is another thing altogether to *do* it, pausing in the midst of the most terrifying situation of one's life to look around and see what opportunities or means might exist—any little thing we might have forgotten about—that could yet save us from an otherwise certain death. It is very difficult indeed, but nonetheless, we must try.

And if we stop to look bravely around Wendy now, we will see that there is, in fact, one such thing that we might have overlooked, had we not kept our wits about us. Only it is not such a little thing at all. It is, in fact, a rather substantial Newfoundland dog named

Nana, who has been waiting for quite some time to rejoin the battle and who cannot help but feel that now, at long last, would be the perfect time to do so.

Ignoring Wendy's earlier command—or perhaps deciding that it should no longer apply under these new circumstances, which amounts to the same thing—she thrust herself bodily between her mistress and her enemy, rearing up on her hind legs to snap viciously at his neck.

"Nana, no!" Wendy shouted, and she grabbed desperately at the dog, trying to pull Nana's massive weight out of danger.

"Oh, for the love of heaven, I'm not going to hurt her," the everlost growled, his tone making it perfectly clear that he found the very idea insulting.

"Behave," he said to Nana, and he plucked her away from Wendy as though the Newfoundland monster were nothing more than one of those pampered *bichons* favored by Parisian ladies, tucking her neatly beneath his arm like an overstuffed handbag.

Nana was so surprised by this that she immediately fell limp, blinking and gazing about herself in confusion, trying to comprehend her new situation and searching for her dignity all the while, which she thought she must have dropped somewhere by accident within these last few moments.

"Strange words from the likes of *you*, I dare say," Wendy remarked. She had never been one to shy from danger, and Nana's bravery had inspired her. If they were going to die, which still seemed probable, Wendy could at least choose not to do it like some terrified child, cowering before the headmaster's switch.

"Is it truly so strange not to harm an innocent animal?" he shot back, hoisting Nana a bit higher on the word 'animal,' as though proffering her as a reference. "Are they murdering pets in

the streets now? Is that what your precious England has become? Not that it would surprise me."

Nana remained suspended in midair, looking back and forth between the two, trying to follow the conversation.

"Not *that*," Wendy clarified. "I meant that it's strange for you to invoke the name of heaven, of course. You, one of the everlost, a creature without a soul."

Perhaps, if I can keep him talking long enough, she found herself thinking, *I might discover a way to get us both out of this.* Under the circumstances, it certainly seemed worth a try.

"Ah ha!" he exclaimed, his face lighting up in sudden realization. "A creature without a soul! Ergo, lost forever to heaven! Ergo, 'the everlost'! Well, that explains it, finally. I've always wondered." He smiled at Nana and rubbed her head merrily as though she were sharing in his private revelation.

"But ... how could you not have understood the meaning of your own name?" Wendy blinked in surprise.

"Don't be absurd. It's not *my* name. It's *your* name. *You* made it up. Why would I call *myself* the everlost?" He regarded her the way a child might scrutinize a particularly baffling puzzle lock from the East, as though she were an exotic treasure of unfathomable mystery. "*You* might lose me, to be sure, but one can never lose oneself. The very idea is ridiculous. I'm always right where I am!"

What a truly odd creature, indeed, Wendy thought, but she was not about to say so, given her situation. "But it isn't about having lost your *person*," she said instead. "It's about having lost your *soul.*"

Of course, this was not a very polite thing to say either, now that Wendy thought about it, and she cringed a little, but only on the inside. On the outside she squared her shoulders and looked

him straight in the eye, hoping he wouldn't take enough offense to kill either her or Nana, who still dangled calmly at his left side, supported under her chest by his forearm.

"I haven't lost my soul any more than you've lost yours," he said lightly. If he felt insulted, he didn't show it. "I've only lost my shadow. Have you seen it, by chance?"

"You've lost your shadow?" she asked, bewildered. "But how could you possibly lose a shadow?"

"I don't know," he said, smirking now. "But I've looked for it every single night for months, and I can't find it anywhere." With this, he actually winked, and then Wendy found herself trying not to smile, which annoyed her immensely. As a result, she ended up scowling at him and looking exceedingly cross.

"Oh, come on," he chided. "That was a good joke. You know, because you can't see your shadow at night! Admit it. I'm quite clever."

"I most certainly will not admit any such thing."

"Well, why not? It's the simple truth. All the boys think I'm clever. They tell me so all the time. In fact, they tell me I'm clever *so* often that most days I wander about the island even in the midst of my many responsibilities singing, 'Oh, the cleverness of me!'" He crowed this rapturously, singing the words just to demonstrate.

"What island?" she asked innocently.

"Oh, no you don't," he shot back. "Never mind about the island. Tell me why you won't say I'm clever."

"Well, why should I?" she asked, her voice finally rising with emotion. "Why would you think I would be nice to you at all? You just killed my friends!"

"*You* just tried to kill *me*, and you don't see me holding it against you," he pointed out.

"But you didn't actually die," she retorted, tears finally threatening to overwhelm her. "My friends *did.*"

He regarded her for a long moment without saying anything, holding Nana under his left arm and absently scratching her behind the ears with his right, which Nana had decided to enjoy as long as he wasn't threatening anyone.

"If I fix it, will you admit to my cleverness then?" he asked.

"If you ... what?"

"Come on," he said, putting Nana back down on the ground and turning toward the carnage that the everlost had left behind. "I'll show you. But then you really must admit that I'm clever. It's the least you could do."

CHAPTER
11

W endy stared down at Reginald, the pious man from
Yorkshire. Or rather, she stared down at what *used* to
be Reginald.

His pale body lay battered and broken some distance from the
church. His red hair, splayed out across the grass, appeared gray
beneath the stormy night sky. His narrow features were locked in
a grimace of pain. His right leg—severed nearly clean through.
This last detail appeared to be what had killed him, judging from
the voluminous pool of dark blood in which his body lay.

A single tear fell from Wendy's left eye, making its way gracefully down her cheek and catching at her chin, where it hovered for
a poignant moment, building up its courage before finally letting go
and plummeting away into the great unknown.

"There, there," the everlost said to her, not unkindly.

Only now he was not the only one.

He and Wendy stood side by side over poor Reginald's body,

surrounded by the rest of the everlost, who had arranged themselves in a loose circle around them now that the platoon had
sheltered itself within the ancient walls of Saint Mary.

"He fought bravely," one of them offered, by way of consolation.

"Good form," another agreed.

"What would *you* know about it? *I* killed 'im," a third pouted,
and Wendy shot an accusing glare in his direction. He had a huge
mop of light brown hair that fell across his eyes and just the faint-
est hint of a beard. He puffed out his chest with pride when he
announced himself to be poor Reginald's murderer, but under
Wendy's angry gaze he shrank back into himself, looking at first
confused, and then embarrassed, and then altogether repentant.

"Be quiet, Curly," the brown-haired statue scolded him.

"Sorry, Chief," Curly mumbled, casting his eyes to the earth
and scuffing his toe sheepishly in the grass.

Wendy silently took in this new information. Apparently the
one she had been fighting was their leader.

"Is this the only one?" the leader asked of everyone and no
one in particular.

"Aye, the others made it in there," the first one answered,
thrusting his chin in the general direction of the church.

"How long?"

This time, nobody offered up a reply.

"Curly?" he prompted, trying again. "You may speak long
enough to answer my question. How long ago did this man die?"

"'E was the one what screamed 'is bloody 'ead off," Curly
muttered. He eyed Wendy cautiously, as though concerned that
she might take new offense at this rather graphic admission, but
she continued to stare at him in stony silence, her expression unchanged.

"Oy, make 'er stop lookin' at me like that, Chief!" Curly begged.

"You killed her friend, Curly. She is upset with you. That is how ladies look at you when they are angry. They don't like people killing people."

"Not *ever*?" Curly asked, somewhat incredulous.

They both turned to Wendy for confirmation, who had apparently come to represent all of womankind at some point during the past few moments.

"Not ever," she agreed. "It is wrong to kill people. Didn't your mother teach you that?"

"Never 'ad a mother," Curly admitted, rather shyly.

"You never had a mother?" Wendy exclaimed.

She looked at him again, and for just the very briefest of moments she couldn't help but think of Charlie. She found herself taking pity on the creature, almost forgetting that he had killed poor Reginald. But then, of course, she remembered what he had done, and she became quite vexed all over again.

"That is still no excuse," she declared. "You should not go around killing people, whether or not you ever had a mother to tell you so."

"But 'e was tryin' to kill *me*," Curly protested.

"Yes, well ... he was only defending himself, which is different," Wendy explained. "One is permitted to defend oneself when one is attacked."

"Well, I'm in the clear then," Curly said, his face brightening significantly. "I was defendin' myself! 'E attacked me first! That's a fact, it is!"

Wendy was preparing to launch into a rather angry lecture on territorial boundaries and invasions and the like, but the leader obviously saw it coming and decided to nip it in the bud.

"That's enough, Curly," he said.

"But—"

"That's enough!"

"Aye, Chief," Curly grumbled, and he fell silent again.

"The point is," the leader continued, "that the man hasn't been dead that long, which means there's still hope for him. Curly, put his leg back right and hold it steady."

"Aye, sir." Curly moved toward poor Reginald's body, walking right up to Wendy and clearly expecting her just to step out of the way for him, the rudeness of which made her significantly less inclined to do so.

"Say, 'Excuse me,' Curly," the leader said, sighing.

"What's that?"

"She is waiting for you to say, 'Excuse me, miss.' Once you have done so, she will move."

"Truly?" Curly asked, eyeing Wendy strangely. "Lotta *rules* women come with, eh? Seems a bloody nuisance, if you ask me."

"Curly, I assure you, a good woman is more use than twenty men."

Wendy narrowed her eyes suspiciously at the brown-haired, blue-eyed leader, expecting to find some indication of sarcasm or humor in his expression—or that condescending look men often give to women when they are only saying nice things to try to get themselves out of trouble, even though they don't really believe a word of it.

But there was no such trace to be found. Wendy saw nothing but sincerity in his ice-blue eyes, and she found herself wanting very much to know where he might have come from, or what events he might have witnessed, to make him realize such value in her gender.

"Excuse me, miss," Curly said, interrupting her thoughts.

"Hmm? Oh! Oh, yes, of course," Wendy said, and she took several steps away from poor Reginald so that Curly might have enough room to kneel by his injured leg.

"Huh," Curly grunted. "Looks like you were right, Chief."

"That's why I'm the chief," he replied, nodding solemnly. "There now, hold him steady."

While Curly held poor Reginald's leg back where it was supposed to be, the leader snatched a dagger from his belt and sliced open his own thumb over poor Reginald's mouth, allowing just two drops of blood to fall before removing the knife and allowing the wound to close right over as though it had never been.

"What are you doing?" Wendy exclaimed. "You're going to turn him into a vampire!"

"Don't be ridiculous," the leader growled back. "I'm not a vampire, and I'm certainly not making *him* into one."

Wendy was about to ask more questions when the wound in poor Reginald's bloody leg suddenly disappeared and poor Reginald himself took a huge shuddering gasp and started trying to sit up.

"Away!" the leader shouted. The wings that had disappeared from his back sprouted there once again before her eyes, lengthening and unfurling with a resounding snap, like a sail catching the wind. Before she knew it, the everlost were all rising up together into the night sky and disappearing into the clouds, with only the leader remaining behind, hovering just out of reach.

"He'll be virtually invincible for a day or two," he advised her. "But he'll be perfectly himself after that, so do tell him to be more careful."

Wendy stared up at him with her mouth open, saying nothing. The events of the evening had all proven to be a bit too much for words.

"But now, you must admit that I'm clever," he continued, "and you must tell me your name. You promised!"

Wendy did not recall promising any such thing, but she found herself answering him nonetheless.

"I admit you're clever," she conceded. "And my name is Wendy. Wendy Darling. But now you must tell me yours as well. It's only polite, after all."

"Mine?" he exclaimed, and Wendy thought he looked rather disappointed that she didn't know it already. He began to rise higher into the air, following the others, but he answered her even as he flew away.

"Haven't you heard of me? Why, I'm Peter!" he called out, disappearing into the night. "Peter Pan!"

CHAPTER

12

A nd then he said his name was Peter. Peter Pan."

Wendy had been pacing in front of the hearth in John's private office while she recounted her story, but now she stopped with both hands on her hips, her eyes bright, her face flushed with excitement. She glanced back and forth between John and Michael, each of whom stared back at her mutely, entirely at a loss for words.

They wished they could share with each other a certain look that would say, "What on earth do you make of *that?*" but they didn't dare attempt it while she was watching them.

Instead, they looked down at Nana, asleep near Wendy's feet, as though the dog might wake at any moment and offer up a less controversial view of the night's events. But it had all been too much for her. By the look of things, she was likely to sleep through until morning right there on the rug.

Wendy, on the other hand, was thoroughly awake. She had

come to rest just next to the hearth, and she reached a distracted hand out toward the mantelpiece, commencing her most
contemplative sort of drumming. It was entirely arrhythmic as far
as anyone else could tell, her fingers deftly performing the *grands
battements* of the ballet, accompanied by the secret orchestra of
her own private thoughts.

John, meanwhile, was seated at his desk, his chair having been
relocated as far as reasonably possible away from the still-shuttered
window. His quill stood poised, unmoving, over a nearly pristine
sheet of paper, his elegant script covering barely two lines before
the words trailed off into thin air.

Michael, for his part, had sat through the whole tale perched
on the edge of the same desk, his expression a study in polite,
credulous attention. Each man, in his own way, was trying to
figure out how to respond to Wendy's story without invoking the
dreaded March of the Executioner.

"Why aren't you writing that last bit down?" Wendy demanded. In truth, John had stopped writing several minutes ago, but
she had been so animated in relating her tale that she had only just
now noticed the omission.

"Well—" John began, but Michael interrupted him before he
could make the mistake of blurting out the truth too harshly: that
the events as she had described them were entirely too outlandish
to report up the chain of command. The platoon would look like a
gaggle of superstitious fools.

"What we mean to say is that the Home Office," Michael
tried, "not having seen what we all saw together, by which I mean
a whole host of flying men falling out of the sky, might not be prepared to accept the full gravity of the situation."

"Well, that's ridiculous," Wendy scoffed. "The Home Office
knows perfectly well that the everlost practice all manner of magic.

It's the very reason Nana and I were assigned to the Fourteenth, for heaven's sake. To alert the men to precisely this sort of ... well, to this kind of sorcery, for lack of a better word."

"That's true ..." John reluctantly admitted, but his pen remained right where it was.

"Yes, but there is a difference in ..." Michael tried again, "in the ability of the average mind to accept a flying man—after all, there are many other creatures that fly—and in its ability to accept the idea of casual resurrection, which seems far less ... er ... likely ..."

"Are you trying to say you don't believe me?" Wendy asked, her eyes narrowing at Michael suspiciously.

"No!" he said, perhaps a bit too quickly. "No, of course not. I'm saying no such thing. I'm saying only that the Home Office ... that is ..." Michael had no idea how to elaborate his position without ending up in a world of trouble, so he stopped speaking altogether and cast his eyes toward the floor.

John cleared his throat. "It's always better to offer several accounts rather than relying upon a single eyewitness," he suggested. "I don't suppose that Reginald would attest to these events as you've described them?"

"Well, he was dead for most of it," Wendy pointed out.

"Of course," John agreed, sighing a little. "There is that, yes."

At this point the two men couldn't help but share the look they had been trying so hard to avoid.

"He was *dead*," Wendy insisted.

"Well, I suppose Reginald could corroborate at least that much for us," John mused.

Michael shot him a look that said, "You can't seriously be considering—" But Wendy interrupted his glance before it could finish the thought.

"I don't think he can, actually," she said quietly.

"How's that?" John asked.

Wendy paused a long moment before answering.

"I don't think he remembers it at all," she finally admitted. "By the time he had fully come around, the everlost were gone. He asked me what happened..." At this she lifted her right shoulder in just the barest, most ladylike hint of a shrug.

"You didn't tell him," John surmised.

"Well how *could* I? I mean poor Reginald had *died,* John. I couldn't tell him that! It would only upset him even if he did believe me, and for what purpose?"

"Perhaps so that he might avoid doing it again," Michael muttered.

Wendy glanced at him sideways, pursing just one corner of her mouth—the one with the secret kiss, as it happens—and she raised one genteel eyebrow just a hair above the other.

"Leaving aside the matter of Reginald's death, just for a moment," John said, clearing his throat again, "there are other concerns when it comes to an official report. A report being quite different, you know, than casual conversation."

"I've read enough reports, John," Wendy retorted, "to know the difference very well, I dare say. There is nothing wrong whatsoever in what I've said."

"I don't disagree, of course," John was quick to reassure her. "I don't disagree at all. However..."

Wendy's defiant eyebrow shot up at the word 'however,' and John gulped nervously. But he forged ahead nonetheless.

"However, there is a difference between stating the facts incorrectly—which, again, I agree you could not have done, knowing you as I do—and *interpreting* those facts to imply various conclusions, a practice which falls more properly within the realm of hypothesis than observation."

"And what, pray tell, would you say that I have *hypothesized*?"

"Pray tell," Michael echoed, smirking at John with the confidence of a man who has just been catapulted miraculously out of trouble by someone else who has had the great misfortune of stumbling into it.

"Well, for instance," John said, looking more uncomfortable by the moment, "you've suggested that the everlost did not attempt to enter Saint Mary because this Peter Pan creature had decided to impress you. But isn't it also possible, if not even more likely, that they were turned away by the sanctity of holy ground?"

John took a deep breath and continued before Wendy could object.

"The *fact* is that they departed without further aggression. The *reason* for that, however, is subject to interpretation, and is therefore not proper to include in a formal report."

"You have also," he said even more quickly, as Wendy began tapping out the dreaded March of the Executioner on the mantelpiece, "suggested that this everlost raised Reginald from the dead, when it is also at least *possible*—and I ask you to maintain an open mind here—that Reginald had merely lost consciousness due to the exertions of battle, only to awaken when the everlost began to treat him roughly."

"He awoke and healed his own severed leg spontaneously, I suppose," Wendy suggested, "or had you forgotten that particular *fact* already?"

To this, John made no reply.

"Perhaps if you had written it all down ..." Michael added, tapping the paper helpfully.

"I know what I saw," Wendy asserted, "and the severed leg is a fact. It is equally factual that Peter Pan raised poor Reginald from

the dead. If your final report says anything different, John Abbot, it is solely because you lack faith in me and for no other reason."

Wendy ceased her drumming abruptly, crossed her arms over her chest, glared defiantly into John's eyes (an expression which had the unfortunate effect of hiding her secret kiss entirely), and raised her eyebrow in an outright challenge.

"But, Wendy," John protested, "of course I believe you. I just ... A report of this nature will surely be read by Captain Hook himself. Are you absolutely certain—"

"All the more reason to make sure that it is both accurate and complete," Wendy declared. "I shall begin again at the beginning, and this time I expect you to write it all down, leaving nothing out. Are you ready?"

"Ready," John said with a sigh, and at long last he touched his pen to the paper before him.

Miss Wendy Darling, he wrote, *the diviner assigned to the Fourteenth Platoon of the Nineteenth Light Dragoons, having come into direct contact with the everlost within the immediate environs of Dover Castle, and having therein witnessed certain magical events, does hereby offer and affirm this missive, swearing to the testimony set forth herein under solemn oath before God and King.*

CHAPTER

13

Wendy couldn't sleep. She lay on her simple cot and stared up at the bare ceiling, a thousand thoughts and memories swirling through her mind like a rainbow of glittering debutantes, each new idea more enticing than the last, all jostling for her attention.

The everlost! Sword fighting! Death! Magic!

And, of course, Captain Hook.

Thanks to her gender, Wendy had been assigned to her own quarters in Dover Castle. It was only a humble servant's room, with rough-woven baskets for her clothing and no window, but still—it was a luxury compared to the overcrowded nursery at the almshouse.

And it gave her a quiet place to think.

About the everlost. About poor Reginald lying on the battlefield. About a creature with perfectly sculpted features who could bring men back to life. But more than any of these, about Captain Hook.

And about everything that one name could finally mean for her.

Captain James Hook was the most illustrious captain in all the ranks of the Home Office—commander of *The Dragon*, a Bellona-class, two-deck, seventy-four-gun fighting ship, sold "out of service" in 1784 to enter the clandestine fight against the everlost. No captain had done more than Hook to defend England's shores against the scourge of the blood drinkers.

To be assigned to his ship, to be assigned to *The Dragon* herself! Wendy had never even allowed herself to imagine it.

She tried very hard to keep her dreams realistic, you see, so as to have some hope of achieving them. Her early years had taught her that, as a defense against the cruelty of life—to dream in small, manageable increments. Learn sword fighting. Memorize the stars. Perform scientific experiments. Stop daydreaming about life at sea, and attend to the here and now.

It wasn't that she had given up her plans. Far from it. She just forced herself to keep her eyes focused on what she had to do today, and no farther.

Over the past year at Dover Castle, her dreams had gone something like this: Rise through the ranks of the Home Office over several years, slowly but steadily. Earn (eventually) a humble position on a small scouting vessel—as a diviner if she were lucky, or as a galley maid if that were all she could manage. See what she could of the English coast, and form new plans from there.

Never in her wildest speculations had she imagined sending a report to Captain Hook himself, let alone a report so monumental that he couldn't possibly ignore it. Yet even now, a young man on horseback was racing through the night, carrying that report, *her* report, across the English countryside, headed for London.

Carrying her destiny. She was sure of it.

And she would be prepared for it when the answer came.

She would need a second pair of fighting breeches. And a proper dress, of course. For her introduction. And a luggage chest. She would have to ask John for leave to shop in Dover tomorrow.

Not that she could afford anything fancy. The Home Office paid its female diviners poorly, to say the least. But her needs were simple, and she had saved what she could. If she spent it carefully, it would be enough.

There were plenty of sailing families in Dover. And she knew people. People who had been kind enough to loan her books. People who shared her interest in science. She would ask around to see who might have a secondhand chest they would be willing to sell. And a simple day dress from last season. Something no longer quite in fashion, but still more than suitable for her needs.

To wear when she met Captain Hook.

Wendy rolled onto her side and reached one arm down for Nana, who was sleeping peacefully on the floor next to the cot. "This is our chance, Nana," she whispered, gently scratching the dog behind the ears. "I just know it."

For one moment, she allowed herself to imagine it—standing on the deck of *The Dragon*, with the wind in her hair and the ocean all around her, as far as the eye could see. One precious moment of indulgence, but no more. Then she forced herself to focus on more immediate plans.

How could she get to Dover without letting John and Michael know what she had in mind? What excuse should she use when purchasing a second pair of men's breeches? And whom should she approach about a dress? Should she wear the new garment when asking about the sea chest, or would she get a better price in humbler clothing?

Thoughts of tomorrow pushed her bigger dreams aside—allowing Wendy to forget also, as she finally drifted off to sleep, the intoxicating scent of magic. And a haunting pair of ice-blue eyes.

D over! Defending London has proven difficult enough! Now they're attacking *Dover*? These outlying platoons are supposed to be advance scouts at best, not true fighting battalions. We don't have the manpower to defend all of England against this wretched scourge!"

The first thing one noticed about Captain James Hook, without exception, was his exceedingly fashionable mane of shoulder-length black hair—the foremost pride of an undeniably handsome countenance. He wore it pulled back at the moment in a loose, rugged sweep that framed his aristocratic nose and squared-off chin to the best possible advantage.

The second thing one noticed, to be sure, was the steel hook that had taken the place of his right hand. But make no mistake about it, even this unusual appurtenance could not upstage the hair.

"At least the scouts were in place, thank heaven. We learned of the attack immediately, and without any deaths or kidnappings to frighten the populace."

This reassurance was uttered by Sir William Collingwood, the head of the Home Office's covert mobilization against the everlost. He had been granted knighthood by King George III, in recognition of his exemplary career and service to his country. His *coiffure*, however, was entirely ordinary and did not hold a candle to Hook's.

"No *permanent* deaths, anyway," Hook growled. "Honestly, where are we finding these sorry diviners? Can we do no better than this?"

At only twenty-four years of age, Hook was a ferocious tactician. His brilliant military gambits had turned the tide of many a battle in England's favor. There were whispers that he would make admiral before he turned thirty. He had no patience for fools.

Sir William, by contrast, was thirty-seven and an excellent strategist in his own right, but far more cautious in his methods. Where Hook was bold, Sir William was cunning. Where Hook was brave, Sir William was wise. Together, they had held back the evil tide of magic from His Majesty's shores.

By any means necessary.

"It is regrettable, of course," Sir William admitted, "but it cannot be helped. Many of them hail from the countryside, which even the long arm of science has still barely touched. Besides which, they are women, so of course they hold little aptitude for any advanced subjects, let alone empirical reasoning."

"Our best warning system," Hook lamented. "Women and dogs."

"If only the dogs were more reliable," Sir William commented.

"The same might be said of the women," Hook quipped, holding up the offending report and brandishing it about with his good hand.

Sir William chuckled. "Be that as it may, I think we must take the bones of the report seriously. The everlost attacked Dover Castle, to be repelled only by the holy grace of Saint Mary. We were lucky. This time."

"Agreed. But we're on the defensive far too often. We can't depend on luck forever. We *must* find a way to strike at their very heart. We *must* learn where they're hiding! Did you see this bit about the island?"

"Yes!" Sir William exclaimed. "I noticed that! At least this Lieutenant Abbot had the wherewithal to include the reference. Assuming it's accurate, of course."

"We need to learn more, to question them directly about the encounter." Hook paced restlessly back and forth, which was how he did his best thinking. "Especially the woman. Where is this island? Did the everlost give it a name? A direction? A distance? Guided by a man's superior intellect, her memory will no doubt be far more fruitful. We must glean the truth within the feminine hysterics."

William nodded, having come to the same conclusion. "I couldn't agree more. I'll order them to London at once."

"Women and dogs," Hook repeated, finally coming to rest and shaking his head sadly. "Women and bloody dogs."

CHAPTER
15

The reply to John's report arrived in the evening, two days after the everlost had stormed the shores of Dover. The platoon was enjoying a late supper in the barracks mess when a government courier burst in, brandishing a sealed missive. Its pristine white gleam proclaimed the wealth and importance of its source even before the boy, who appeared to be twelve or thirteen years old, could announce it.

"Message for Lieutenant Abbot!" he called out, but his voice cracked at the end, followed by a subdued eruption of coughing throughout the mess.

The Home Office did not entrust important dispatches to just anyone. The boy was obviously the son of someone important, and no one wanted to offend that someone, whoever they might be. This is why the men hid their amusement by coughing behind their napkins rather than laughing out loud—which, after all, is the real reason napkins were invented.

"Here," John replied, rising from his seat.

The boy raced to him, held the letter out in the air, and buckled over to rest his other hand on his thigh, his chest heaving.

"They told me ... to see that ... it got to you directly ... sir," the boy reported, his head still bent toward the floor as he tried to catch his breath. "In person, that is. To be opened immediately. It's from Sir William Collingwood."

At this, John's eyes opened wide, and he looked to both Michael and Wendy across the table. When John didn't take the letter right away, the boy looked up and followed his gaze, which was how he finally noticed the presence of a woman in the midst of the platoon.

"My apologies, miss!" he exclaimed. He snatched his hat from his head, stood upright, and bowed. "I should have taken better notice of the room."

"That's quite all right," Wendy assured him. She rose to offer the boy a polite curtsey. "Matters of military importance cannot always accommodate civilian propriety. I am here on official assignment, so I understand the urgency."

"You're the diviner, then!" he blurted out. "You're Wendy Darling!"

"I am," she agreed, her expression clearly registering her surprise.

"Well, then ..." the boy trailed off, looking around the room at the rest of the platoon, aware that he now held their rapt attention. "Perhaps you'd best just read the note," he finished, lowering his voice and turning to address this last comment to John.

"Of course. I'll take it to my study," the lieutenant replied, plucking the note from the boy's hand and hiding an uncharacteristic grin beneath his habitual veneer of decorum. (He had, unfortunately, left his napkin on the table.) "In the meantime,

I'm sure you're hungry. You've had a long ride from London. Please, take full advantage of our hospitality. I'll look over this message and then send for you if I need you."

"Thank you, sir," the boy said, eyeing the plates of roasted quail and fresh-baked rolls. "I *am* hungry, I don't mind admitting."

"Michael? Wendy?" John waved the boy toward the serving platters with one hand and held up the sealed note with the other. "If you would both join me, I have no doubt this reply will impact us all."

"Well? What does it say?" Wendy demanded as soon as John had shut the office door behind them.

"Why, I don't know, of course. I have to read it first," he said.

John had always been an extremely literal sort of man. If you had said to him, for example, "Isn't it about time for supper?" hoping that he would take your meaning and offer you a bite to eat, he would instead have opened his watch to see whether you were correct. It was not that he wanted to deprive you of your meal if you were wrong. He was just trying to answer honestly.

Proceeding to the business at hand, he cracked open the wax seal and began to read, holding the expensive paper with a care that bordered on reverence, his eyes silently scanning the page while Wendy and Michael watched him intently.

At long last (which was in truth only a few brief moments but which felt like forever to Wendy) John looked up from the sheet, his expression carefully neutral. He glanced back and forth from Wendy to Michael, saying nothing.

"And?" Wendy demanded.

"It looks like we're going to London," John said.

"I knew it!" Wendy exclaimed. "What's gotten into you, John? This is wonderful news! We're being called to London to report directly to Sir William! Perhaps even to meet with Captain Hook, himself! Why aren't you smiling?"

But John didn't answer, sharing a look with Michael instead.

"Because we aren't all going," Michael finally told her, tilting his head and looking at Wendy with a small grin of resignation.

"What?" Wendy demanded. "Don't be silly, Michael. Of course we're all going."

"He's right, I'm afraid," John confirmed. "*I* wrote the report, and *you* are the eyewitness. They want us both in London—to answer their questions, I'm sure. But Michael ..." John trailed off, unwilling to say the words aloud.

"With John in London, someone has to lead the men here," Michael explained, his voice gentle. "I'm the platoon sergeant, so that job falls to me. It's just how things are. Especially now."

No one had slept easily after the attack. (No one except Nana, that is, who had just now stayed behind in the barracks mess, hoping the newcomer might be a dependable source of table scraps.) John had posted watches all through that night and the next, and Wendy had remained keenly aware of every new scent in the sea-touched air. Although there had been no sign yet of their enemy's return, the entire platoon remained on edge.

Michael was right, Wendy realized. Someone had to stay behind to lead the men. But it didn't make the news any easier to bear.

"It isn't fair," she protested.

"Fairness has nothing to do with it," Michael assured her. "Only one of us can go. If I were the one heading to London, then it would be John staying here, and I wouldn't like that any better."

"But you'll miss the whole adventure!" she cried, and she pouted so prettily on his behalf that Michael thought he would have forgone a dozen grand adventures just to see her look at him that way each time.

"Nonsense," he said kindly. "I'll have *you* to tell me everything just as soon as you return. And if I know you at all, Wendy Darling, hearing about it will be a hundred times better than being there. You've always told the best stories. All the men say so."

"They do? Do you mean it?" Wendy asked, resting one hand lightly on his arm and staring up at him in the most fetching way.

"They most assuredly do say so, and I most assuredly do mean it," he confessed, looking down at her fondly. "But I shall miss you while you are away, and I mean that, too. So you must promise to think of me the whole time you are in London."

Hearing him say so, Wendy realized immediately that she would miss him very much as well. So even though it was far from proper, she threw her arms around him and hugged him with all her might.

"There, you see? It's worth staying behind already," Michael murmured in her ear, and Wendy couldn't help but blush a little.

"Besides," he said, as she finally stepped away, "you won't be gone more than a few days, and then we'll have all the time in the world. It's not as though you'll be traveling to London once a fortnight."

"I'm quite sure you're right," John grumbled. "With my luck, I'll never leave Dover again after today. We'll all be stuck here until we retire."

"Well then you should try to enjoy the one trip you're going to get," Michael said, grinning wryly. "Godspeed, John. Take care of her, won't you?"

"You may count on it," John promised.

But Wendy had no intention of being stuck in Dover forever. *One trip is all I will need,* she vowed to herself. *One chance to impress Captain Hook—to convince him that I don't belong in Dover. I know I can do it.*

Which is the problem, of course, with the magic of intention. One must always be specific.

CHAPTER
16

L ondon!
 Wendy and John reached the outskirts of the city late in the evening, more than twenty-four hours after the arrival of their orders (travel being what it was.)

"Does it feel good to be home?" John asked, as the carriage forged its way through London's bustling streets.

"Home?" Wendy echoed. Her words were soft, more murmured than spoken, almost lost in the clamor of the evening's final passersby, the clanking of the street peddlers packing up their wares, and the rickety clatter of the carriage itself. "I don't suppose I know where that is, but it isn't here."

"Surely you must have fond memories though," John suggested gently. He hated to see her look even remotely sad. "Of the city. Of your childhood here."

"Of course!" she said immediately, perking up a little. "Of studying under Mr. Equiano. And with Charlie. Navigation and

fencing and mathematics. And so many books! But a memory isn't a home." Her voice fell away again, so that he almost missed what she said at the last: "You can't live in your memories."

"I suppose not," he agreed, and the look on her face was so poignant, the secret kiss in the far corner of her mouth so carefully tucked away, that he did not ask her about it again.

It was surprising, she thought, how much could change in a year. Not that London itself was especially different, but the streets that had once felt familiar now seemed strange ... distant. As though she had never truly belonged here at all.

Which, she supposed, she hadn't.

She tried to imagine dropping by the almshouse for a visit. But Charlie was gone, of course. And Mrs. Healey would have new babies to hold. New mouths to feed. Besides, it wasn't as though Wendy could tell anyone what she had been doing for the past year. Not even Olaudah Equiano, no matter how much she might want to.

He would have questions. Simple, friendly questions about her life and her journeys in the world. But in asking them, he would introduce a conversation she had no idea how to approach. It wasn't until that moment that she realized how truly John and Michael and Nana had become her only family—the only people she could be herself with.

She turned to John and smiled then, for no reason that he could see, which made him blush and drop his head, raising his left thumbnail to examine it intently, turning it this way and that, as though some speck of lint had just now lodged beneath it, in sudden and desperate need of extracting.

Fortunately, he was saved from further embarrassment by their arrival.

The headquarters of the Nineteenth Light Dragoons were lo-

cated in an unassuming building in the heart of London's bustling trade district, where the comings and goings of its various affiliates would not be considered noteworthy by the general public. The gray stone edifice squatted unobtrusively between a fine boot maker's establishment and a men's tailoring shop, looking so unfashionable by contrast as to be held in general disdain by the average passerby, which helped a great deal in deflecting any unwanted attention.

It was so late by the time the carriage came to a stop, the street now all but deserted for the night, that John and Wendy both expected to be assigned to their respective sleeping quarters and ushered off to bed until morning. But this only shows how little they knew of the illustrious Captain James Hook and the fervor with which he pursued the responsibilities of his command.

It was not at all uncommon for him to work well into the night in his efforts to track the enemy's movements, arranging various reported sightings by both place and time, hoping to find some pattern that might lead him to a point of origin, but always to no avail.

One entire wall of his private office consisted of floor-to-ceiling bookshelves, while the other three displayed an overwhelming collection of maps—so many, in fact, that they had all come to overlap each other, making such a jumble of the world's geography as to place the tigers of India within the deserts of Egypt, or the elephants of Africa within the American plains.

Only Hook knew anymore what any of it meant, and he wasn't the sort to share his thoughts with anyone until he was ready.

This, then, was the scene into which Wendy now entered, with John by her side, to meet the great James Hook for the very first time. She gazed about herself in wonder, feeling as though she must have fallen asleep back in the carriage, quite without realizing it,

and had embarked upon one of those impossible dreams in which one walks directly from one's bedroom into the Taj Mahal, even though one's real bedroom and the real Taj Mahal are, of course, located nowhere near each other.

She had barely begun to take in the cartographical chaos when Captain Hook himself rose from his desk to greet them, and in that sudden moment she had eyes for nothing else. He wore his hair loose, as he usually did after the dinner hour had passed, and its soft black cascade provided such a contrast to his chiseled features as to take her breath away.

"Lieutenant Abbot, I presume," he said, returning John's salute with his steel hook.

"Yes, sir. And I present to you Miss Wendy Darling, diviner of the Fourteenth Platoon of the Nineteenth Light Dragoons. Sir."

"Yes, very good, lieutenant. That will be all." Hook stared at John, clearly waiting for him to leave.

"I... yes, sir. Of course. I was told you wished to speak with us immediately. My apologies."

"Not 'us,'" Hook said before they could turn to go. "Her."

"I'm sorry?"

"You said, 'us.' Implying both of you. I am correcting that misapprehension. I wish to speak with only one of you immediately. Specifically, Miss Darling. She will stay. You are dismissed."

Throughout this conversation, Captain Hook had not so much as glanced in Wendy's direction, and she found her initial fascination with the man turning quickly to annoyance. She had not imagined that a well-bred gentleman could be so ill-mannered.

It doesn't matter, she reminded herself. *You need him to like you. You need to impress him. Be polite.*

"Don't worry, John. I'll be quite all right," she said. Her voice

remained cheerful, but her eyebrow drew itself up a bit, watching Hook with just the smallest hint of mute disapproval.

"Yes, well … I'll be right outside if you need me."

"And why would she need you?" Hook demanded sharply. "You have delivered her safely into my care. Your job is done. I am a decorated captain in His Majesty's military service. Do you imagine me incapable of protecting this woman within my own private office? By all means, speak freely, lieutenant. I'm genuinely curious."

His voice, however, was cold and hard and held not an ounce of curiosity within it, so despite Hook's words, John held his tongue.

"Chaperones are for parks and parlors, Lieutenant Abbot," Hook finally continued. "This is a military debriefing. You may wait for us in the hallway, but only because I wish to question you as soon as I am done questioning *her*. *Not* because we are, in any way, in need of your oversight. Have I made myself clear?"

"Yes, sir."

"Then you are dismissed. Again."

"Yes, sir."

John pivoted on his heel and strode out of the room, shutting the door behind him, leaving Hook to glare suspiciously at Wendy, and leaving Wendy to smile innocently back at Hook, the two of them locked in a battle of wills that already had both the tigers and the elephants running for cover.

iss Darling," Hook began, "I have called you to London because I have several questions regarding the details of Lieutenant Abbot's report. I understand you had the rare opportunity to speak with the everlost directly."

He did not return to his chair. Instead, he plucked John's letter from the desk with his good left hand and held it up, staring at her expectantly, as though his every statement were to be taken as a question until further notice. There was no attempt at civility, no offer of a seat, not even so much as a cup of tea after her long journey. But Wendy was determined to make a good impression, whether he deserved the effort or not.

"I did," she affirmed.

She met his regard with a confident, upward tilt of her chin, and discovered in doing so that his eyes were the exact blue of the forget-me-not. This irked her considerably. It wasn't right that such an indecent man should have such a memorable gaze. But the

very thought of it reminded her of her promise to Michael: to tell him the entire story of her London adventure just as soon as she saw him again. Like it or not, Hook was critical to the tale.

She scrunched up her mouth, until the secret kiss in the corner was pressed as small as possible, and she set about memorizing the man. His sparkling hair. His handsome countenance. His aristocratic posture. His dashing, knee-high boots. She wanted to be able to describe him accurately. (Or perhaps with just the slightest bit of exaggeration, but only for the purpose of accentuating the truth, which is the hallmark of any good raconteur.)

"What is it?" Hook demanded.

"Pardon?" she asked, continuing her examination by scrutinizing the polished steel hook that had taken the place of his right hand.

"Does it disturb you?" he asked stiffly. "I can remove it if you find it unsettling, but you might find its removal to be even more so."

"What? Oh!" she exclaimed, suddenly realizing how rude she herself was being, to stare openly at his disfigurement. "No, of course not! I mean, whichever is your preference, of course. It doesn't disturb me in the slightest. If anything, it is a badge of honor. A testament to your dedication in His Majesty's service."

She drew herself up straight and looked firmly into his forget-me-not eyes. Remembering at last whom she was speaking to, and remembering his distinguished position (not to mention his *ship*), she resolved again to overlook his inconsiderate nature.

"Yes, well," he said, making an obvious effort to recompose himself, "my intention this evening, Miss Darling, is to walk you step by step through your encounter with the everlost. Although your memory of the event has omitted several critical details while embellishing others—which happens even to *men*, by the way,

under the stress of battle, and is therefore only to be expected in *your* case—direct questioning should produce a more accurate account."

Wendy clenched her jaw. *The ship. Remember the ship.*

"Of course," she finally managed to reply.

"Very good." Hook's eyes fell to the report, scanning the lines of John's careful penmanship. "Here. Describe for me your initial sense that the everlost were present. What warning, or warnings, made you aware of them?"

"There was a scent in the air," Wendy said immediately. "It smelled like green and the taste of pickles."

"I'm sorry, it smelled like ... green?"

"Yes. And the taste of pickles. And like a clear pool of water in the back of a cave on a hot summer day. All of those together. That's all in the report, by the way. That part is quite accurate, I should think."

Hook shifted his jaw to the left and blinked at Wendy twice, watching her suspiciously. She returned his gaze without a word, her feminine smile unimpeachable. Even her eyebrow had agreed to hold its tongue—complicit, at least for the time being, in her show of innocence.

"So, you knew they were coming because you could smell them," he finally said.

"No, I don't think so. I mean, yes, that's what they smelled like. Even up close. But I don't see how I could have been smelling them directly. They were still in the clouds, you see. And the men couldn't smell it at all. Just Nana and myself."

"Nana?" Hook asked, clearly perplexed.

"Oh, 'Sheba,' you would call her. The platoon's dog. I call her Nana. Because she takes such good care of us. She's listed in the report as 'Sheba,' of course, which is the name on her official papers."

"I see," Hook said, and his lips twitched with just a hint of smugness before he asked his next question, which was this: "And how do you know that the dog could smell this same scent? How do you know she wasn't just responding to your own unease?"

"I don't, of course," Wendy replied. "Which is why, if I might say so, written reports are always preferable to verbal ones. In a written report, one must consider one's words very carefully before committing them to paper. My *written* report only describes the dog's actions. It does not assume anything about her motivation."

Hook furrowed his brow and held up the report again, rereading the pertinent section and then frowning.

"Well, Miss Darling, your report also suggests that the everlost refused to follow the platoon into Saint Mary due to their sudden infatuation with you. Given the holy nature of Saint Mary in Castro, surely even you can see another, more likely explanation."

"I most certainly did *not* claim any such infatuation," Wendy protested, her cheeks flushing. "I said only that they were fascinated with me, which is another thing entirely. It was as though some of them had never met a woman before! They were curious about me, and Peter Pan promised to save poor Reginald on my behalf. *That* is why they did not pursue the men."

"He promised to save the dead man," Hook stated, and his eyes were cold and hard now, glittering in the lamplight. It was another question that was not really a question, his voice dripping with condescension.

"He did," Wendy said. Her jaw thrust forward at a decidedly stubborn angle. "And then he accomplished it. He healed poor Reginald's leg and returned him to life. Just as it says in the report."

"After severing it clean through and killing him first, lest we forget," Hook growled, and his eyes flashed dangerously, a warning that Wendy did not find herself inclined to heed.

"It was a battle," Wendy found herself arguing, "as you said yourself. Yes, his men killed poor Reginald. But still, Peter didn't have to save him afterward. He was the enemy, and Peter showed him mercy."

Hook sucked in a sharp breath and stood perfectly still for a long moment. When he spoke again, his voice was utterly devoid of emotion, every word pronounced with clipped, military precision.

"The everlost made us the enemy, Miss Darling, when they attacked our homeland. They made us the enemy when they kidnapped our children. They made us the enemy when they killed my men, sending their bodies home for their mothers and their widows to bury. And Pan made himself the enemy when he cut off my hand. As you can see, he did not show me any mercy on that day."

Wendy gasped as he raised the steel hook before him, the lamplight gleaming over its polished surface, reflecting her own visage back to her, wild and distorted by the curve of the metal.

"Do not be fooled by a single kindness shown to a pretty young woman whose favor he might wish to curry for any number of ignoble reasons," Hook finished quietly. "Pan is the enemy of His Majesty's Kingdom of Great Britain, and you would do well to remember it."

Wendy had not known it was Peter who had severed Hook's hand from his body, but after what she had seen at Dover, she knew he was capable of it. The miraculous resurrection of poor Reginald had also made her forget—at least temporarily—the many reports from London of kidnappings and missing children. And of the dead who had tried to protect them.

Staring now at Hook's cold, steel hand, she thought back on the first time she had seen Peter Pan, when he and his band of everlost had only just descended from the clouds. She remembered

his wolflike canines, shining in the darkness. And the hardness in his ice-blue eyes. The captain was right—she had forgotten, in the charm of Pan's manners and the allure of his magic, that he was their enemy.

She would not forget again.

Their conversation afterward veered toward Peter's words that night, which Wendy provided as directly and exactly as she could remember—managing, with extreme effort, not to comment on Hook's continuing disparagement of her gender. She realized at some point that he didn't even know he was insulting her, but she wasn't sure whether that made matters better or considerably worse.

Yes, she told him, Pan mentioned an island. No, he did not give the name of the island, nor a distance, nor any particular direction for it. Yes, she was quite certain. Yes, even she, a mere woman, was familiar with compass points and with the essentials of land measurement.

Yes, she understood also that resurrection was medically impossible, as was the restoration of a fully severed limb. Yes, scientifically impossible. Yes, empirically impossible. Nevertheless, that was precisely what had occurred. Yes, she was absolutely certain. No, her feminine sensibilities were not commonly subject to either shock or hysteria.

The interrogation went on for a surprisingly long time until Wendy was fighting just to keep her eyes open, having eventually slumped (still uninvited, mind you) into an armchair, propping her

head up on one hand in a decidedly unladylike manner and watching Hook pace tirelessly back and forth, his energy never flagging.

No matter how many questions she answered, however, Hook never seemed satisfied, and she began to wonder whether he could tell that she was holding back certain details, the divulgence of which she felt would only lead to trouble.

She did not mention, for example, that she had disobeyed a direct order in following the men out to Saint Mary. She also failed to mention the doffing of her dress and her protracted sword fight, both of which she had agreed with John and Michael to omit from the report as a matter of propriety. A decision for which she was now exceedingly grateful.

Throughout their discussion, Hook's countenance remained devoid of any further expression, so she had no way of knowing whether he was taking any of her answers seriously. She suspected, however, that he was not. By the end of it, she couldn't help but feel as though the entire exercise had been a lost cause from the very beginning.

There was no way she could ever impress the man. Her gender alone had blinded him thoroughly to her abilities. She had finally met the renowned captain of *The Dragon*, and what did she have to show for it? Nothing but a sympathetic tale to tell Michael when she returned to her post, destined to stare wistfully out to sea for all the rest of her days.

"Thank you, Miss Darling," Hook said finally, interrupting her sad reverie. "This first interview has been quite productive."

Wendy sat up straight.

"I'm sorry," she said carefully. "Did you say, 'first' interview?"

"Why yes, of course," he assured her. "Surely you did not expect us to extract all the important details of your encounter in a single evening?"

"I had thought your questions to be quite thorough," she replied, which was a rather delicate way of phrasing it, given what she wanted to say—which doesn't bear repeating.

"Be that as it may," he said, nodding at what he believed to be a compliment, "there is more to be discovered here, I think. New developments may arise over the coming weeks—"

"Weeks?" she interrupted, but she was speaking mostly to herself.

"Yes, weeks. As I was saying, new developments may arise over the coming weeks that could raise new questions. And your insights, given your direct contact with the everlost, could prove to be more valuable than you think."

You mean more valuable than you *think*, Wendy thought bitterly, but of course she didn't say this out loud either.

"To that end," he finished, "I should like you to stay reasonably close to this office for the immediate future. Accommodations will, of course, be provided."

"But, I—"

"Miss Darling," he said darkly, "the direct order of a superior officer is not a matter for negotiation. Have I made myself clear?"

"Perfectly," she replied quietly, and she meant it in more ways than one. But at least she could try to make the best of it.

I suppose I can do some good while I'm here, she thought to herself. *The Foundling Hospital can always use an extra hand. And perhaps I might pay a quick visit to Mr. Equiano, if I can figure out how to handle the niceties. James Hook will realize soon enough that my account of the incident isn't going to change.*

But as Wendy was soon to discover, Hook's idea of "reasonably close" and Wendy's idea of "reasonably close" were not, in fact, reasonably close to each other at all.

CHAPTER

18

H ertfordshire!"
This was the first word Wendy spoke when she stepped off the coach at St. Albans. It was also the first word she had spoken when she had stepped *onto* the coach back in London, and it was the only word she had spoken since.

There was simply nothing else to say.

Hook was sending her to stay at his family's estate in Hertfordshire. Where she would be safer than she would be in London, he explained, and yet still close enough that he could speak with her again as new questions arose.

Safer! The very idea that he should need to protect her was absurd. Was she not an agent of the Home Office, attached to the Fourteenth Platoon of the Nineteenth Light Dragoons? Hook could have at *least* let her join a platoon in London until he was ready to return her to Dover! Now she would be stuck in Hertfordshire, trapped like some delicate hothouse flower beneath an

insipid garden cloche—with no platoon at all (not to mention no *ship*), and even farther away from Dover than she was before.

Wendy hated this plan.

Nevertheless, that was where she was going, and there was nothing whatsoever that she could do about it. To disobey him would have meant an immediate dismissal from the Nineteenth Light Dragoons, and then she would *never* get back to John and Michael and Nana, let alone win her place on a ship. Doomed instead to take the first miserable position she could find. Probably as a milliner.

No. That alternative was simply unacceptable.

All she could do, in the end, was keep her chin up and hope that Hook decided sooner rather than later that she had nothing useful to tell him. But that didn't mean she had to like it. She had boarded the coach in London with a grim countenance indeed, and her mood had not improved since.

Throughout the entire journey, she had sat across from a slightly plump woman with a kind smile, impeccable manners, and an impossibly large yet fashionably debonair yellow-feathered hat. The woman had prattled on cheerfully about her husband and her children and her first grandchild on the way, beaming with pride, to which Wendy had smiled as best she could. She even nodded at the most important bits whenever she felt prompted to do so, her expression gracious but distant, her eyebrow lying low, lost in its own quiet melancholy.

But whenever the woman began to hope that Wendy might offer some comment upon her soliloquy—some word of encouragement or approval regarding her husband or her children or her grandchild-to-be—Wendy would lean forward as though preparing to share some observation of the utmost importance and would say again, both eyebrows raised momentarily for emphasis,

"Hertfordshire!" before slumping back in her seat once more, the moment having passed.

Then the woman would tsk-tsk in sympathy and reach forward to pat Wendy's knee, waiting politely to see whether she might have anything more to offer on the subject. When she did not, the woman would launch once again into a litany of her own invention, which made the hours pass by a bit more quickly for them both, truth be told, despite Wendy's lack of enthusiasm.

"Miss Darling? Miss Wendy Darling?"

The boy who approached her as she disembarked in St. Albans could not have been older than twelve, but he wore the livery of a coachman nonetheless.

"I'm Wendy," she admitted, sighing a little.

"Colin Medcalf, at your service," he replied. "They sent me to get you."

"So you're one of Hook's cousins or nephews or some such, I suppose?" She tried very hard to keep any trace of annoyance from her voice, as it was hardly this boy's fault whom he was related to, but she found the effort more difficult than she would have liked.

"Oh, no, miss. The family lives up in Yorkshire. The estate here is more of a hunting retreat. It's just the staff most of the time. I'm the cook's son. It was Huxley who sent me."

"Well then, I'm very pleased to meet you, Colin," she said, her voice warming considerably. "But who is Huxley?"

"Oh, sorry. He's the butler. He runs the place. He's good people, miss. Don't you worry. You'll like him. Everybody likes Huxley."

"I'm sure I will," she agreed. "And who's this then?"

The 'who' was a dog—a Dalmatian, to be precise. She had slunk up behind the boy and was now hiding behind his legs, craning her neck around them to look up at Wendy with interest.

"Athena!" the boy exclaimed, following Wendy's gaze and discovering the dog behind him. "You know better than that! If you're here with me, who's guarding the carriage?"

Athena's ears pricked up at her name, but she made no move to return to her post. As there was nothing in the carriage worth stealing at the moment, and as it was so very interesting to meet new people, she couldn't help but feel that this was a much better use of her time.

"Athena's our coach dog," Colin explained. "*She's supposed to guard the coach when we go places.*" He said this last with a distinct rise in volume, and he stared at the dog as he said it, but the comment didn't seem to faze Athena in the slightest.

"Perhaps she isn't meant to be a coach dog," Wendy suggested. "People don't always end up being what's expected of them. Look at me, for example. Nobody thought I could be a … a nurse, and yet here I am."

She had wanted to say that no one had thought she could be a member of a secret platoon, fighting supernatural forces in the name of the king. But technically, no one thought that to this very day, as it wasn't something she was allowed to admit to anyone who thought otherwise.

"Well, that's all well and good for a person, I suppose," Colin countered, "but a dog's supposed to be what a dog's supposed to be."

Wendy knew, however, that sometimes the best way to win an argument was not to engage in it. So she dropped the subject entirely, turned her luggage over to Colin, and then followed him dutifully to the carriage. But when they were all ready to go and Colin had climbed up into the driver's seat, Wendy snuck open the carriage door for Athena, who was perfectly happy to jump inside rather than running along next to the horses like a proper coach dog.

"I think you're very beautiful," Wendy told Athena as the dog curled up on the seat next to her. Athena thought that was very nice of her to say, and she laid her head upon Wendy's lap, hoping for a proper scratch behind the ears.

"I don't think it suits you to be a coach dog, though. Do you?" Athena couldn't have agreed more. It wasn't so much that she disliked being a coach dog; it was just that the coach hardly ever went anywhere, so it really wasn't much of a job at all.

"On the other hand," Wendy continued, "you make a lovely companion. Quite fetching. And soothing too. There's a dog waiting for me back in Dover, you know. She has a very important job there, watching over the men, so she had to stay behind. I think you would like that sort of job very much."

Athena closed her eyes blissfully while Wendy stroked her head.

"Would it be all right if you were my companion dog while I'm here in Hertfordshire? And perhaps if I called you something else, more suited to the position? Your lovely spots remind me of a field of poppies. Not that I've ever seen a field of poppies," Wendy admitted, "but I saw a painting of them once. It was almost as beautiful as you are. Would it be all right if I called you Poppy?"

Poppy flopped onto her side and closed her eyes, understanding thoroughly, long before anyone else, that the Hertfordshire estate had just come under new management.

Dogs *always* know.

CHAPTER
19

By the time Wendy and Poppy arrived at the Hook Estate, they had already decided how Wendy was going to spend her time there. First, she would continue her research into the everlost. Second, she would continue her training in both swordsmanship and marksmanship. Third, she would find some way to help the local orphans and foundlings.

She had no idea how she was going to do any of those things, but at least she knew what she *wanted* to do, which is the most important part of any plan—even one that is not entirely worked out yet.

The coach had just pulled up to the grand entrance of the manor house, hardly coming to a full stop before Colin leaped out of the driver's seat and scrambled around to open the door for his lovely passenger. He held Wendy's hand, blushing a bit, as she stepped down from the carriage, and he was just about to shut the door behind her when Poppy poked her head out and jumped down after her.

"Athena! What were you doing in there? Bad dog!" Colin said sharply. He turned to Wendy with a look of profound chagrin. "I'm so sorry, miss. She's never done that before. I don't know what got into her!"

"Oh, now don't be cross with her, Colin. Poppy didn't do anything wrong," Wendy assured him. "I invited her to ride with me. For the company."

"Poppy?"

Colin looked down at the dog, confused, while Poppy looked up at Wendy obediently, awaiting her orders.

"That's right," Wendy affirmed with an approving smile. "Come along, Poppy. I'd like very much to meet this Huxley I've heard such nice things about."

"I'm Huxley, miss. It is a pleasure to make your acquaintance."

Huxley had been standing at the grand entrance this entire time, and Wendy had already suspected that he was Huxley due to his proper butler's uniform and his excellent posture. But she had found in the past that it tended to set things off on the right foot for a new acquaintance to overhear something complimentary about themselves before proper introductions had even begun.

"Huxley!" she exclaimed. "I am Wendy Darling, and I am very pleased to make *your* acquaintance as well. The estate is just lovely, I must say. Captain Hook has made a fine choice indeed leaving it in your care."

"Why, thank you, Miss Darling," Huxley said. And then he smiled. It was a very small and proper smile, of course, but a smile nonetheless. He was a slight man—in his mid-forties, Wendy suspected, and hardly any taller than she was herself. But despite his stature, he carried himself with the confidence of a man who had been in charge of things quite successfully for a good number of years.

"We only just this morning received word of your arrival by courier," he continued, "and I'm afraid there were no instructions regarding your preferences, so if anything is not to your liking, please be sure to let me know. Dinner will be served at six o'clock. If you missed lunch, Mrs. Medcalf will be glad to see to that as well. There is a room made up for you in the east wing. Colin can escort you there, and then he will be glad to show you about."

If Colin seemed more than pleased to be assigned that particular duty, Wendy was polite enough to pretend not to notice. She was also genuinely glad to have his assistance, as the estate house was so large that she might have gotten lost in it without him. The fact that this was not the family's primary estate spoke volumes about their wealth, as did their library, which was the very first thing Wendy asked to see after Colin had deposited her luggage in her room.

From the moment she stepped through its grand double doors, Wendy couldn't help but feel that she might remain in that library quite happily for the rest of her life—if only she could take it with her on a ship, that is. (And *then* she wished she could at least take it back with her to Dover Castle, which would better accommodate the space than any ship could ever hope to.)

Hook's collection was so extensive as to fill not just one story but two, with a spiral staircase in one corner that led up to the second level, where a balcony made of iron railings ran all the way around the room. There was a large fireplace for warmth and south-facing windows for light, as well as lamps for the evening hours. There were armchairs near the hearth for pleasure reading and a massive table in the center for more serious study, the latter of which Wendy claimed for herself immediately, at least in her own mind.

"Oh! It's magnificent!" she exclaimed.

"Why thank you, miss," Colin said, grinning from ear to ear. "I thought you'd like it. It's why I was so pleased when you asked about it. It's Captain Hook's pride and joy, it is. He only comes to the house once every month or two, but when he does, he always asks me what I've read since he left. He lets me pick whatever I want, but somehow he always knows the book. I think he knows every one of them! Can you imagine? He asks me questions and such, just to make sure I read it carefully. For my education, he always says."

"Does he?" Wendy asked.

"Aye, he does. My father makes sure I learn the groundskeeping, and my mother makes sure I learn proper manners for a nice household like this one. So I can find a good position of my own one day. But Captain Hook makes sure I read. 'Books allow everyone a traveler's education, Colin,' he always says."

"Well, I'd have to agree," Wendy admitted, albeit grudgingly. She was surprised to discover anything that she would agree with Captain Hook about, given her current circumstances.

"Whenever he travels," Colin continued, "he brings back new books from wherever he went. There are volumes here from France and Spain and even from the Far East. All kinds of books about all kinds of things!"

"Are there?" Wendy asked quietly.

With a library this extensive—especially when that library was curated by Captain Hook himself—there might well be hidden within it a treasure or two that could finally provide her with some insight into the true nature of the everlost. If they weren't vampires, as Pan had claimed they were not, then it was her duty to find out precisely what they were.

And how to kill them.

CHAPTER
20

As soon as the shouts rang out that John's carriage had been spotted on the road, returning from London, Michael and Nana raced to meet it. Michael was dressed for the occasion in a pair of tall black boots, an impeccably white shirt, and a blue riding coat. The boots were polished to such a shine that they could have turned Medusa herself to stone if no mirrors were handy, and the coat was his very best—which is to say, the one upon which he received the most frequent compliments from the ladies.

Nana, of course, wore a blue ribbon to match.

They arrived at the front entrance even before the carriage had come to a full stop. Michael stood smartly upon the curb, his heart swelling with anticipation as John clambered down from the vehicle. He smiled expectantly—a smile that turned to puzzlement and then descended into an outright frown when the carriage failed to produce anyone else from within its depths. Not even after several long moments of awkward stillness.

"Where is Wendy?" he finally demanded.

John could hardly look him in the eye, staring instead at his own booted foot, which he shuffled forlornly in the street, looking for all the world as though he had just lost his best friend. Which, truth be told, was precisely what had happened.

"Well?" Michael demanded again. "Where is she, man? What did you do with her?"

At this John looked up sharply. "What did I do with her? What kind of question is that? It isn't as though I threw her to bandits somewhere along the road, for heaven's sake. I didn't do anything with her!"

"But where *is* she?" Michael's voice was perhaps a bit more stern than it should have been in speaking to a superior officer. But Nana was of the opinion, if anything, that he did not sound quite stern enough. She had the exact same question, you see, and she kept jumping into the carriage, turning all around within it, leaping back out to stare accusingly at John, and then jumping right back in to repeat the process all over again.

"That's enough, Nana," John said, and the dog leaped out one last time, cocking her head at him with a deeply worried brow, demanding an explanation.

There was no good way to say it, so John expelled a long sigh— puffing out his cheeks with the exertion of it—and then forged ahead bravely, which is the best way to proceed when one is forced to say something that one absolutely *must* say but would honestly rather not.

"She's in Hertfordshire."

"Hertfordshire?" Michael replied, his tone incredulous, and then he said it again, only now he sounded more than a bit cross. "Hertfordshire!"

"There wasn't anything I could do," John protested, shrugging his shoulders dramatically and raising both hands in the air as though that were any sort of proof of the matter. "She left under Captain Hook's orders! If I had tried to stop them, they would have thrown me in irons!"

Michael said nothing, continuing to glare at him in silent reproach, a response with which Nana wholeheartedly agreed. No matter how many times she had been chained up in the yard for her trouble, that had never once stopped her from trying to do what she knew was right in the excitement of the moment.

Never even *once*.

"Look, don't worry," John tried. "She's perfectly all right. Hook's family has an estate there—a rather fine one, I'm told."

"She's staying at Captain Hook's private estate?" Michael all but wailed.

"He just wants to ask her a few more questions—"

"I bet he *does* want to ask her something, and I bet I know *what*," Michael grumbled, but John ignored the interruption.

"And then he'll send her back to us," John continued, trying to sound confident. "You'll see. She's out in the country, nowhere near the everlost."

"If Captain Hook's taken a liking to her, the everlost are the least of our problems," Michael growled, to which John made no reply at all, as this was the exact same thought that had been torturing him along the entire journey back from London.

After supper, John sat in his private office trying to attend to the accounting that had piled up while he was away, his eyes running over and over the same lines of figures while his mind stubbornly ignored them. Instead, his brain insisted on replaying his time in London, trying to come up with some way—*any* way, no matter how implausible—in which he could have prevented Wendy from being whisked off to Hertfordshire.

He could (for example) have knocked on her door in the middle of the night and convinced her to tie their bedsheets together, climbing down the side of the building and fleeing into the anonymous throng of London's poor. Or he could have clothed himself in one of her most voluminous dresses, hidden his face beneath a floppy hat, and stoically taken her place on the coach to St. Albans. Or better yet, he could have challenged Captain Hook to a duel—and he could have won, obviously, as long as he was imagining things, inspiring Wendy to swoon gratefully into his arms.

It was an entirely useless exercise, as there was nothing he could do about it now even if he *were* able to arrive at some reasonable alternative. But still, he couldn't seem to give it up.

It didn't help any that Michael was also sitting in John's office, slumped over Wendy's desk, resting his cheek upon his arm and idly tracing the grain of the wood with his index finger, leaning down every so often to pat poor Nana on the head and say, "There, there," in a sad, commiserating sort of way, while the dog lay forlornly on the floor at his feet, beyond consolation.

When Michael started imitating Wendy's mournful sort of drumming—thumping out the slow, miserable cadence with his third and fourth fingers together—well, that was the last straw. John was just about to say, "*Please*, Michael," in a tone very much like Wendy herself would have used, but that was also the exact moment in which Nana's head shot straight up into the air. A

growl began deep in the back of her throat, rising steadily in volume until she was snarling viciously at the window.

John thought immediately that he had never felt so relieved in all his life. He would rather face the possibility of death itself than be forced to suffer even one more moment of their combined melancholy.

"Where is Wendy?" Peter demanded.

"You must be joking," John muttered under his breath.

This is not, of course, how things had started out. When Peter Pan had *first* arrived—alone this time—diving through the night sky to hover ominously over Dover Castle, John had shot at him. As had every other member of the Fourteenth Platoon of the Nineteenth Light Dragoons of the British Home Office.

The bullets, however, had not had their desired effect. Peter had sat through the entire ordeal patiently—or rather, *hovered* through it patiently—until the men were all quite finished with their first volley and were stuck reloading their muskets. (Which is more of a bother than you might think if you have never reloaded a musket yourself.) It was into this relatively quiet interlude that he finally spoke, demanding to know the whereabouts of Wendy Darling.

"I am most certainly not joking," Peter assured them. "Where is my Wendy?"

"She's not *your* Wendy!" Michael snarled. "She's not *your* anything!"

"Where is *your* Wendy then," Pan tried again, addressing Michael this time.

"She's not his either," John snapped, perhaps a bit too quickly. Michael furrowed his brow and shot him a rather nasty look, but John refused to meet his eye, pretending not to notice.

"Fine! Not my Wendy. Not your Wendy. Where is *the* Wendy? You must tell me at once!"

"Fire!" John shouted, the musket reloading having been accomplished by this point.

They all fired. Peter waited through it again, looking somewhat less patient than the last time. His body flew backward through the air just a bit, due to the sheer momentum of the ammunition, but otherwise the second volley had no greater effect than the first.

"Tell me!" Peter shouted.

"Reload!" John ordered his men. "Clip his wings this time!"

"This isn't over!" Peter warned them, but a powerful down-beat of those very same wings propelled him higher into the air, and another one higher still, continuing on until he had flown so high as to be entirely out of sight.

"We must get word to Wendy!" Michael paced so vigorously back and forth across the carpet in John's office that it seemed in danger of being worn out within the span of a single evening. Not that John could blame him. He felt the same way, in fact. To be so far from Wendy when she was so clearly in danger was a torture the likes of which he had never known.

"I'm already writing the letter," John assured him. "What did you think I was doing?"

"By special courier," Michael insisted.

"Of course," John agreed.

"But not to Hook. To Wendy."

"Of *course* to Wendy! If we sent a letter to Hook, God only knows where he might move her, and then we'd have no idea where to find her."

Michael stopped in his tracks and stared intently at John. "Maybe we *should* go find her."

"And abandon our posts? Absolutely not." If John were the type to abandon his post, he would have done so in London, where he might have convinced Wendy to run off with him alone. Not that he was about to share that thought with Michael.

"No, you're right. Of course, you're right." Michael's shoulders fell in helpless resignation, and he resumed his pacing. "Nana, *please*. I'm tense enough as it is!"

Nana was standing up on her hind legs with her front paws propped against the windowsill, trying to look outside. She had not stopped growling ever since Peter Pan had flown away, and it was beginning to set Michael's teeth on edge.

"A special courier. You *promise*," Michael said again. It was not exactly a question.

"As I've said," John promised.

"To be carried to Wendy *directly*, at Hook's estate in Hertford-shire. Not via the London office."

"To Wendy directly," John assured him.

"Oh, thank heaven!" Michael exclaimed, which was very much something Wendy would have said, had she been there herself, but he said it only partly in reply to John's words.

It was *mostly* in response to the fact that Nana had just in that moment settled back down onto the carpet, the growl in her throat falling mercifully silent—now that the tiny, magic-scented wings outside the window had finally flown away.

CHAPTER
21

High up in the night sky, Peter hovered above the clouds, holding a miniature, living dragon in the palm of his chiseled hand. She spoke to him in the fairy language, which sounded more than anything else like the vigorous jingling of a thousand tiny bells. It might have seemed odd—a palm-sized, golden dragon speaking in a symphony of delicate chimes—but Peter was used to it. The dragon's name was Tinker Bell, and he knew her very well indeed.

One might even suggest that he knew her a bit too well for his own good, but that remains to be seen.

He knew, for example, that she was not a dragon at all. Tinker Bell belonged to that rarest and most precious of fairy species (known as the *innisfay* by those who still remember such things) who can turn themselves into any sort of animal at will. In their natural form they look a bit like you and me, with a few significant exceptions.

One, they possess wings. Two, they approximate the size and jeweled brilliance of your average hummingbird. Three, every last one of them is devastatingly beautiful (which makes them quite vain as a general rule.)

Tinker Bell, as it happens, was *particularly* proud of herself at the moment, having discovered the whereabouts of the Wendy for Peter (whatever a Wendy was) through a very clever deception, in which she had disguised herself as a bat and dangled upside down above a particular window of Dover Castle, eavesdropping in a very literal sense on the conversation within.

It is a special peculiarity of the innisfay that the color of their hair (or their fins, or their scales, or what have you, depending upon their form) always reflects their mood. This is why it is sometimes said that the innisfay cannot lie.

On the contrary, they can lie extraordinarily well, spinning such elaborate and magnificent yarns at the drop of a hat that you would have a very hard time disbelieving any of it. Because *how could anyone invent such a preposterous and complicated set of circumstances on the spur of the moment*, you would think to yourself. And in any event you would not *want* to disbelieve it, as it would all be so much more interesting and entertaining than the truth.

When they are engaging, however, in such calculated exaggerations, their hair (or feathers, or fur, or what have you) turns a distinct shade of gray, ranging anywhere from a light, ashen color if the lie is a relatively innocent one, to an ominous hue of thick, choking smoke if the deception is born of cruel intentions.

So, had Tinker Bell been lying to Peter about finding the Wendy, he would have known it immediately. Just as he would have recognized a sorrowful shade of blue if she were sad, or a nasty, envious shade of green if he had something she wanted.

Instead, her bright, golden hue reflected her profound sense of pride, so Peter knew she was telling the truth.

(In point of fact, Tinker Bell exhibited a dazzlingly golden hue—of hair, or fur, or feathers, or scales, or fins—a vast majority of the time.)

But knowing the truth of her report did not make it any easier to bear. Peter's eyes narrowed dangerously, his teeth grinding together as he snarled a single word into the darkness.

"Hook!"

With that, he tossed the little dragon unceremoniously into the air and shot away through the night to the northwest.

Tinker Bell, of course, was not harmed in the slightest, as she was more than capable of flying quite well on her own. She was, however, a bit miffed not to receive an exuberance of praise for her cleverness or even so much as a thank you for her trouble, and she turned an angry sort of red—cursing after him in the most delightfully lilting trills, the translation of which shall not be attempted here, on certain magical principles regarding the safety of all concerned.

The curses of the innisfay are not to be trifled with.

But when Peter made no attempt to counter her tirade, continuing to fly away even as she hurled egregious (albeit melodious) insults in his general direction, Tinker Bell's curiosity got the better of her. She ended her stream of invective abruptly as a new color flashed over her from nose to tail.

Had Peter been watching, he would have recognized it, and he would have known that in Tinker Bell, it could only mean trouble—the shimmering, moonlight shade of pearlescent silver that lies at the heart of all great inquiry.

But, sadly, Peter was not watching. So there was nothing to stop her when she took off after him.

CHAPTER
22

T he very next morning, Wendy stood in the kitchen of the Hertfordshire estate, watching Mrs. Medcalf as the kind-hearted cook kneaded the dough for their afternoon tea scones. Mrs. Medcalf, you'll remember, was Colin's mother, and Wendy had liked her from the moment they met. She was a robust woman, with bright red hair, warm brown eyes, a plump midsection, and arms that reflected hours upon hours of scraping and chopping and slicing and basting. Not to mention kneading and rolling countless lumps of dough by hand, just as she was doing now.

She did it all without complaint, fueled by the considerable love she obviously felt for Mr. Medcalf and Colin and even Huxley—and now fueled even further by the newfound responsibility she clearly felt toward Wendy.

Take the scones, for example.

The scones were the only request Mrs. Medcalf had so far managed to wrestle out of Wendy, and the woman had been happy

to oblige her in it every afternoon since. Which was perhaps a bit more often than Wendy had intended.

They had been visiting with each other for quite some time on this particular morning, Mrs. Medcalf finally having worked up the courage to ask a few pointed questions of their new guest. She had her suspicions about Wendy's sudden presence at the manor and had finally broached the subject head on, clearly hoping to learn what to expect from ... well, from the woman she believed to be the future lady of the house.

Wendy, needless to say, was at a loss.

(Poppy, for her part, lay at Wendy's feet, clearly hoping for snacks, but so far none had been forthcoming.)

"Mrs. Medcalf," Wendy was saying, blushing wildly, "I can assure you, the captain has no intentions toward me whatsoever, whether honorable or otherwise."

"Why, of course his intentions are honorable!" Mrs. Medcalf exclaimed, pausing with her hands deep in the dough and snapping her head up to gaze at Wendy in a shocked sort of way.

"I'm not trying to question his honor," Wendy assured her quickly. "That isn't the point. What I'm *trying* to say is that I'm quite certain he has no intentions toward me at all."

"Oh, don't you worry about *that*," Mrs. Medcalf replied, her features relaxing into a sly grin. "Now, it shows your fine character that you wouldn't assume. That it does. And I can see why the captain is fond of you. But he wouldn't invite you to stay here without a reason. He *has* intentions. I can promise you that!"

The cook smiled reassuringly and started back in on the dough, her motions firm and efficient, while Wendy furrowed her brow in confusion, trying to sort out how to respond. On the one hand, she didn't want people getting the wrong idea. But on the other, she

wasn't free to tell anyone the truth, given the clandestine nature of her appointment in the Nineteenth Light Dragoons.

It only made sense that they would make certain assumptions.

Mrs. Medcalf interpreted Wendy's puzzled silence to be an embarrassed confirmation of those assumptions and chuckled merrily to herself, beaming at the prospect of a wedding. Perhaps this summer, or maybe even later this spring.

"And what is your view on cake, my dear?" she asked Wendy, seeming to change the subject (although of course she wasn't really.) "I've always had a particular fondness for lemon myself. Do you like lemon?" Her voice held a distinctly hopeful tone, but Wendy was spared further difficulty by Colin's sudden breathless appearance in the doorway.

"A courier, Miss Darling!" he exclaimed, his eyes wide. "With a letter for you! He says he'll speak to no one else. He wouldn't even let Huxley take it!"

"For me?" Wendy echoed. "I'll come immediately, of course!" Never in her life had Wendy felt so relieved to exit a kitchen. She followed Colin out the door at a fast clip, with Poppy trotting at her heels.

Later that night, despite the warning from Dover, Wendy could hardly believe it when she smelled the taste of pickles in the air. It had been wonderful to hear from John and Michael and Nana, but she didn't see how Peter Pan could possibly find her here. The whole point of sending her out to the countryside had been to keep her safe (much to her annoyance.)

Nonetheless, she had been studying in the library, as had become her habit after the dinner hour, when Poppy's hackles suddenly rose straight up along her spine, and the dog stalked toward the windows with a menacing growl.

"No! Here? But how could he have found us?" she asked Poppy, who had no answer for her, continuing to snarl instead at the darkness outside the manor.

"Come along then," Wendy said, bracing her shoulders and rising from her seat at the table. "We must not allow this threat to breach the house. Huxley and the Medcalfs have nothing to do

with this fight, and we shan't bring the everlost into their home. Whatever happens, we must face them out there."

She gulped, and for just a moment her face betrayed her nervousness. But then her eyebrows set themselves into a grim line of determination—both of them at once, in a splendid show of solidarity.

"Poppy, you have no obligation to follow me. I think it best if you stay here to guard Colin and his parents."

But Poppy, of course, would have none of that. She padded to her mistress and sat firmly by her side, putting an end to any further discussion on the matter.

"Oh, I must admit I'm relieved you feel that way." Wendy smiled gratefully at the Dalmatian, who looked up into her eyes with such tender loyalty that Wendy felt very moved indeed. "All right. Let's both go, then."

They tiptoed through the house toward the grand entrance, moving as quietly as they could so as not to disturb the staff, and as they passed the trophy room (as Colin had called it during his tour of the manor), Poppy paused and whined softly. This was, after all, the Hook family hunting estate. The trophy room held an impressive array of guns and ammunition.

"No, Poppy," Wendy replied, understanding her immediately. "Although I certainly do appreciate the suggestion. Guns won't help, I'm afraid. They will only alert the others without doing us any good. But never fear. We have our wits, and we have each other. We must pray they will be enough."

Poppy thought she would rather put her faith in her teeth than in her wits when it came to ominous scents in the night, but she could see how Wendy might feel the opposite. At any rate, they possessed both teeth and wits between the two of them, which seemed better than having either one alone.

As soon as they were free of the house, they sprinted across the lawn, through the pasture gate, and out into the open fields. Looking from there up toward the clouds, Wendy could already see a lone everlost plummeting toward the earth, his giant hawk-like wings folded close around his body. She kept expecting him to open his wings and catch his fall, but he continued to drop like a stone until he was so close to the ground that she thought he would surely crash into it.

"Oh!" Wendy exclaimed, opening her eyes wide and covering her mouth with one horrified hand. But at the last possible moment, he snapped his wings out dramatically, one knee and both hands slamming into the grassy earth of the pasture, absorbing an impact that would have crushed human bones into shards.

Wendy exhaled and regained her composure, patting the waist of her dress primly back into place. But Poppy decided right then and there that she did not like men falling out of the clouds. She did not like it at all. She began to bark as loudly as she could, but Wendy ordered her immediately to be silent, afraid that Colin would come to investigate and place himself in danger.

"Did I frighten you?" Peter asked, paying no heed to the dog, who continued to growl at him, albeit quietly. He tried to stand up, but the deep holes he had just made in the soil with his landing prevented him from doing so with any dignity. Surveying his situation in a detached sort of way, he finally stepped up out of the depressions and crossed his arms proudly across his chest, the awkwardness of the moment not seeming to faze him in the least.

"You most certainly did not," Wendy replied, placing her own hands on her hips and glaring at him sternly.

"Then why did you shout?" he demanded, tilting his head and curling his lips into a smirk.

"I did no such thing," Wendy retorted.

"Oh!" Peter shot back. He spoke in a falsetto that captured her voice just a bit too well for her liking, opening his eyes wide and covering his mouth with one hand, mimicking her reaction perfectly.

"I was startled, at best," Wendy declared, hiding her annoyance behind a matter-of-fact sort of tone. "But only that you found me, not that you might have been hurt. I can assure you, your safety means nothing to me."

"Ha! I found you easily! And all by myself!" Peter boasted, ignoring the second bit and also conveniently forgetting any role that Tinker Bell might have played in the matter. "I followed your courier! Oh, the cleverness of me! Did you know he rode straight through the night? He must have changed horses at least half a dozen times, but I'm faster than all of them! I flew ahead and chased the clouds. More than once you know, just to have something to do while I waited. I bet *you've* never touched a cloud!"

Unfortunately for Peter, the two things in the world that Wendy Darling had the very least patience for were acts of unkindness— especially when directed toward children—and incessant bragging. And Peter Pan was guilty of both (even if there did not happen to be any children present at the moment.)

She drew herself up to her full height, squared her shoulders, narrowed her eyes dangerously, and addressed him with such venom that Peter raised both of his own perfectly sculpted eyebrows in the air and took half a step backward in surprise.

"What are you doing here, Peter?" she spat at him. "Why are you following me? Because *I* certainly have no interest whatsoever in speaking with *you*! You are the enemy of the crown. You and all your kind!"

"What am *I* doing here?" Peter echoed, his own eyes narrowing in response to hers. "What are *you* doing here? Why are you at Hook's family estate?"

"That's none of your business!"

"Hook *is* my business!" he shouted back, his voice filled with gravel in its sudden intensity. "Hook is my enemy! He is *death* to all my kind! All of us! What is he to *you*?"

They stared at each other for a long moment, Peter's nostrils flaring, his chest rising and falling in anger with every breath.

"He is my countryman," she said finally. Her voice was soft, almost reluctant, but she looked him directly in the eye when she said it, understanding the wall she was building between them with that simple truth and regretting it somehow, despite her irritation.

Much to Wendy's amazement, Peter clenched his fists, tensed his arms, thrust his chest forward, and roared at her—an inarticulate, anguished howl that echoed through the night.

Wendy's eyes flew wide and she took a step back as Poppy bravely leaped in front of her. But he made no move to harm them. His scream finally fell away and he stood a moment longer, his chest still heaving, his gaze locked onto hers, with the most heart-wrenching look of betrayal on his face that Wendy thought she had ever seen.

Then, without another word, he burst into the air and flew away.

Wendy watched him shrink into the distance until he finally disappeared altogether into the night, marveling all the while at the strange trickery of the wind as it rustled through his feathers— making them sound for all the world like the distant, improbable jingling of tiny bells.

CHAPTER
24

By the next evening, Hook had returned to Hertfordshire.

Wendy had been reluctant to inform him of Pan's appearance—not being in any hurry to see the captain again—but in the end, she had spent half the night drafting a complete and accurate report, depositing it with Huxley at dawn and asking that it be delivered to Hook personally in London as quickly as possible. It was her sworn duty to crown and country, and she took that duty seriously.

Which made the captain's current accusation all the more galling.

"What did you tell him?" he demanded.

Wendy was seated at the table in the library, with Poppy resting loyally at her feet, while Hook paced back and forth. A leopard in a cage of books. She watched him in fascination, amazed that it was he himself who had cultivated the vast collection of tomes that surrounded her. He seemed so much more a man of action than of

quiet reflection or study—unable to sit still even long enough for a simple conversation.

"I assure you, Captain," she said calmly, sitting ramrod straight, shoulders back, chin tilted proudly in the air, defying his implication with her very posture, "I told him nothing of any significance."

"I don't mean *this* time," he countered, coming to a sudden halt and scowling at her. "I mean the *first* time. Obviously he came looking for you here, hoping for more information. You must have told him something back in Dover."

"What makes you think he was looking for *me*?" She made the question sound as innocent as she could. John and Michael had taken a significant risk in writing to her at Hook's estate. She wasn't going to admit she knew anything about Pan's *second* appearance in Dover, whether or not Hook was aware of it himself.

"Do you think I'm stupid?" he demanded.

"No, Captain. Of course not." She folded her hands before her on the table and stared directly into his eyes. He stared back for a long time before speaking again.

"Surely even you can see that his sudden appearance here, so soon after your arrival, is an unlikely coincidence. Especially given your earlier encounter."

"Even me?" Her eyebrow rose in a silent warning—a warning that would have given him pause had he known her better.

Unfortunately for Hook, he did not.

"Yes, you. A woman. Designed by our Creator for the tender care of children rather than the strategic calculations of war, the rational pursuit of science. But even you must surely recognize that he is somehow following you. The natural deduction is that you are providing him with useful information, whether you realize it or not."

"Oh, I see. Even me." Another long silence extended between them during which Wendy fought to maintain her composure, while Hook presumed she was trying to follow his reasoning.

"Well?" he said finally.

"I apologize for the delay," Wendy said evenly. "It's just that your previous statement is incorrect on so many levels that I'm having trouble deciding where to begin my rebuttal. So as to approach it in the most *logical* fashion."

"I—"

Wendy closed her eyes and raised a gentle but preemptive hand, an action that surprised Hook so deeply he fell silent on the spot. When she was certain she had his attention, she opened her eyes again and began to speak.

"Firstly, you said that Pan's appearance here was an unlikely coincidence. On that much, we agree. But being unlikely is not the same thing as being impossible. A true logician must allow for the *possibility* that it was, in fact, a coincidence, albeit an unexpected one.

"Secondly," she continued, "you stated that he must therefore be following me, and that the natural deduction—I believe those were your exact words—is that I have been acting as a traitorous informant."

"Now wait just a moment, I never called you a traitor—"

"Yes, of course. You presume I am too stupid to be a traitor. That I have been *accidentally* committing one of the worst crimes imaginable before God and King."

"That's not what I—"

"It is very much what you implied, whether or not you said it directly. *That* is a logical deduction. What is *not* a deduction is the preposterous leap from 'not here by coincidence' to 'gaining traitorous information.' At the very most," Wendy forged on, hardly

taking a breath, although her voice remained imperturbably calm, "if we *presume* Pan's presence here *not* to be a coincidence, then clearly he must be here for a reason. Which, by the way, is a rhetorical tautology rather than a deduction. But that still provides us with no indication as to *what* that reason might be. The idea that he is gathering useful information from me is a *supposition*, certainly not a deduction, and only one of several possibilities that a good logician must consider."

Hook said nothing, merely staring at her as though she, not he, had become the exotic creature on display in the library zoo. A tiger crouching upon a tree limb, pontificating to its prey.

"For example," Wendy continued, gaining momentum, "Pan might have been searching for your family's estate. You yourself admitted that the two of you share a particular enmity. Perhaps *you* have been the target of his pursuits, not I. Or he might have been hoping to learn something from me precisely because he has not yet been able to do so. He might see it as a challenge. Or, speaking of challenges, he might have enjoyed matching his wits against my own, having been unable to find a worthy adversary among the king's *men.* There are many reasons for which he might have paid a visit to this estate, but again I assure you, it was not because I have *ever* helped him in any way!"

As Wendy said this last, she rose from her seat until she was glaring at Hook across the table, both of her hands planted firmly upon it, her elbows locked, her eloquent eyebrow raised in defiance, daring him to challenge her again. Hook still did not know Wendy very well, but he certainly knew her better now than he had even a few moments ago. He recognized what that eyebrow was trying to tell him, and he chose finally to heed its warning, skirting the confrontation by approaching her from a new angle.

"Well then, what have *you* learned from *him*?" he asked.

"I'm sorry?" She continued to lean menacingly across the table, but her face now registered confusion alongside its original hostility.

"Presuming, for the moment, that you are correct—that he has not gained any useful information from you, and that your wits have bested his at every turn—then surely *you* have managed to learn something useful from *him*, yes? Something, Miss Darling, *anything*, that we might use to turn the tide of this war."

As he said it, Hook mirrored her posture, calmly placing both his hand and his hook on the table directly across from her and leaning toward her. His thick, raven locks were tied back behind his neck, and his eyes of forget-me-not blue locked onto hers in a way that made her uncomfortable for more reasons than she would have wanted to admit.

She straightened back up and tidied her dress demurely.

"Perhaps if you would treat me like an actual member of the Nineteenth Light Dragoons," she suggested, "and brief me on our current initiatives rather than hiding me away on your family's hunting estate like some sort of swooning romantic interest, I might be in a better position to help the cause."

A hint of a smile played across Hook's lips. "Swooning? I can hardly imagine anyone mistaking you for a swooning anything, Miss Darling."

"Yes, well ... Mrs. Medcalf is quite certain that you and I are soon to be engaged," Wendy reluctantly admitted. "I would vastly prefer it if you would take steps to correct that misapprehension."

"Is she?" Hook said, and his eyes danced with a cruel sort of humor. "I must admit I hadn't considered the likelihood, but it's as good a cover story as any. And better than most. As an *actual* member of the Nineteenth Light Dragoons, you should expect to hide your true purpose from the world, should you not?"

"Be that as it may—"

"No. It is best that you continue to act in that capacity." Hook stood and nodded to himself, the matter clearly settled. "You shall henceforth pretend to be my *swooning* romantic interest. I dare say it will be an excellent test of your *wits*, and it gives me a perfectly good excuse to keep you here as long as needed."

"As long as needed! But—"

"I am still your superior officer, Miss Darling. Unless, of course, you no longer wish to be an *actual* member of the Nineteenth Light Dragoons?"

Wendy merely glared at him in silence.

"As to briefing you regarding our current initiatives," he continued, "if my *hypothesis* is correct—if Pan is indeed seeking you out—then the less you know of our plans, the better. All you need to know is that I want as much information as you can learn. Specifically, I would be very interested to discover the location of Pan's island. I'm tired of defending our shores, Miss Darling. I would like very much to take the battle to our enemy. And the sooner, the better.

"I will send a few men to stay with you here. Not only for your protection but for the house. As you say, this is my family's estate. No one will question my decision to see to the safety of my bride to be."

Wendy blushed furiously but refused to rise to the bait. "Fine," she said. "Then send me the Fourteenth Platoon. I am their diviner, and they should not be without me. I shall be safe here in their care."

"This is not a negotiation, Miss Darling," Hook replied evenly. "The Fourteenth has its own post to attend to. I will, instead, be sending my own men from London. If you wish to be reunited with the Fourteenth Platoon in Dover, then find me the location of

that island. Once I know where it is, I shall be far too busy hunting the everlost to maintain a fiancée in Hertfordshire."

A challenge, Wendy thought. *Ha! Two can play at that game! On your guard, then, Captain. Maintaining a fiancée in Hertfordshire might be more trouble than you'd expect!*

But, of course, Wendy kept that thought to herself. Instead, she took a bold pace toward him. Two paces. Three. Did he honestly believe he could intimidate her? Make her uncomfortable by forcing her to act as his fiancée? She held up her hand, clearly inviting him to take it.

"Until we meet again then, darling," she said.

He eyed her warily for a long moment, but then his mouth twisted into a cold, calculated smile. Instead of taking her hand in his own, he brought his steel hook up to rest it beneath her delicately curled fingers, its tip—sharp and deadly—just inches from her chin.

"Oh, I haven't left yet, Miss Darling." He spoke quietly, his voice deep and rasping. "I'm afraid you won't be rid of me that easily."

His eyes locked onto hers, and he pulled her hand gently to his lips. The leopard once again, toying with its catch. But Wendy only held his gaze, saying nothing.

We will find out soon enough, she thought to herself, *just who is toying with whom.*

Hook spent three days at the Hertfordshire estate, and for Wendy, every one of them felt like an eternity.

He insisted that she join him on long rides through the countryside each morning. (With Colin tagging along as chaperone, staring sullen daggers at Hook when he wasn't looking.) Every afternoon he propped his boots up on the table in the library and leered at her as she tried to read. During dinner he held her hand captive throughout the meal, his eyes never leaving hers as he skewered bits of meat with his steel hook.

And all the while she had to play the part of the swooning girl, blushing at his ardent attentions, knowing they were meant to be intimidating.

But Wendy wasn't intimidated. She was just biding her time. If Hook insisted on this ruse, she would use it to her advantage. Unfortunately, she couldn't put her plan into motion until he left,

and that didn't happen until the two lieutenants had finally arrived from London. On his way out the door, he issued them strict orders not to leave Wendy unattended—which was just going to make everything that much more difficult.

But of course, not impossible.

"Good morning, Mrs. Medcalf!"

Wendy found the cook just where she had expected: in the kitchen, preparing the morning's biscuits, even as the first pink light of dawn was beginning to grace the sky.

"Why, good morning, Miss Darling! You're up early, I dare say. Even for you! Someone has a reason to be happy, I'd wager?"

Mrs. Medcalf loved fishing for information almost as much as she loved lemon cake. It was a trait Wendy's new plan relied upon heavily.

"A small reason, Mrs. Medcalf," Wendy replied, careful to look hesitant. "Nothing momentous yet. Not a promise ... but a hope, at least."

"Are you *certain* there hasn't been a promise?" Mrs. Medcalf asked wistfully. "I thought surely ..."

"I'm afraid I can't be certain of anything!" Wendy wrung her hands together, then hesitated. Had that been too much? No, watching Mrs. Medcalf's expression, she decided it was perfect. "I have so little experience with this sort of thing ..."

She allowed her voice to trail off and then sighed. Unless she missed her guess, Mrs. Medcalf would not need much prompting.

"Oh, my dear! Of course you don't! Tell me everything! We'll figure it out together." The woman brushed her hands against her apron and turned to Wendy, her eyes wide, cheeks flushed, all thoughts of biscuits apparently forgotten.

"Well ... if you think so ..."

"I absolutely insist! What did he say?" She leaned so far forward in her eagerness that Wendy feared the woman might topple right over.

"Mrs. Medcalf, he was the perfect gentleman, of course. But he *did* profess a ... well, a certain romantic fondness for my company. I'm embarrassed to say more—I'm sure you understand— but you were right about *that.*"

"Of course I was, dear! Oh, how exciting!" Mrs. Medcalf clutched her hands together beneath her ample bosom and inhaled sharply.

"There was no talk of a wedding, though." Wendy did her best to look worried. "No specific ... question ... *but...*"

Mrs. Medcalf grabbed both of Wendy's hands in her own. "Yes? But what, dear? But what!"

"Well, that's just it! I don't know! I thought he would ... or at least, I thought he might ... but all he said was that he couldn't say more—something about military secrets!"

"Military secrets!"

Wendy paused, giving Mrs. Medcalf sufficient time to gasp and release Wendy's grip, raising her hands to her mouth instead.

"That's what he said," Wendy affirmed. "And then he said that soon he might be too busy to maintain a fiancée in Hertfordshire."

"Oh!" Mrs. Medcalf began to bounce up and down, her eyes opening wider and wider until she burst forth with an actual squeal of excitement and grasped Wendy's hands again. "Oh, my dear! That's why he hasn't asked! Oh, it all makes sense now! He's afraid you'll be lonely if he has to go off to sea right away. Always so thoughtful. He's a true *gentleman*, he is!"

"Yes. Yes, that's what I thought, too," Wendy agreed. "So, you see, there's nothing official. A *hope*, as I said. But not a *promise.*"

"Oh, my goodness! No, dear, that's as good as a promise from our Captain Hook! There's no doubt about it now! I'm quite sure!"

"Do you think so? Really?" Wendy didn't have to act hopeful. The feeling was entirely genuine. This was exactly how she had hoped this conversation would go.

"It's just a matter of time!" Mrs. Medcalf exclaimed.

"Are you absolutely certain? Because if you're *absolutely* certain, then I really should begin to appear in charitable circles, don't you think? To put forth the *best* possible image. To uphold his reputation in the *community*, you understand. So that people will approve of the match?"

"Yes! Oh, yes!" Mrs. Medcalf was already nodding emphatically. "That's very good thinking. *Very* good. We must arrange for you to meet—"

But Wendy placed a gentle hand on the woman's arm, stopping her before she could suggest anything in particular. Wendy had her own introductions in mind.

"I have always had such a tender place in my heart for orphans, Mrs. Medcalf," Wendy suggested. "Is there an orphanage, perhaps, in Hertfordshire?"

And, of course, there was.

As it happened, there were several almshouses in St. Albans, and Wendy toured four of them that very afternoon along with her retinue of two lieutenants, one coachman (a position she attributed to Colin, which pleased him immensely), and Poppy, whom

she introduced as a companion dog, rather than a coach dog. As though that explained why the animal should be allowed inside the buildings.

At their *fifth* stop, however, Wendy was informed that she could not tour the premises. A fine lady such as herself, they said, should not have to witness the sad conditions in which these particular orphans lived. The poorest almshouse in all of St. Albans barely managed to keep a roof over their heads, with nothing left over for extravagances like food or warm blankets.

Wendy assured them that she understood *completely*, and if she could perhaps see a list of what they most desperately needed ...

So back they went to the center of town, where the wealthy shopped for mutton and pastries and fine haberdashery, and where Wendy knew she could find just what she was looking for.

"He brought it on himself, Poppy," Wendy said. They rode together in the carriage, with the lieutenants following along behind on horseback. "I can't let him keep me from my platoon. You understand, don't you? He's never going to take me on for *The Dragon*. The least he can do is return me to my post, where I have *some* chance of moving up in the world."

Poppy licked Wendy's hand in sympathy.

"I know it's a bit underhanded, but he's the one who said I could leave if I made it worth his while."

Poppy rested her head on Wendy's lap and closed her eyes. That wasn't exactly how Poppy remembered the conversation, but she wasn't one to quibble.

"I have no idea how long it will be before Pan comes back. Or even *if* he's going to come back! Finding that island is an unfair condition to place on my freedom, don't you think?"

Poppy snored a little, and Wendy jogged her knee to wake the dog up.

"Don't you think?" she asked again.

Poppy barked obediently.

"Yes, I quite agree. So if I'm forced to make my stay in Hertfordshire inconvenient for him, well then it's his own fault. He should have just let me go back to Dover in the first place."

Poppy was perfectly happy for Wendy to go wherever she liked, especially if she could ride along in the carriage. She was a bit irked at Hook anyway for failing to understand that he was no longer in charge. He had insisted on calling her 'Athena' for the entire three days of his stay, and frankly, it had rankled.

"Yes, that's right. Three dozen blankets," Wendy said. "The warmest you have. Preferably in cheerful colors."

The shop was located in the center of the wealthiest section of St. Albans, and the proprietor flicked his tongue across his lips as he mentally tallied the profit on his thirty-six most expensive blankets. Then he brushed his hands together and watched Wendy closely as he asked the crucial question. "And how does the lady wish to pay?"

"I presume the credit of the Hook Estate will be acceptable?"

The man's eyes widened. Wendy's dress was not the finery of a wealthy woman. It was far too practical. But then again, there were the two lieutenants standing behind her in full dress uniform. (It would hardly have been appropriate for Hook's "romantic interest" to be escorted about town by two civilian men of no relation to her.) The lieutenants did nothing to interfere, and Wendy had arrived in the estate's coach ...

"Of course! Of course!" He bowed deeply. "Whatever the lady needs!"

"And as many of the items on this list as you have, please." When the merchant's eyes widened to the size of saucers, she added, "It's for the orphans."

"Ah!" he exclaimed. "Such a *fine* family, the Hooks! True pillars of the community! It is a *pleasure* to assist you, my lady. A genuine pleasure!"

Behind Wendy's back, the lieutenants shared a look that would have reminded her very much of John and Michael had she seen it, and it said this: "Do you think we should be trying to stop her?"

But as each man had intended to ask the other, neither received an answer. They merely watched as the bill continued to grow, dutifully following their orders—which, after all, had only been to protect her. Nothing had been said about preventing her from spending Hook's money.

Still, it *felt* as though they should be doing something, which is why they overreacted when the French gentleman suddenly opened the door and stepped in off the street.

"*Bonjour*," the man said.

Leaping to Wendy's rescue, the lieutenants charged the man together, one holding a sword to his chest while the other demanded answers.

"Who are you? What is your business here? Declare yourself!"

He was an older man, though certainly not *elderly*, Wendy decided. His silver hair was receding, but he was still surprisingly fit. His dark brown eyes showed hints of both intelligence and humor in equal measure, and he never lost his cheerful demeanor as he addressed the soldiers who had confronted him.

"*Messieurs*, I am Antoine Dumas. I do not represent the first wave of a British invasion, I assure you. I am here to buy a hat."

Wendy was appalled. It was one thing for the lieutenants to follow her around in case the everlost showed up. It was another thing altogether for them to accost innocent hat buyers.

"Boys!" she said sharply. "That's quite enough."

The lieutenants looked around at her, clearly startled. She was younger than they, but she had used such a firm, maternal tone that each had been reminded for a moment of his own mother. The one with the sword looked down at it in his hand and then back at Wendy as though to say, "What? No. Of *course* I wasn't going to hit Antoine with it. I was just holding it, like this. See?"

He put the sword away but continued to glare at Antoine. *This* look said, "Now you've done it. You've gotten us all in trouble!"

"Monsieur Dumas," Wendy said. "I apologize for my lieutenants. I hope they have not done you any harm."

"No, mademoiselle. Thank you. But the apology is entirely unnecessary. We live in troubled times, and there is no love lost between our two lands. I understand the precaution. There was a time I would have done the same."

"Oh? Were you in the military?" Wendy decided that he did, in fact, have a military bearing about him, tempered by time and experience.

"I was," he acknowledged. "But that was years ago. Now, life is quiet. I raise goats. I read books. Occasionally, I buy a hat. It has been a pleasure to meet you, Miss ...?"

Books! she thought. Wendy had planned on doing three things with her time in Hertfordshire. The bit about helping orphans was going very well indeed. Her marksmanship training, however, had been foundering, and she had turned up nothing new about the everlost. If this man had both military training and a library ...

"Wendy Darling, Monsieur Dumas! I must say, it is a great pleasure to meet you! A great pleasure indeed!"

Visiting Monsieur Dumas turned out to be much more difficult than Wendy had expected.

For one thing, he was French, so the good people of Hertfordshire treated him with tremendous suspicion just for standing on English soil rather than staying on his own side of the Straits where he belonged. As long as Wendy was pretending to be Captain Hook's fiancée, she could not be seen socializing with the wrong sort of crowd. It was one thing to spend Hook's money, of which he seemed to have plenty. It was another thing altogether to stain his honor.

Not that speaking to Monsieur Dumas should have placed any sort of stain upon either her own name or Hook's, in Wendy's opinion. He seemed like a kind man, and *refusing* to speak to him struck her as a sign of very poor manners. But she understood that some people will gossip about things they ought not to worry over

at all, that this is just "how things are," and that the best thing to do about it is simply to avoid the situation altogether.

Which can usually be managed by sneaking around and doing what you wanted to do in the first place, just with less attention. (A process with which she was perfectly familiar, thanks to several years of sneaking out of the almshouse for her training with Olaudah Equiano.)

This cloak-and-dagger solution to her first problem, however, only raised a second one. The Hook Estate was no mere almshouse, and she had two lieutenants following her everywhere she went. Even worse, thanks to her shopping spree, they had now been commanded in no uncertain terms (via orders sent from London and written in Hook's own hand) not to allow her to leave the premises.

The lieutenants could only assume this meant they were to follow her everywhere she went even within the estate itself, so they greeted her at her bedroom door every morning and then followed her to the kitchen and to the library and to the gardens and so on, all day long. Apparently, Captain Hook had not appreciated the bill for the orphan's supplies.

Unfortunately for Wendy, he had *not* been unhappy enough to send her back to Dover. He had instead taken steps toward "reining in the unruly filly," which was the exact phrase he used in his letter, comparing Wendy to an ill-tempered horse.

Needless to say, this was a poor choice of words.

Wendy had attempted straightaway to send Colin out in her place to spend more of Hook's money, on the orphans' behalf and with a *much* longer shopping list. But the boy had reported sadly, with his hat clutched in both hands and his eyes downcast, that Hook's letter had been quite clear on the matter. Wendy had no

authority to spend the money of the Hook Estate, and therefore Colin could not do so at her request.

Mrs. Medcalf, having been apprised of the request by her son, went to comfort Wendy and found her in her room, which was the only place in which she could escape the lieutenants. The kindhearted cook recognized the depth of the young woman's disappointment immediately. Wendy sat on the edge of her bed, looking down at her hands in her lap, doing nothing. She didn't even look up and smile when the older woman opened the door, which wasn't like her at all.

"Oh, my poor dear," Mrs. Medcalf said, rushing to her side and sitting next to her, taking one of Wendy's hands between her own and patting it gently. "It's going to be all right."

"Is it, Mrs. Medcalf? I don't see how, I'm afraid," Wendy admitted sadly, although each woman was speaking of something altogether different than the other.

Mrs. Medcalf assumed Wendy was worried because Hook was angry with her, afraid this might mean the end of his affections. In fact, Wendy had hoped he might be a bit *more* angry than he was—angry enough to send her back to her platoon and be done with this false engagement. She was only sad that her plan had backfired, leaving her with even less freedom than before.

"Of course it is, dear," Mrs. Medcalf assured her. "He'll get past it. He has to. The captain has always been careful with his money. *Too* careful, if you don't mind my saying so. He understands finance well enough, but he doesn't understand *society*. One has to keep a proper appearance in town, and that means donations to the Church, of course, and alms for the poor. If a wealthy man fails in these things, eventually people will talk. You were only protecting his reputation. He will come to see

that, when he returns to Hertfordshire and hears the kind words people say to him regarding his generosity."

Even though Wendy wasn't concerned about any of that, she found the older woman's fond attention and plump, steady presence—which always smelled delightfully of apples and cinnamon—so comforting that she began to take heart, nonetheless.

"Do you really think so?" Wendy asked. "He'll get past it, and he'll let me go out again?"

"Let you go out again? What do you mean? What's this then?"

"Oh, Mrs. Medcalf! Then you don't know! The letter wasn't just about the money. He commanded the lieutenants to follow me everywhere, even here at the estate, and to prevent me from leaving at all, ever again!" (The "ever again" part was a bit of an exaggeration, but that was how it felt to Wendy, so that was how she said it.)

"What?" Mrs. Medcalf exclaimed. "Why, I have half a mind to write to the captain myself! It's one thing for a man to choose how he wants to spend his money—even if he's wrong about it— but it's another thing altogether to try to lock his fiancée away like a prisoner! There's no call for *that*. It isn't as though you'd go against his direct wishes, now that's he's made his position clear."

"Of course not," Wendy agreed. "I would never!"

It went through her mind that the very first thing she did was try to get Colin to spend more of Hook's money, a fact of which Mrs. Medcalf was perfectly aware, and Wendy winced a little— but only on the inside. Outwardly, she maintained a look of wide-eyed innocence. She hadn't been *successful* at it, so to claim that she would not do so from now on seemed reasonable enough.

"But truly, Mrs. Medcalf," Wendy continued, "I would not want you to interfere. You and your family have been so kind to

me. If you were to risk your position here at the estate, I would never forgive myself."

"There, there," Mrs. Medcalf said. She was touched that Wendy would be so considerate, especially when she was being treated so wrongfully herself.

"I only wish I could find some way to go out, just for a bit. Not to spend any more money of course," she added hurriedly, "but only to represent him in a positive manner. To visit the local parsonage, for example. So that when he comes back, as you say, everyone will be speaking well of me."

"Of course, dear. That would be an excellent thing to do. If only it could be managed, that is. It is always best, I've found, to prove a man wrong by one's actions, rather than by one's words. They tend not to listen to us, I'm afraid. But when faced with evidence, the good ones always come around eventually."

"I have found the exact same thing, Mrs. Medcalf."

Mrs. Medcalf beamed proudly. (Between her husband and Colin, not to mention Huxley and even Captain Hook, she had been surrounded by men for a very long time. Although they were good men, in her opinion, and she adored them all, it was still nice to have another woman in the house. And such a sweet young woman at that, to listen to her advice, and even to agree with her point of view.)

"Do you think, Mrs. Medcalf," Wendy asked, watching her closely, "that if there *were* a way in which I might get out for a while, to go visit the parson's wife, for example, that I might be able to count on your help?"

"Of course, dear! Why, I would even bake a lovely tart for you to carry with you, by way of introduction. But I don't think we can convince the lieutenants to allow it."

"No, I don't either. But the letter never said that Colin couldn't

drive me in the coach. It didn't say that *he* had to keep me here, or that *you* had to keep me here. It only said that the *lieutenants* had to keep me here. It was very specific."

"Was it now?" Mrs. Medcalf asked, and then she smiled. It was a devious sort of smile, with a wicked gleam in her eye that revealed, just for a moment, the spirited girl that Mrs. Medcalf herself had once been—now almost forgotten in the midst of cooking for the estate and comforting a husband and raising a child.

Almost forgotten, but not quite.

Wendy had been quite fond of Mrs. Medcalf from the beginning, but it was in this very moment, with this particular smile, that she came to love her.

CHAPTER
27

Wendy's visits with Monsieur Dumas began with an elaborate plan of escape, or rather a *series* of escapes, the first of which involved eleven mice and a lot of high-pitched shrieking by Mrs. Medcalf as she hopped from foot to foot, clutching her bonnet to her head with one hand and directing the lieutenants with the other.

"Look there! Another one! Eeeeeek! No, there! Get that one!"

By the time the rodents had all been gotten, Wendy and Colin were nowhere to be found.

The lieutenants were reluctant to report the incident. After all, Wendy returned unharmed, having been chaperoned by Colin the entire afternoon, and they didn't see the point of getting themselves in trouble for nothing. So their weekly letter to Hook left that bit out.

But the first escape was followed by three others, each new scheme more carefully orchestrated than the last, involving after-

noon tea; poppy seeds; a croquet mallet; two of the estate's trained peacocks; Mr. Medcalf's old, battered bugle; a thoroughbred stallion; a honeycomb from which the bees had not been properly removed; and eventually a broken window, which even Mrs. Medcalf admitted privately had probably gone a bit too far.

Wendy, however, wasn't sorry for any of it. It was the lieutenants' fault, not hers, that they refused to report her absences. She enjoyed her time with Monsieur Dumas well enough, and he was exceedingly grateful to have found a friend. But the whole point of these shenanigans was to get Wendy out of Hook's glorious hair by sending her back to Dover. If the captain didn't know what was happening at home, the plan didn't have a chance.

The lieutenants were only forcing her to escalate things, and heaven only knows how far things might have gone if it hadn't been for Pan.

There was something intriguing about the Wendy, Pan thought, and he had decided to keep an eye on her even though he was still a bit irked.

He couldn't watch her directly, of course. She had too good a nose for magic, and she had a dog with her besides. So he sent Tinker Bell to do his dirty work for him. (Tinker Bell did not think kindly of this, and she had several other unkind thoughts besides, but it is probably best not to repeat them.)

Now, Tink had the scent of magic upon her just as Pan did himself, but she was smaller, which made the effect more subtle — in the same way that you might ignore a single tree in the midst of

a city block, but you could hardly miss the sudden appearance of an entire forest. Being small also gave her more places to hide, and if Wendy was being followed by a distant golden bird, flitting from tree to tree across the countryside of Hertfordshire, neither she nor Poppy took any notice.

This affected Tinker Bell in a very unsettling way. On the one hand, she was proud of her ability to sneak about undetected. But on the other, she was annoyed that anyone could fail to notice her exceeding beauty, no matter how hard she was trying to hide it. As a result, Tink's feathers took on an intriguing shade of red-burnished gold—an angry sort of pride. Still beautiful, mind you, but far more natural in effect than either red or gold would have been alone, which only enhanced her ability to blend in among the robins and the finches.

She would watch as Wendy evaded the lieutenants and ran off to visit Monsieur Dumas, shooting at targets and reading books in the garden whenever the weather allowed it. Reporting back to Pan, Tink would embellish these events by dragging out every detail of each escape—she couldn't help herself, Pan's rapt attention being almost intoxicating to her ego—so that before she knew it she had made Wendy out to be larger than life. A brilliant military strategist with the speed and endurance of the ancient gods.

Looking back on it, this made Tinker Bell even madder. She didn't know exactly how the Wendy had tricked her into such embellishments, but Tink vowed to have her revenge, one way or another. (This was just like the innisfay, who believe to their very core that nothing is ever their own fault—one of the many reasons why it is best to avoid them whenever possible.)

Wendy, however, didn't know this, which is why she reached out her hand toward Tinker Bell the very first time she saw her.

Wendy was reading in the garden behind the modest home of Monsieur Dumas, a lovely cottage surrounded by an explosion of flowers that masked the subtle, pickle-green scent hiding within it. When a tiny hummingbird of red-burnished gold burst forth from among the bellflower leaves to hover in the air before her, Poppy raised her head and barked even before she had fully comprehended the danger.

But Wendy ignored the dog's warning, reaching out in wonder toward the little bird, its wings a blur of motion, its body impossibly still, radiant in the late afternoon sun. That's when Tinker Bell turned back into a dragon and bit her.

"Oh!" Wendy exclaimed, but she said nothing else for the moment as she was already sucking on the tip of her injured finger. It was bleeding, albeit just a little, the metallic taste of it sharp against her tongue.

Poppy sprang into action, trying to snatch the creature out of the air, but Tink only flew higher, chattering away amidst her jingle bell laughter.

"Pan," Wendy said, putting two and two together. "He sent you, whatever you are."

Tinker Bell's chiming stopped cold. She hadn't planned on the Wendy figuring that out. Tink came from a place where magic was common—where there was no particular reason why the appearance of one magical creature should remind you of another, any more than your next-door neighbor dropping by should make you think of the baker. She had not accounted for the fact that people

in England were aware of very few magical creatures, so that the arrival of one might remind them of the only other one they had ever met.

Naturally, she blamed the Wendy for this oversight.

Launching back into her melodious tirade, Tinker Bell dove straight at Wendy's eyes, intending to gouge them out. Wendy threw her hands up in defense, but Poppy was already on the move, leaping with all her might to gnash at the tiny dragon, her teeth snapping together wickedly in the empty air, having just barely missed the creature's tail.

Tink trilled out a lovely screech and sped off toward the distant trees, leaving Wendy with little doubt as to where Pan was hiding. Monsieur Dumas was due back with their tea at any moment, so Wendy set off at a run through the fields before he could return, following Tink as best she could, with Poppy trailing eagerly behind.

They soon lost sight of Tinker Bell in the forest, but by then the scent alone was enough to track Peter Pan. Wendy realized, standing among the trees and the light undergrowth that tugged playfully at her skirts, that he smelled very much like the forest itself (except, perhaps, for the taste of pickles). In fact, he smelled even *more* like the forest than the forest did. It was as though she were constantly moving toward its richest and most vibrant depths—where it was most alive—as though Peter Pan stood always at the heart of it.

When they finally found him, he was standing in an oak tree scolding Tinker Bell, who perched somewhat above and away from him, looking blue. Literally. Peter stood with his left foot on one branch and his right foot on another, his back leaning casually against the trunk, his arms folded across his chest, his chin thrust angrily toward the small creature.

"I told you not to let her see you," he said.

Tinker Bell chimed back in a protesting sort of way.

"That isn't the point," Peter told her.

More chiming.

"Excuse me," Wendy called up to him, "but is he actually speaking? Why, that's remarkable!" The fact that the small creature spoke in jingle bells seemed even more amazing to Wendy than the fact that it looked like a miniature dragon, which tells you just how much she had been coming into contact with magical creatures lately.

"She," Pan corrected Wendy, accompanied by the sound of several dozen strands of Christmas bells all being shaken at once.

"Oh. I'm sorry," Wendy apologized. "She's very beautiful. Does she always change color like that?" The dragon had morphed into a fiery red, glowering down at Wendy from her high branch.

"Her color matches her mood, of course," Peter replied. "All the innisfay do that. Don't you know anything?"

"The innisfay?" Wendy asked, ignoring the implied insult.

"You don't even know what they *are*?" Peter asked, his tone incredulous.

"Well, I know *she's* one," Wendy said, sounding a bit defensive. "So at least I know what they look like."

"Ha! You know nothing!" Peter moved away from the trunk and began to pace back and forth along one of the two branches he

had been straddling, staring down at her all the while. "The inn-isfay can look like any creature they please! Birds, foxes, sprites, dragons! That's how she's been following you!"

"Following me!" Wendy exclaimed, and Pan stopped pacing, his expression sobering just a bit. He obviously hadn't meant to tell her that part.

"Yes," he declared, as though he had intended the conversation to take this new direction all along. "And she has told me everything. How you come here to shoot. How you've been running away from Hook's men. That's why I decided we could be friends again. You're a prisoner of war. I respect that."

Wendy almost corrected him, but she had only followed Tinker Bell because of Hook's promise: She could return to Dover if she could find out where Pan's island was. Perhaps if Pan thought they were on the same side, he would be willing to confide in her.

"Thank you," she said, straightening her shoulders and tilting her chin upward in stoic dignity. "It has not been easy, as you can imagine."

"Does he beat you?" Pan asked, but he sounded more curious than sympathetic.

"Well, no. No one beats me," Wendy admitted.

"Do they chain you to the wall, forcing you to watch while they eat their rich dinners, your empty stomach growling in agony?"

"Of course not," Wendy protested. "Nobody chains me up, and Mrs. Medcalf feeds me very well."

"Hmph," Pan muttered. "Then he's not a very good jailer. That's what *I'd* do if *I* had any prisoners."

"Well then I'm glad I'm his prisoner and not yours," Wendy snapped. The very thought of anyone being treated in such a way made her angry.

"You should be." Pan's face darkened and he stepped out of the tree, opening his wings just before he slammed into the ground. He landed mere inches away from her, staring down into her eyes. "But you are *his* prisoner, so we are on the same side after all. Come away with me. I shall grant you asylum."

"What? No!" Wendy said, her mind racing. "No, I can't. I'm using the situation, you see. To gather information. To learn about the strength of his forces—where his ships are, how many men he has. That sort of thing."

"Ah!" Pan exclaimed. "Yes, of course! That's very good thinking!"

"But I don't know enough yet," she continued. "Let me learn everything I can, and then I'll steal one of his ships and come to your island. You just have to tell me where to find you."

"Ha!" Pan laughed. "None of *his* ships can find *my* island. It's impossible!"

"Impossible?" Wendy asked. "Why is it impossible?"

Peter drew himself up to his full height and looked down at her proudly.

"Because none of *his* ships can fly!"

T hat night, Wendy couldn't sleep. Instead, she sat in a chair by the window in her room, her feet tucked up underneath her, and she stared out at the stars.

A flying ship!

She tried to imagine it—a ship full of winged men sailing through the sky. Their voices calling to each other in the night. The deck bucking in the wind. Nothing but an explosion of stars above their heads, strewn across the heavens. It felt as though all the dreams of her childhood had been magnified a thousand fold and then wrapped up like a gift, just for her.

Come away with me.

Despite his handsome features and athletic form, his chiseled hands and the scent of the forest upon him, it was the ship that had tempted her. To join the crew of a flying ship! To live a life of adventures more magnificent than any she had ever imagined, seeing all the world from above!

But Peter hadn't said anything about being a part of his crew. That hadn't been the offer. If it *had* (and assuming she had believed him) she thought for just a moment that she might have gone with him. Despite the fact that she was his sworn enemy. Despite the fact that he had chopped off Hook's right hand. Despite the fact that he and his crew had kidnapped orphans and murdered their caretakers.

Blood drinkers.

No. She shook her head, even though there was no one there to see. Not even Poppy, who lay fast asleep on the floor next to her chair. No, she knew she could never join them, no matter how tempting the idea of sailing among the stars.

If it was even true. If there even *was* a flying ship.

A tiny line formed between her brows as she considered it. *Was* it true? If there was one thing she had already learned about Peter Pan, it was that he had a tendency to exaggerate. But then again, look at poor Reginald. The man had *died*. Peter had claimed he could fix it, and then he *had* fixed it, bringing poor Reginald back to life. She never would have believed *that* claim either if she hadn't seen it with her own eyes. Was a flying ship really so hard to accept?

Then again, he might be feeding her false information on purpose, expecting her to report it back to Hook. And *that* thought brought up a whole new problem. *Should* she report it?

She could certainly think of several reasons not to.

First, if Pan were lying just to throw them off his trail—tricking the Home Office into searching the skies while he and his men snuck through the dark alleyways of London right beneath their noses—then reporting the idea of a flying ship to Hook would only be helping the everlost to carry out their plan.

Second, she risked looking like a fool. Or worse—losing her

position with the Home Office. After all, Hook hadn't believed her report about poor Reginald. That was what had gotten her stuck here in Hertfordshire in the first place. But at least he had thought she was *mistaken* about poor Reginald, not purposefully *lying*. If Hook came to believe she was inventing false information, he would dismiss her from the king's service altogether, and *then* what would she do?

Third, she couldn't report the conversation without admitting she had escaped from her lieutenant chaperones. Even if she didn't mention Monsieur Dumas (which, of course, she never would, so as not to cause trouble for her friend), it would still be clear that the lieutenants had not been present in the woods when she had found Peter Pan. Hook would question them, and they would be forced to admit that she had evaded them several times now.

Even if Hook didn't dismiss her from the Home Office on the spot, her escapades would be over. Hook would send more men. Crueler, more devious men. And Wendy would be Hook's prisoner after all.

Wendy sighed deeply. Poppy opened one eye to look up at her, then rolled onto her back, bending her head to one side to watch Wendy from a more quizzical angle. Wendy smiled sadly and brought her feet down to the floor, tucking them under Poppy's back for warmth.

"There's only one reason I can think of to write any sort of report at all about this afternoon," she told Poppy, "but I'm afraid that one reason is more important than all the reasons against it put together."

Poppy wriggled on the floor, scratching her back against Wendy's feet and making a low, guttural sort of sound that went something like this: "Rauuuauuuwauuu."

"That's right," Wendy agreed. "Duty. Exactly. As a sworn member of the Home Office, I have a duty to report any encounter with the everlost. I'll just have to report the entire conversation exactly as it occurred."

Of course, Poppy hadn't been thinking "duty" at all. Instead, she had been thinking, "Oh, it feels so good to scratch one's back on the floor. You really should try it." And because Wendy hadn't understood her, she decided to try again.

"RauuauuRAUUwauuauu."

"Well of *course* I'm not going to tell him *where* the conversation happened," Wendy assured her. "I'll just say I found Peter in the woods here on the estate. It's the conversation *itself* that matters."

Poppy blinked twice at her mistress, waiting to see whether the itch on her back was going to return, but thankfully it did not. Sighing in relief, she rolled onto her belly, curled up into a ball, and fell promptly back asleep.

Hook sat in his London office, turning the pages of Wendy's latest report over and over in his hands as though there might be some sort of trap waiting for him on the back of the exquisite stationary. Some danger that he hadn't yet discovered. A tactile poison, perhaps. Or an army of trained insects. Each tiny, cruel heart named after a delicate flower.

Dandelion. Lavender. Poppy.

He grimaced.

There had to be a trick in it somewhere. The woman was devious to her very core. How many times had she managed to evade her guards before Peter Pan had found her? Or before she had found him. Whichever.

If she had even spoken to him at all.

Hook eyed the report suspiciously and then dropped it on the desk, opening a drawer to retrieve a long sharpening stone. Staring at her fine handwriting all the while, he slowly drew his hook back

and forth across the stone, tilting it first this way and then that, honing it to a cruel point.

Scree... scree... scree...

She was toying with him. That much was obvious. Flying ships? Tiny dragons that could sit in the palm of your hand? Did she think him a fool? What game was she playing?

Scree... scree...

It occurred to him that she might be trying to look ridiculous on purpose. If the full report was ever discovered by the Home Office, she would be discredited entirely—as would anyone else who associated with her. He would be forced to release her from the Hertfordshire estate. But Wendy Darling didn't strike him as the kind of girl to play the fool. Not even to get what she wanted. Besides which, she clearly didn't intend to leave the Home Office in disgrace. If she had wanted as much, she could have simply run away.

No, the trap was more clever than that. It had to be.

Scree... scree... scree... scree...

He would have burned the entire report to ash and returned it to her in a snuff box, just to make a point, but he couldn't quite bring himself to do it. Tiny dragons. Flying ships. The whole thing was preposterous. A flying man was implausible enough, but a ship? The sheer weight of the thing alone!

Still, it made a strange kind of sense. A man might be able to swim, but that didn't mean he could swim all the way to France. And even if he could, that was no way to wage a war. The ships of men carried weapons, ammunition, provisions. The ships of men carried the spoils of battle back home.

Wouldn't the everlost want ships to do the same? To carry their stolen goods, their pilfered sheep, their kidnapped orphans? He had always assumed the children were carried away for their

blood, to be fed upon later in some terrifying ritual. They were small, relatively helpless. Easy prey. Like lambs taken by wolves.

But the everlost only came every few weeks. Sometimes even months would go by without any sign of them. Surely they needed more than just a meal or two in all that time. He tried to think only of flour and sheep, but there were too many missing children to ignore. Far too many for the everlost to carry kicking and screaming in their arms across the vast leagues of the sea.

Scree… scree…. scree… scree… scree…

A flying ship made sense. But Wendy Darling *wanted* it to make sense. Or at least she wanted it to *seem* as though it made sense. Which is why he didn't trust it.

Just a few short weeks ago he would have written off the entire thing as the overactive imagination of an uneducated child, but now he wasn't so sure. She had escaped from his best men—not just once but apparently at will (a fact that they had finally been forced to admit)—turning his groundskeeper's family to her own purposes, resilient in the face of his plans to keep her in Hertfordshire.

Perhaps that had been a mistake.

No! That was what she *wanted* him to think!

He slammed the sharpening stone down on the desk and ran his good left hand though his hair. He was overthinking the whole thing. He needed a clear perspective. Someone who hadn't met the woman. Someone who wasn't engaged in her cat-and-mouse games. Someone who could help him separate fact from fiction.

He needed Sir William.

Sir William had barely even opened the door when Hook shoved Wendy's report toward him across the desk with a look of disgust.

"Flying ships!" Hook growled.

Sir William rolled his eyes. "Give it here."

Hook handed the pages over and then leaned back in his chair, folding his arms on top of his head, his left hand grasping the stump of his right wrist just below the razor-sharp metal.

"This is ridiculous," Sir William muttered, his eyes scanning the elegant lines. "Women and dogs. First resurrection and now flying ships? Why haven't you cut that diviner free and sent her back to Dover already? Never mind, don't answer that. I know perfectly well why you haven't."

He thrust the report back toward Hook without looking beyond the first page, but Hook made no move to take it.

Sir William narrowed his eyes. "It's one thing to indulge a girl in dresses and draperies, Hook. It's another thing altogether to indulge her *ideas*. You might as well spray this nonsense with rose water and call it a love letter. She just wants your attention."

At this, Hook barked out a laugh. "I assure you, she wants no such thing."

"Of course she does. They all do. Attention, social standing, and children. And not necessarily in that order."

"Not this one," Hook said. "At least not from me."

Sir William snorted. "You're a commissioned officer, favored by the king, with an honorable family and overflowing coffers besides. If she acts like she isn't interested, she's just a better actress than most. Those, by the way, are the ones to watch out for."

Sir William dropped the papers back onto Hook's desk, but Hook only leaned forward, lowering his hands—or rather, lowering his one hand and his one hook—to slide the first page off the stack and pick up the second.

157

"*Although he refused to reveal the island's location,*" he read aloud, "*Pan admitted that it is too far from London for most of the everlost to reach by flying under their own power.*"

Sir William said nothing, but he pursed his lips in reluctant interest.

"*He boasted several times that he is more than capable of flying the distance himself, but stated that the rest of his 'crew' is not. Instead, they traverse the ocean via flying ship, a voyage that takes 'many moons.'*"

Sir William scowled again, but Hook raised his shining metal appendage in the air, twisting it so it caught the candlelight. The older man held his tongue, in deference to his sacrifice.

"*I presume this was an exaggeration,*" Hook continued. "*Everything Pan says contains some manner of embellishment, making it difficult to determine the precise truth contained within any of it.*"

"You see? Even *she* admits that it's nonsense!" Sir William declared.

"*There are, however, several facts that did not change, no matter how many times I questioned him. These are the following. First, the everlost live together on an island. Second, the island is located far out to sea—a voyage of several days from any known port. Third, they use at least one ship to travel between the island and England, anchoring it offshore as a base of operations for their raids. Fourth, as strange as it sounds, Pan insisted at every turn that this ship can fly.*"

With each number, the captain tilted his hook forward just a touch and then withdrew it again, as though it were a flesh-and-blood hand upon which he was raising imaginary fingers one at a time. When he had finished, he lifted an eyebrow at Sir William, waiting for a response.

Now, Sir William had never seen Hook make this precise expression before. Nor had he ever seen an eyebrow poised so ele-

gantly and yet so challengingly at the same time. He took half a step backward, despite the safety of the desk that stood between them, and then he stepped forward once again, ready to put the younger man in his place.

"Let's pretend, just for a moment, that it's all true," he growled. "If anything, it would be the worst possible news! An uncharted island in the middle of the bloody ocean. An enemy with flying ships—"

"Wait," Hook interrupted, his eyes flying wide. "It's not uncharted!"

"What?" Sir William paused before he could really get going, glancing around at the countless maps plastered over the walls.

"No, you're right," Hook clarified, and he swiped his hook through the air as though clearing the maps away. "*We* haven't charted it. But that's not the same thing as being *uncharted.*"

Now Sir William's lips curled into a triumphant smirk. "Of course! *They've* certainly charted their own island!"

"Exactly! Steal their ship—" Hook began.

"Whether or not it flies," Sir William added.

"Steal their maps!" Hook finished.

He didn't have to find the island after all. He just had to find that ship. Hook grinned at Wendy Darling's report—a wicked grin that promised vengeance for the king, vengeance for England, and vengeance for his own right hand all at once. Whatever game she thought she was playing, she would be no match for him.

And it was time for him to make his next move.

CHAPTER
30

Two days later, a letter arrived at the Hertfordshire estate ordering the lieutenants to report back to Hook immediately—seats had been arranged on the afternoon coach from St. Albans. Colin was all too happy to load the two men up in the carriage and drive them off, although the lieutenants themselves did not look happy about it at all.

It was several hours before Colin returned, but when the carriage finally neared the manor house, it was accompanied by the sound of a very particular bark that had Wendy flying toward the main entrance even before the new arrival could be properly announced.

And Nana was not the only familiar face to greet her.

"John! Michael! Nana!" She froze at the door of the manor for just a moment, taken by surprise—both by their sudden appearance and by their military uniforms—but then she raced down the steps to hug all three, in the same order.

"But ... how? And where are the others?" she asked. She had not expected Hook to return her to the platoon so quickly, and she could hardly believe her good fortune.

"It's just us," Michael said.

"There's much to tell," John confirmed. "But we mustn't keep you from your supper." He looked over Wendy's head toward Mrs. Medcalf, who was standing with her arms folded at the top of the stairs, watching the reunion with a distinct air of displeasure.

"Oh!" Wendy exclaimed. "Oh, Mrs. Medcalf, I'm so sorry. I had no idea they were coming."

"It's not your fault, my dear," Mrs. Medcalf assured her. "If the captain chooses not to prepare the house for guests, that's his business. We'll make do."

"Of course," Huxley agreed. He had appeared out of the shadows of the house without a sound, as good butlers will, sensing that his presence was needed. "Colin, please escort these gentlemen to the west wing."

Mrs. Medcalf nodded, looking somewhat mollified. Wendy, of course, was staying in the *east* wing.

"We will delay dinner for one hour to give them a chance to settle in and wash up," Huxley continued. "Mrs. Medcalf, will that be sufficient for the kitchen to make the necessary arrangements?"

"It will, thank you," she confirmed.

"I'm so glad you're here!" Wendy exclaimed, hugging both men one more time, road dust and all, and the look on each of their faces made Mrs. Medcalf scowl all over again.

As for Poppy, she wasn't sure how she felt about Nana's arrival either. She had followed Wendy from the house of course, and she growled just a bit to see Wendy treating the newcomer with obvious affection.

"Poppy!" Wendy chided. "Poppy, this is Nana. She's the dog I told you about. The one I had to leave behind in Dover. Nana, this is Poppy. She's been my lovely companion here in Hertfordshire."

Has been? Poppy wasn't sure she liked the sound of that.

Lovely companion? Nana wasn't sure she liked the sound of *that*.

The two eyed each other warily, but they said no more about it in Wendy's presence.

"When do we leave for Dover?" Wendy asked.

She was seated at the library table next to Colin, with John and Michael sitting across from her. They had retired there after dinner, and Colin had been sent in by his mother as a trusted chaperone. Poppy and Nana lay at Wendy's feet—Poppy on her left side, closer to Colin, and Nana claiming the right.

"We can trust him," Wendy added, meaning Colin, when neither man answered her. More importantly, she trusted *them* not to say anything in front of Colin that could compromise their mission. Or their own vows of secrecy. Still, she wanted Colin to understand the depth of her faith in him.

"Colin," she said, "what you are about to hear could be of the utmost importance to both king and country. You must swear on your life—and quite possibly on my own as well—not to reveal anything said here tonight to your parents or to anyone else. Not for any reason. Do you swear it?"

"Yes, ma'am! I swear it on my life! On both our lives! I would never betray you!" Colin agreed, his eyes wide as saucers. John

and Michael's uniforms clearly marked them as military men, a necessary change since they were being offered up as Wendy's new guardsmen. Unlike the last two, these men clearly had Wendy's respect, and that had already earned them Colin's as well.

"There, you see?" Wendy said, returning her attention to John. "So then, when do we leave for Dover?"

John and Michael shared a glance that said, "You answer her. No, *you* answer her." But of course Wendy was watching them and saw the whole thing.

"John," she declared, and John frowned while Michael grinned triumphantly. "What is it? When do we leave for Dover?"

"We're not going back to Dover," he admitted, staring down at the table.

"We're not? Then where are we going? Remember, Colin, not a word."

Colin nodded mutely—a rapid, stuttering sort of nod—glancing at Wendy and then returning his gaze to John, awaiting his reply.

"We are all to remain here until further notice."

"What?" Wendy exclaimed. "But the platoon!"

"Has been assigned a new lieutenant," John explained, "with his own second-in-command, and his own ..." John glanced at Colin. "His own attachment. His wife, as it happens." He watched Wendy closely as he said this last bit. "They work together."

If he was trying to feel Wendy out on the subject of diviners marrying their lieutenants, she missed the cue entirely.

"You've been removed from command?" Wendy demanded. Her own eyes flew wide, ranging back and forth between John's gaze and Michael's.

"It's all right," John assured her. "We've just been reassigned. That's all. We're glad to be here."

"But the platoon!" Wendy said again, and her left eyebrow began to look dangerously cross, followed immediately by the other.

"It isn't as though we've lost our rank," Michael reassured her. "We were glad to get the assignment. We both were. We've been worried sick. Besides, we have a way to get back."

"Oh, well thank heavens! Why didn't you just say so?"

"It's not quite as simple as he's making it sound, I'm afraid," John retorted, glaring at Michael.

"What? I never said it was simple," Michael protested. "I just said we had a way."

"What way, exactly?" Wendy wanted to know.

"Here," John said. "It's in the note."

"Note?"

He reached into a small messenger satchel that hung at his waist and handed Wendy a note, addressed to Wendy Darling. She knew immediately from the handwriting on the envelope that it was from Hook. She would have recognized that arrogant scrawl anywhere.

"Oh, what now?" she demanded.

"Just read it," Michael said, grinning wickedly.

"It's not funny," John growled.

"It's a little funny," Michael said, and he winked at Colin, who giggled.

"But how do you know what it says?" Wendy asked, moving to break the seal, but she soon realized it was already broken.

"You broke the seal on official orders?" Wendy demanded, brandishing the evidence with an angry flourish.

"Nana did it," John and Michael both declared at once, pointing under the table.

Nana growled and Colin laughed more loudly this time, but Wendy only sighed.

"We had to know what it said," John protested.

"In case he was moving you again!" Michael added.

"Oh, just let me read it."

Wendy silenced any further protest with one delicate hand. She read the note without a sound, moving her lips just the smallest bit as she read, so that the secret kiss in the corner danced in and out of view, making both men and even Colin want to sigh a little, although none of them did.

My Darling Wendy,

I trust you won't try to run away from these two. I'm sorry to have to send them, but you left me no choice. I can hardly have my fiancée running about the countryside unescorted. I have had to replace them in their posts, of course, but that arrangement need not be permanent. Find me the location of an everlost ship, and what I have done shall be undone just as easily. I will gladly return you and your escorts to the platoon at Dover immediately upon proof of true delivery.

Yours in earnest,
Captain James Hook

"How dare he?" Wendy cried. "I knew this was my fault! And to hold it over my head like some kind of ... some kind of ... wait, what part of this is funny?"

Colin looked back and forth among the others, trying to guess from their reactions what the note had said.

"Some kind of ransom?" John suggested.

"The part where he calls you his fiancée, obviously!" Michael declared, answering her question. "He *is* joking, isn't he?"

"Teasing me mercilessly, yes," Wendy affirmed.

Colin grinned, taking this in. He had never agreed with his mother's opinion on the likelihood of an engagement—although he had been wise enough to keep that counsel to himself.

"See? I told you it was a joke!" Michael crowed this triumphantly while thrusting his chin at John in a taunting sort of way.

"I never said otherwise!" John declared.

"But you didn't agree with me either," Michael pointed out.

"Oh, hush, both of you," Wendy said, and the two men fell silent. "How on earth are we going to get him to tell us where his ships are?"

"Who?" But from the threatening look on John's face, he already knew the answer.

Wendy glanced briefly at Colin. "You know who," was all she said.

"He's been here?" Michael's own expression now mirrored John's, sending a bit of a thrill through Wendy, whether she wanted to admit it or not.

"Just twice," she said.

"*Twice?*" they shouted together.

"Hush," Wendy admonished them again. "You'll scare Colin's parents. Yes, twice. Once after I first arrived, and again just recently."

"But how did he even find you?" John demanded.

Wendy was far too kind to admit that Pan had followed the courier John and Michael had sent.

"He has a spy," she said instead.

"A spy! Inside the regiment!" John curled his hand into a fist on the table before him.

"No, no. A spy of his own," Wendy said quickly. "Just ... well ... a very small one."

"A very small spy? What does that mean?" Michael cocked his head and rested his chin in his hand, awaiting her reply, his eyes already twinkling in anticipation. Wendy always did tell the best stories.

"It's an innisfay," she said, watching Colin out of the corner of her eye.

"And what, pray tell, is an innisfay?" John wanted to know.

"It's a magical creature," Wendy finally blurted out. "It's very small, and it can look like any creature it chooses, but it was a dragon when I saw it." Colin's eyes opened even wider, but he showed no sign of disbelief—a fact that both worried and comforted her at the same time.

"A tiny dragon spy," John said, trying to take that in.

"Yes, she's been following me. Oh!"

Wendy planted both hands on the table and thrust herself to her feet all at once, causing both men and both dogs to do the same. Not to be left out, Colin followed suit immediately. When Wendy turned and ran for the rear garden, they all trailed behind her in a line behind from smallest to largest: Poppy, then Nana, then Colin, then Michael, and then John.

As soon as she was outside, she cupped both hands to her mouth and called into the night, accompanied by a low growling from Poppy and Nana.

"Oh, innisfay! Little innisfay!" She was embarrassed to realize she had never asked the tiny creature for its name. "I know you're out here! Tell your friend we need to speak with him, please. It's very important!"

"Wendy, I don't think—"

There were quite a few things that John might have thought. He might have thought that calling to magical creatures in the night was not the best course of action, for example. Or that Wendy

couldn't be certain the little spy was anywhere nearby. But Wendy cut him off before he could say exactly what it was he *did* think, so now we will never be certain what it was.

"Tiny dragon-person-innisfay!" she called again. "Do you hear me? Go now, please. Go on! Go find him!"

As though in answer, there was a sudden explosion of tiny, jingling chimes, rising into the night out of a lovely patch of bell-flowers and fading rapidly into the distance.

"There now," Wendy announced, and she placed both hands on her hips, clearly satisfied. "He'll come to us. All we have to do is wait."

(As for what Tinker Bell thought, well, it's probably all for the best that we will never be certain what *that* was either.)

CHAPTER
31

While they waited, Wendy admitted to John and Michael that she had told Peter Pan she was Hook's prisoner, which both men felt was closer to the truth than they would have liked. She had tried to convince Peter to tell her where his island was, claiming she intended to meet him there later, but he had refused to do so, insisting there was no point in it. She would not be able to get there without his help.

But he would not explain any further.

They all wondered about that for a bit, but the *point* of the story, Wendy reminded them, was that Pan still thought she was a prisoner who had to sneak away from the house, and he would surely know something was amiss if he found her waiting for him in the garden with two guardsmen and a member of Hook's personal staff. Not to mention two guard dogs, she added hastily, so that Nana and Poppy would not feel left out.

"We're not leaving you alone out here," John declared, and

Michael stood a bit straighter beside him, setting his jaw and crossing his arms over his chest, making it perfectly clear whose side he was on about *that*.

"Well *of course* I'm not asking you to go inside," Wendy assured them. "But you can't stand out here in the open either."

"And what would you have us do then?" Michael wanted to know.

"I'm afraid you're going to have to hide somewhere," Wendy said, looking around for ideas. "Like over there behind the bushes."

"You can't honestly expect us to cower in the bushes like ..." John stopped himself and looked down at Nana, who was watching him suspiciously. "Like cowards!" he finished. Satisfied, Nana turned back to Wendy, waiting for the answer.

"Of course not like cowards," she said. "Like members of a ..." Now Wendy looked at Colin, who was watching her face and listening very attentively. "Of a certain office ... who occasionally have to behave in ... in unusual ways."

John glared at Wendy, and Wendy glared back at him, all the while darting her eyes meaningfully at Colin. Colin looked back and forth between the two, thinking how much more interesting this was than reading or practicing his mathematics before bed.

Michael ran his thumb and forefinger across his chin and finally said, "You know, John, she might have a point. It could be dangerous." And now *he* darted his eyes down to Colin and back again, willing John to catch his meaning. Which was that maybe they shouldn't leave the boy out in the open while they were awaiting the arrival of a kidnapping blood drinker.

"Thank you, Michael," Wendy said. She smiled and placed a grateful hand lightly on his arm, at which Michael smiled in return and blushed wildly.

"Fine. Stay with him then. From now on, he's your responsibility." John growled this at Michael, who replied that of course he would be more than happy to, holding Wendy's eye all the while and taking her hand gently in his own to kiss it.

"Over there!" John ordered, pointing at the bushes.

Michael winked at Colin, making the boy giggle, and the two headed off to duck behind the foliage.

"I still don't like it," John said, once he was sure they were out of sight.

"Don't worry, John. You won't be far. I'm sure I'll be quite all right."

"At least keep the dogs with you."

Nana and Poppy looked up at Wendy, clearly agreeing with him.

"Oh, I couldn't," Wendy said, and both animals hung their ears in disappointment. "They have a natural dislike for magical creatures. They'll only bark and wake up the house if they're out in the open. I need you to stay with them, to keep them quiet."

Nana and Poppy looked at each other as though to say, "This is *your* fault. *I'm* the trustworthy one."

"Oh, you *both* growl at Peter. You know you do," Wendy chided them. "After all, it's your job to warn us when magic is nearby, and you're both very good at it." Mollified, the dogs puffed out their chests proudly, but they continued to eye each other with suspicion whenever Wendy wasn't looking.

John didn't look any happier with Wendy than the dogs did with each other, but he did as she asked and took the dogs with him to hide where Michael and Colin had already settled in. Wendy sat on a stone bench to wait.

She did not have to wait for long.

Soon enough there was a taste of pickles in the air, followed by

a low growl, which John managed to silence almost immediately. Colin's sharp gasp—a natural reaction upon seeing a flying man descend from the sky—was a bit louder than the growl, but Peter was too busy making an impressive entrance to notice.

He came in so fast and landed so hard that he slammed one knee into the ground. Again. Ever since the first time he had done so (which had been a bit of an accident), he had been practicing the move, trying to make it faster and even more heart-stopping every time and leaving knee-shaped depressions all across the southeastern fields of England.

"Peter," Wendy said, hardly batting an eye.

"The Wendy," Peter said, and he bowed.

"It's just Wendy," she corrected him.

"I know that, of course," Peter proclaimed. "I only say it that way to indicate what you are not. Not my Wendy or someone else's Wendy, but your own Wendy. The Wendy. Obviously."

In truth, he had forgotten until just now how that whole thing had come about, and he had begun to think of it as a title. The Wendy of Dover. The Wendy of Hertfordshire. But Peter spent a lot of time with Tinker Bell, and the innisfay never admit to being wrong about anything, as you already know. Unfortunately, more than one of her bad habits had rubbed off.

As for Wendy, she rather liked the idea of being her own Wendy. So much so that she almost regretted correcting him.

"Well, when you put it that way ..." she said.

Peter watched her for several long moments, waiting for her to finish, but she said nothing else.

"When I put it that way, then what?" he finally asked.

"Well, I mean I don't mind it so much, now that I understand it," she admitted. "If you want to call me the Wendy, that is."

"Tinker Bell is very angry at you," he said, giving her no indication as to what he would or would not continue to call her.

"Oh," Wendy exclaimed, "the innisfay! Tinker Bell! What a lovely name! Is she angry? I'm truly sorry." Her mouth pursed in concern, and a tiny line formed between her brows.

"She's not your scullery maid to order about, you know," Peter told her. He placed both fists on his hips when he said it and leaned forward at the waist, looking more than a bit cross.

"Oh my goodness! I didn't mean—"

"Her words, not mine," Peter said, interrupting. "I was told to tell you." He dropped the angry expression, stood up straight, and turned his hands upward in a helpless shrug. Apparently, his posture had been part of the message.

"I see," Wendy replied slowly. "Well then, tell her for me, please, if you would, that I was not trying to order her about. I just didn't know how else to find you."

"You can tell her yourself if you like," Peter offered.

"Oh! Is she here?" Wendy looked around and listened very hard for the sound of jingling bells.

"No. She's back on the ship. She's sulking. Like I said, she's very angry."

On the ship! Wendy thought.

"On the *flying* ship?" she asked, careful to sound skeptical.

"That's right," Peter affirmed.

"Why, I don't believe you," Wendy declared. "A flying ship would be quite impossible."

"Haha!" Peter crowed. "That shows what you know! I have a whole *fleet* of flying ships!" (This was a bit of an exaggeration. In point of fact, he had two flying ships, and only two, but that was still infinitely more than England had.)

"I don't believe you have even one," Wendy maintained, and she drew herself up to her full height, tilting her chin into the air, taunting him. "I don't believe you can make a ship fly."

"I'll prove it to you!" he declared. Quick as a wink, he pulled a small leather pouch out from beneath the armor that covered his chest, opened it up on the palm of his hand, and blew upon it boldly. Its contents, which consisted of a small pile of golden dust, exploded into the air before him, glittering as it fell gently upon Wendy's hair and spring riding coat.

"What was that?" Wendy demanded, somewhat alarmed.

"Fairy dust!" Peter declared. "You can fly now. Go ahead."

"I ... what?" Wendy looked down at her feet, which had not raised even one inch into the air, and then glanced back at Peter suspiciously. "How does it work?"

"Think happy thoughts," Peter said. "The happier the thought, the higher you'll go. To come back down, think of something sad. It takes the wind right out of your sails."

"Um, all right," Wendy said. She closed her eyes and thought of every happy thing she could remember. Mr. Equiano and Charlie. John and Michael. Nana and Poppy. Her new friendships with Colin and Mrs. Medcalf. And, of course, books. Shelves and shelves full of books. But it was all for nothing. Her feet remained firmly on the ground.

"It isn't working," she finally said. She opened her eyes to find Peter grinning.

"What is it?" she demanded.

"I was only teasing you," he admitted. "What did you think of?"

"That's none of your concern!" Wendy was very angry at being made to look the fool and was not about to tell him any of her happy thoughts. Not even one.

"Well, you looked very lovely thinking them anyway," Peter said. "Standing there in the moonlight. I just wanted to see you smile. That's all. I didn't mean to make you angry."

It wasn't the first time Wendy had been surprised by Peter's mercurial nature, but somehow, this seemed like a very different side of him than she had ever seen before. Suddenly, she didn't feel angry with him at all.

"So the fairy dust doesn't work?" she asked, sounding more than a bit disappointed.

"Oh, it works," he assured her. "Just think in the direction you want to go. Up, down, sideways. Loops and swirls and as you please. It's as simple as that."

She narrowed her eyes, not sure she should trust him after the last time, but still, it would be such a lovely thing, to be able to fly. To *really* fly.

If it were true.

She closed her eyes again, and this time she imagined jumping into the air, just a little. And when she opened them back up, it was as though she *had* jumped, all at once, without moving her legs at all—because she found herself hovering steadily, with nothing to catch her, about knee height off the ground.

CHAPTER

32

"Oh! How extraordinary!" Wendy exclaimed, and then she giggled like a schoolgirl, clapping one hand over her mouth when she remembered that John and Michael and Colin and Nana and Poppy were all still watching.

"Extraordinary?" Peter replied, sounding less than impressed. "Why, you're hardly flying at all! I do *ten* things more extraordinary than *that* before breakfast!"

To prove his point, Peter launched himself into the night sky and performed several fast loops through the air, twisting and spinning all the while.

"You're right, of course," Wendy called up to him, lowering herself back to the ground so she could think. (Flying was a brand new adventure and therefore terribly distracting.) "I've seen you fly plenty of times. It really isn't very impressive."

"Now wait just a minute—" Peter started to say, but Wendy interrupted him.

"A flying *ship*, on the other hand," she clarified, "*that* would be extraordinary. But this proves nothing. This would never work on a ship."

"It most certainly does," Peter shot back, sounding even more put out.

"For one thing, a ship is far too big," Wendy continued, as though Peter hadn't even spoken. "You couldn't possibly fit enough dust in that tiny pouch of yours to cover an entire sea-going vessel. And for another, a ship can't think. So even if you did manage to cover the whole thing, it still wouldn't lift even one inch off the ground."

"It would so!" Peter declared. "It would and it does!"

"It couldn't possibly." Wendy was careful to sound very firm on the subject. "You're just making that up."

"I'd show you, but I doubt you can fly far enough yet," Peter said, suddenly looking smug. "It takes a lot of practice to fly well, and to maintain one's concentration for so long."

"For *you*, maybe," Wendy countered. "It seems easy enough to *me*."

She looked up at the roof of the estate house behind her and focused on moving in that direction. Without any physical effort whatsoever, she did exactly that, traveling much faster than she had intended. She tried to slow down, but that only distracted her from her target, and she ended up catching her foot on the edge of the roof, tripping, and sprawling face first onto the steep slate.

Unfortunately, there was nothing for her to hold onto, and— reverting in her surprise to her lifelong habit of *not* flying—she slid right back off, falling rapidly toward the ground below.

Three things happened then at the same time, or at least in such quick succession that it was hard to be sure afterward which had happened first and which had happened last.

One was that Wendy screamed in fright. Another was that John and Michael and Colin and Nana and Poppy all burst from the bushes at once, yelling and barking like mad. And another was that Peter Pan, having anticipated this sort of accident, flew to Wendy's rescue and caught her somewhere between the first floor and the ground. If he had intended to deposit her gently in the garden, the sudden ruckus below made him reconsider, and instead he rose into the air with Wendy cradled in his arms.

This gave Wendy just long enough to compose herself and regain her wits, quickly inventing an explanation for her friends' sudden appearance.

"Oh no! Peter! They've found me!" she yelled, much more loudly than was necessary since Peter's ear was now located mere inches from her mouth.

John and Michael, staring up at them from below, could only watch in horror. But Colin had never heard anything about kidnapping or blood drinking or the like. As far as he was concerned, this was yet another of Wendy's rollicking escapes, and he knew a thing or two about helping her with those. So he was the first of the three to understand what she needed them to do.

"Come back with our prisoner!" he shouted, waving his fist at Peter. "Bring her back this instant!"

Nana and Poppy were already barking as loudly as they could, so Colin ignored them, aiming a stern look at John and Michael while he continued to shout.

"Come back, I say! She's *our* prisoner! Do you hear me?" He added this last bit while staring intently at the two men, who finally came around.

"That's right!" John shouted halfheartedly. "Bring our prisoner back here!"

"You can't have her!" Michael yelled, sounding a lot more like he meant it.

Peter looked down at them and then turned to Wendy, his ice-blue eyes locking onto hers.

"Are you ready to come with me to the ship?" he asked, his voice more gentle than she had ever heard it.

"But you were right," she pointed out. "I can't fly well at all."

"You'll learn," Peter assured her. "I can show you how. In the meantime, I can carry you, if you like."

"You have to promise me something first," Wendy said.

"And what's that?" Peter asked with a grin. (He found it amusing that she was making demands, given the current situation.)

"You must promise to take me wherever I want to go after I've seen it," Wendy told him. "I refuse to be anyone's prisoner again, especially so soon after the last time. I'm sure you can understand."

"And when you refused to be *their* prisoner, how did that go for you?" Peter asked, his eyes twinkling.

"Not very well at all, obviously," Wendy retorted. "But I believe you to be a better man than Captain Hook. Am I wrong?"

Peter's face darkened considerably.

"You're not wrong," he said. "I accept your terms, and I give you my word."

"Then yes," Wendy replied. "I'm ready to go."

So Peter sped off into the night carrying Wendy in his arms, and there was nothing that John or Michael or Colin or Nana or Poppy could do about it.

There you go!" Peter exclaimed. "Now you have it!"

Wendy was already flying much better on her own, although she still wasn't ready to try the acrobatic loops and spins that seemed to be Peter's habit. She had to think specifically of both direction *and* speed to navigate properly—a detail Peter had failed to mention at first—but with a little practice she was starting to get the hang of it.

"How much farther is it?" Wendy asked, although she certainly wasn't flying as though she were in a hurry, taking a leisurely moment to circle a tall tree before moving on.

"Farther than this," Peter said helpfully, "but not as much farther as it could be."

They had passed by London some time ago. Wendy had seen the glow of the city's lamps off in the distance to her right, but then they had crossed over the Thames. It was much harder for her to tell exactly where they were after that. All the farms and

small villages looked very similar to one another, especially at night.

Whenever the moon peeked through the clouds, she amused herself by flying low over the tall grasses of the hunting fields that they passed from time to time, allowing her fingers to brush along the delicate tips of the greenery below. But eventually the clouds would hide the heavens once again, and it would be too dark to take the chance of running into a tree. Then she flew higher, pulling her coat tightly around her shoulders against the cool spring air.

"Peter?" Wendy asked.

"Yes?"

"How do you stay warm on the ship?"

"You mean on the *flying* ship?" Peter asked.

"That remains to be seen," Wendy replied, and Peter chuckled.

"The cold makes little difference to me," he told her, "but the boys often keep a fire going in the stove."

"Oh," Wendy said, shivering a little. She had forgotten about Peter's crew, but of course they would be on the ship, as would Tinker Bell, who was probably still cross with her. Wendy had forgotten about that too, until now.

"Peter?"

"Yes?"

"What should I say to Tinker Bell, do you think? To apologize properly?"

"Oh, it doesn't matter."

"It doesn't?"

"Not really. I don't think she'll forgive you no matter what you say."

"Oh."

Wendy waited to see whether he might elaborate on the subject, but apparently he had nothing further to add.

 181

"Well, why is she so angry?" she finally asked. "Can you at least tell me that? Is it really because I asked her to go find you?"

"*Ordered* her to go find me," Peter corrected her. "But no, I don't think that's it. Or not *just* that. I think she finds you too beautiful. Tink doesn't like humans to be as pretty as she is. It offends her."

"You think I'm as pretty as she is?" Wendy asked, suddenly feeling shy.

"*Tink* thinks you're as pretty as she is," Peter said.

"Oh," Wendy said again, but if she sounded disappointed, Peter didn't seem to notice.

"Look there," he said suddenly, and when he pointed ahead, Wendy's breath caught in surprise.

"Dover!" she exclaimed. The distinctive walls of the keep coalesced out of the night as they drew closer. "It's so beautiful!"

She had never in her life expected to see it from above, and the very sight of it brought tears to her eyes. She remembered how badly she had wanted to come back. But of course that had been to see John and Michael and Nana, and now all three were behind her in Hertfordshire along with Colin and Poppy and Mrs. Medcalf and even Huxley.

But still, the rest of the Fourteenth Platoon lay asleep in the castle, just beyond those walls.

"I wonder how poor Reginald is doing," she mused, speaking mostly to herself.

"He was fine the last time I saw him," Peter said.

"You saw him?" Wendy echoed in surprise.

"Of course! When I came back to see you again. But you were gone, and they wouldn't tell me where you were. They shot at me instead."

"I'm sorry," Wendy told him, and she realized that she really was.

"I didn't kill him," Peter added quickly. "Or any of the others either. I knew you wouldn't want me to, after the last time."

"Thank you," was all Wendy could think to say.

They passed Dover Castle and continued out over the water, veering left and then right after a long while and then left again, turning in places Wendy could only guess at, with nothing obvious below except the vast expanse of the straits and then the wide open sea.

And finally, just as Wendy thought she might drift off to sleep—and wondering whether she would keep going in the same direction or suddenly fall out of the sky if she did—the lights of a ship emerged out of the darkness. A perfectly normal, seafaring ship, resting peacefully upon the water like any other.

Showing no signs of flight whatsoever.

They were hardly within sight of the vessel before a shout rang out from the crow's nest.

"Peter! Peter's back!"

Within moments, the cry had been taken up by a dozen voices, and the everlost crew poured onto the deck in various states of dress (and undress), making Wendy blush before they had even properly arrived.

"Peter!"

"Welcome back, Peter!"

"Good form!"

The one in the crow's nest spread his wings and flew ahead to greet them, shouting as enthusiastically as the rest. This turned out to be Curly, who had killed poor Reginald. Which Wendy had not forgotten.

"Curly," Peter called out, "why are you on watch? I left Tootles in the nest!"

"I got in some trouble after you left," he replied easily, once he had reached them. "On account of Slightly's sock. Someone used it as a handkerchief."

"While it was still on his foot, I'd wager," Peter said.

"Aye," Curly replied.

"Was it you?"

"I don't think so, but you know how it is."

Peter nodded sagely.

"What do you mean?" Wendy wanted to know. "Why would they punish you if you didn't do it?"

"Oh, I'm always doing something," Curly admitted, "so I might as well stand forward. I'm used to it. Some of the others get upset when they're in trouble."

"So you take the blame for *everything*?" Wendy asked.

"Sure." Curly shrugged in midair. "Besides, I knew if someone else took Tootles' place, there was a better chance we'd see Peter back tonight. Nothing exciting ever happens when Tootles is around. He misses everything."

"It's true. That's good thinking," Peter agreed, and without any warning he dove for the deck of the ship, touching down lightly amidst the everlost, who swarmed to greet him. Curly followed, but Wendy continued to hover in the air, trying to stay out of the way.

"Listen up!" Peter shouted. His wings disappeared so he could clasp his hands behind his back, strutting before his crew in a captain-like manner. "I have returned with the Wendy! She is our guest and is not to be harmed! Nor is she to be pushed off the deck, forced to drink seawater, dangled over any crocodiles, or challenged to any duels!"

He said this last bit about the duels while bending forward at the waist and staring pointedly at a set of twins, who pursed their lips in a disappointed fashion.

"Nothing like any of that," he finished, "or you're off my ship for good!"

When the crew began to mutter, Peter removed his hands from behind his back and pointed at them all with a wide sweep of his arm.

"I mean it!" he declared. "You are to treat her like your own mother!"

"A mother!" they whispered reverently, their attitude transforming in an instant. One of the tallest, standing in the back, looked like he was suddenly fighting off a tear.

"Tink!" Peter shouted. "Where's Tink? I don't want any trouble out of that one."

"She left with Tootles to look for sheep," Curly reported.

Wendy thought that they really ought not to be stealing England's sheep. But she also thought this might not be the best time to mention it.

"All right then. Back to the crow's nest, Curly," Peter ordered. "If they return, bring Tinker Bell to me immediately. Don't let her anywhere near the Wendy until I've told her the rules myself. Is that clear?"

"Aye, Peter!" Curly saluted smartly and flew up to watch out for Tootles and Tink.

"So," Peter said, turning toward Wendy with a proud lift to his chin, "what do you think of my ship? You can come down now, you know."

Wendy floated down to settle on the deck next to Peter as the everlost crew backed away, making room for her.

"The ship is lovely," Wendy replied, trying to be polite, "but resting decidedly upon the sea, I've noticed." And then her left eyebrow (which had always been the more outspoken of the two)

lifted itself into the air and added silently, "You promised it would fly."

Peter smiled.

"To your stations!" he shouted, his eyes never leaving her. "Tonight, we sail among the stars!"

Preparing for flight turned out to be a boisterous process, full of much yelling and racing about, but as far as Wendy could tell, there was nothing magical about it. There was a grand unfurling of the sails, and special attention was paid to the security of the hatches. There was also a good bit of swordplay on deck that seemed to have little to do with anything useful.

Eventually the crew settled down to their various places amidst the rigging, and a stillness fell upon them, by which Wendy understood that everything was ready. When Peter moved toward the ship's great wheel, Wendy followed him. She thought he looked quite grand, standing at the helm with a light of adventure in his eyes. But she already knew him better than to say so.

"How will you make it fly?" Wendy asked.

"With a kiss, of course," Peter replied. "Here, I'll show you!"

"What? No!" Wendy exclaimed. If she had perhaps been daydreaming of a kiss only a moment ago—just *if* she was, not saying anything for certain—being faced with it as a real possibility was a different thing altogether.

She took a step away from him, but even as she did so, she realized he was not making any move to kiss her. Instead, he had

reached forward through the spokes of the wheel and opened a small, unadorned compartment that lay hidden behind it. From this cubbyhole he had retrieved a tiny metal bauble, which he was now trying to hand to her, his face full of confusion.

"Don't you want to see it?" he asked.

"See what?" Wendy demanded suspiciously.

"Why, the kiss! It makes the ship fly." Peter shook the small thing in the air between them and tried again to hand it to her.

"But that's not a kiss," Wendy protested. "That's a thimble!"

"It's called a kiss among the innisfay," Peter told her haughtily. "Tinker Bell made it. It's quite extraordinary."

"Tinker Bell made it," Wendy repeated, a light finally dawning. "And she gave it to you, and told you it was a kiss."

"It *is* a kiss," Peter insisted, pushing it toward her a third time.

This time, Wendy took it and held it in her hand. On close inspection, it still looked exactly like a thimble. It felt slightly warm to the touch, if one was paying close attention, but otherwise it seemed perfectly normal.

"And this makes the ship fly?" she asked, sounding doubtful.

"It does," Peter affirmed.

"So the ship doesn't need the dust?"

"The ship *is* the dust!" Peter crowed. "The innisfay imbued every timber with its magic, from the masts down to the keel. Every last speck of wood or cloth." He spun in place with his arms spread wide.

Looking closely, Wendy could see that the ship was glistening subtly in the moonlight, as though every inch were cloaked in a sheen of the finest dew. "Oh!" she exclaimed, drawing in a sharp breath. "It's beautiful!"

Peter's chest swelled in obvious pride.

"But you were right when you said it can't think. The ship,

I mean," he continued. "Or at least, not as far as I know. That's why Tink made the kiss."

"Well, how does the … kiss … work then?" Wendy asked.

"You just hold it in your hand, and then you can think for the whole ship, instead of just for yourself."

"Would it work for anyone? Or does it only work for you?"

"Try it and see." Peter's smile was wide enough to reveal his fangs, which glistened in the darkness. Wendy shuddered, but she reminded herself to be brave. This was for England. And especially for the orphans.

She closed her hand around the thimble, and very carefully, remembering her first flying experience with the roof, she thought *up*, to a distance about the height of a man, and with the slow pace of a casual stroll.

Sure enough, she moved as she had intended, but now the entire ship moved with her. The wood of the hull creaked ominously as it lifted higher in the water, but the deck beneath her feet held firm. They had not yet broken free of the sea, but they were no longer resting upon it either.

"Extraordinary!" she exclaimed.

"Higher," Peter murmured. He was standing close enough now to whisper in her ear, and she shuddered again, although for entirely different reasons.

The massive hull continued to rise until only the keel remained submerged. But now the light, spring breeze, which had seemed so minor before, threatened to topple them. It caught in the sails and shoved at the body of the ship while the keel still anchored it from below, causing the vessel to tilt wickedly to the side.

The crew began to shout, but their voices were more excited than fearful.

"Get us out of the sea!"

"Free the keel!"

"Up! Up! Up!"

Peter gripped her shoulders, steadying her against the pitching deck. "Higher," he whispered again, and as she tipped ever so slightly toward him, his lips brushed lightly against her ear.

In the blink of an eye they were a hundred feet up, and then the sudden halt caused them all to catapult through the air, accompanied by the whooping laughter of the everlost crew.

"Aye, that's it!"

"Good form!"

Their bodies tumbled every which way, but of course a flying man has no fear of falling. Those who found themselves above the sails fell harmlessly into the sheets, sliding down the cloth for fun. The rest extended their wings to glide back down to safety—or to fly back up to it, for those who had been tossed overboard.

Wendy, having no previous experience with flying ships, hadn't been prepared for either the sudden movement or the sharp halt that followed. Much to her embarrassment, Peter caught her in his arms as she tumbled through the air, saving her from herself for the second time that night.

It almost made her feel guilty about what she knew she had to do, but there was no other choice. England could never defeat a flying ship.

For crown and country, for all the orphans of London, Wendy Darling had to steal that kiss.

(Or rather, that thimble.)

CHAPTER
35

S o, the Wendy, where will you take us?" Peter set Wendy's feet lightly upon the deck and then bowed gracefully. "The sky is yours this night!"

Wendy's eyes flew wide. A flying ship! To take where she pleased!

It was not her ship, she reminded herself, and she was not its captain. But still, to navigate through the *sky*, if only for a few short hours—it was as though her childhood dream had come true for just one night, in a form more incredible than she ever could have imagined. Her heart swelled in her chest, and a single tear formed in her eye before she brushed it away.

She could feel the ship's magic deep within her bones, as though it were a part of her. Or she, a part of it. A low vibration buzzed through the deck, and there was a distinct thrumming sensation in the air. But that was nothing compared to the gyrations of the thimble itself. As long as she remained focused on flying, the

delicate metal hissed and spat against her closed fist like a living thing, trying to break free.

This made her think of Tinker Bell, and she marveled at the tiny creature—and all of her kind—who could harness such tremendous power. What wonders could England achieve if it could do the same?

Wendy thought of the orphans, imagining the possibilities. If the innisfay could use the will of the mind to make a ship fly, could they use that same will to heat an almshouse though the winter? Or to grow a seedling overnight into a fruit-yielding tree? She had to steal that thimble. To study its magic. But how?

She needed a plan.

While she stood pondering her options, Peter opened his arms wide and spun around slowly, taking in the entire sweep of the heavens. Soft chuckles and hoots of anticipation rose from the crew, returning Wendy's thoughts to her surroundings. Once Peter had completed the circle and faced her once again, he leaned in toward her and began to sing.

Yo ho! Yo ho!
Where'er you wish to go,
Adventurers of land and sea,
Put down your burdens! Follow me!
Yo ho!

His voice began softly, but he moved away from her to stalk about the deck as the song's energy increased, rising to a hearty bellow by the final "Yo ho," which the crew gleefully shouted out with him. Peter stomped his right foot twice on the deck at that part for good measure. Grinning over his shoulder at Wendy, he launched into the second verse.

Yo ho! Yo ho!
Where'er you fear to go,
Unafraid of moonless night,
We'll sail without a lick of light!
Yo ho!

This time every member of the crew stomped twice, yelling the final words as loudly as they could. The sound of so many everlost boots slamming into the deck at once pounded through Wendy's chest, making her feel in that moment as though her heart were as large as the night itself.

Yo ho! Yo ho!
Where'er you dream to go,
Commanders of both sea and sky,
We'll break the bonds of earth and fly!
Yo ho!

The crew had worked themselves into a fever pitch, breaking into swordplay all around the deck and high up into the rigging as they sang with him at the top of their lungs. After a final stomping "Yo ho," they all burst into a raucous clamor of cheers and laughter, and more than one was bold enough to fly up and clap Wendy on the shoulder before returning to his post.

As they settled down, their glittering eyes watched her in the darkness, eager to know where she might take them.

"How can I decide where to go when I don't even know where I am?" Wendy asked.

The question was genuine enough, but it also occurred to her that she was supposed to be pinpointing the location of the ship for the Home Office. She wasn't entirely sure how she felt about

that particular mission at the moment, but she could always decide what to do with the information later. The key was to *have* the information first.

"You *do* know where you are," Peter said. "You're between *that* star ... and *that* one." He pointed into the night at two different stars when he said it, one over the port side and one off to starboard.

"But that doesn't tell me anything!" Wendy protested.

"Of course it does," Peter assured her. "Look, Dover is obviously that way, directly toward the Dover star, there." He pointed at a third star, this one lying low over the horizon. He smiled down at her fondly, but if he expected her to smile back, he was sorely disappointed.

"There's no such thing as a Dover star!" she all but shouted. "The stars move all night long!"

Peter frowned and folded his arms across his chest.

"Hmph," he grunted. "I didn't know you knew that."

Wendy straightened herself to her full height and glared up (nonetheless) at Peter, who was still a good bit taller than she, no matter how angry she might be at the moment.

"Of course I know that!" she snapped. "I'm not a fool, Peter Pan, and I'd advise you not to treat me like one!"

"You said she was a smart one, Peter," one of the twins interjected.

"Aye, you did, and that she is," the other twin agreed.

"That she is," Peter echoed, staring directly into her eyes in a way that made her blush from head to toe.

Wendy was suddenly glad it was still so dark, but the very thought made her realize she needed to do something quickly. She couldn't fly back over the pastures of England in the light of day.

With or without a ship. Not while keeping her vow to prevent the general public from learning the truth about magic.

If she was going to steal that thimble and leave the ship floating helplessly upon the sea, preferably somewhere the Home Office could find it, she was going to have to do it soon.

"I miss the cliffs of Dover," Wendy blurted out.

"I'm sorry?" Peter asked.

"You asked me where I wanted to go, and I miss the cliffs of Dover. I'd like to see them again."

Peter's features brightened once more into a smile. "Of course. Dover really is that way, at least for the moment." He pointed toward the same star he had earlier.

"Thank you." Wendy held the thimble tightly in the palm of her hand and concentrated as hard as she could. Accelerating carefully this time, without any sudden starts or stops, she began to fly the ship toward Dover.

"We can't really see them from here, can we." Wendy did her best to sound disappointed. "They're too far away."

"What?" Peter asked. "The cliffs? Just fly closer."

"No! We mustn't! They keep sentries posted up and down the coast. We can't let them see the ship. It's too dangerous."

"That's very kind of you," Peter said softly, "to look after my ship—and her crew. Good form, the Wendy. Good form. I knew from the moment I saw you that you were different from the others."

"Yes ... well ..."

Suddenly, Wendy couldn't quite meet his gaze. She had meant, of course, that it would be too dangerous for the sentries. Not to mention for the Fourteenth Platoon, which was still stationed in Dover Castle even if John and Michael and Nana were no longer with them. "Perhaps it would be best to return the ship to the water and fly up to the cliffs ourselves," she finished quietly. "Just to be safe."

"That's good thinking," Peter affirmed.

Fortunately, landing the ship turned out to be far less harrowing than taking off had been. Wendy was already learning to keep it steady in the wind. She descended smoothly but definitively, without hesitation, and in two shakes of a lamb's tail they were floating once again upon the sea.

The sudden absence of magic almost took Wendy's breath away.

It felt a bit like losing one's hat to the wind in the middle of winter. The vibration throughout the deck was present in one moment and simply gone the next, its memory alive only in a soft, vague thrumming of her feet. The hum in the air fell deathly silent, and the thimble came to rest in her hand all at once, with nothing but its subtle warmth to remind her of its power.

"How extraordinary," she whispered.

"Did you like flying the ship?" Peter asked.

"Oh, very much!" she exclaimed, and tears of joy threatened to fill her eyes again, just for a moment.

"Then you must come back and fly it again."

Wendy started. *Fly it again?*

A subtle excitement rippled through the crew, as they waited for her answer.

"Yes ... well ..." she said again. "I'm sure I shall be back very

soon." It was true enough, but it was not the *entire* truth. Wendy was feeling worse about her plan by the minute. The sooner she could get back to John and Michael and Colin and Nana and Poppy, the better.

But the crew cheered at her reply, and she used the sudden outburst of flying acrobatics as a distraction, pretending to put the thimble back in its place while palming it instead and dropping it into the pocket of her riding coat.

"Shall we go see the cliffs?" she suggested to Peter.

"It would be my honor."

They flew together above the white cliffs of Dover, far enough from the castle to minimize the risk of being seen. Wendy even managed to perform one loop-the-loop while holding her arms carefully against her sides, protecting the tiny treasure in her pocket—although it left her feeling a bit dizzy. She landed at the top of the cliff to catch her breath, and Peter touched down lightly next to her.

"Will you really come back to us soon?" he asked, taking her hand gently in his own. "Do you promise?"

"If you want me to, then I shall do my best." *I shall do my best to move quickly,* she thought, *so you don't realize the thimble is missing before Hook can come for your ship.* It was not a happy thought. In fact, it left her feeling even more queasy than flying loops in the night sky.

"I do want you to," Peter said. "Very much."

"Yes ... well ..." she said for a third time. "Goodbye for now, then."

"Goodbye, the Wendy," he replied.

Whatever that look was in his eyes as he let go of her hand, Wendy didn't stay to investigate. Instead, she lifted off the ground at once and flew as quickly as she knew how toward Hertford-

shire. If her eyes filled with tears, she told herself it was nothing more than the windy chill of flight, and she resolved to fashion herself a pair of goggles. Just in case she might need them again.

CHAPTER
36

Wendy flew alone through the cold night, following the main road so she wouldn't have to think about navigating. She knew Peter would have escorted her back to Hertfordshire if she had asked—away from the towns and crossroads, across the fields and over the hunting woods where no man lived. But she didn't want his company. Not now. Not after what she had done.

She finally had what she needed: the location of the everlost ship—the ransom Hook had demanded for her freedom.

No, not *her* freedom. *Their* freedom. John and Michael and Nana had lost their posts at the Fourteenth because of her.

But what would their freedom cost Peter?

And why did it have to *bother* her so much?

She should be *glad* to have the advantage, shouldn't she? The everlost were the sworn enemies of England. This was what she had signed up for! To fight the blood drinkers! The kidnappers! The murderers!

Not that Peter was letting her see their true colors. Oh no, he was too smart for that. But she had no reason to doubt the reports. And she had seen firsthand what he was capable of.

She thought of Hook's missing right hand. Of the curved steel that had taken its place, flashing in the firelight. And she thought of poor Reginald. Lying on the ground in a pool of his own blood, his leg severed through. He would be dead and buried if it weren't for her. The everlost had done that.

But then again, the everlost had saved him too. *Peter* had saved him.

The confusion and frustration of it all finally overwhelmed her. She clenched her fists and yelled at the sky—a single cry, as sharp and plaintive as a hawk's. Then she hurtled herself at the empty road beneath her, wanting more than anything to slam her knee into the ground like Peter would have done. It was only at the last possible moment that she bothered to control the impulse, landing hard enough to send needles of pain through her feet but not hard enough to break any bones.

She stood there in the darkness, her heart racing, her lungs heaving with every breath. More than anything she wished she could fight her way out of this mess. Swords were so much easier than intrigue.

Why did it have to be like this? The everlost treated her with *respect.* They kept their word. They let her fly their ship! It was so much more than she could say for her own countrymen. She had studied harder than any man she knew, from the time she was only ten years old. And for what? Hook was never going to let her set foot on *The Dragon*, let alone sail it.

Unbidden, the taunting voice of Mortimer Black echoed through her memory, singing all those years ago at Bartholomew Fair.

If women ever sail the sea,
They'll scrub the decks for men like me!
They'll marry none but Davy Jones,
And for their children, only bones!

It had been cruel and hurtful even then, but the grown men she reported to now were no better. Hook had treated her like an imbecile from the moment they had met, just because she was a woman. He had imprisoned her in his home, demanding information she didn't have. And now he had practically kidnapped John and Michael and Nana. To punish her for her disobedience, as though she were nothing more than a child.

She hated giving him what he wanted. She *hated* it. But she didn't have much of a choice. She couldn't leave her friends stuck in Hertfordshire. Even if she had been willing to give up her own dream of serving on a ship to live at Hook's estate forever, just to spite him, she couldn't do that to the others.

She would tell Hook where to find Peter's ship—his beautiful, magnificent *flying* ship. And Hook would end up sinking it.

She *knew* it, and it made her ill just thinking about it.

The everlost couldn't be killed by any means she knew. She had seen them shot and stabbed with her own eyes. They would have no reason to retreat. No reason to abandon their ship, even if they couldn't fly it without the magical thimble she had stolen.

But Hook wouldn't let them keep it either.

Rather than let them win, he would sink it—while it lay vulnerable upon the sea, stuck fast to the face of the earth thanks to her treachery—and that would be that. Hook would end up with nothing, and the most beautiful ship she could ever have imagined would be lost beneath the waves, never to sail again. Let alone fly.

But John, Michael, and Nana would have their freedom.

Wendy sighed.

At least she didn't have to worry about Peter. He had other flying ships. He had said so himself. He would be all right. Curly and Tootles and the twins—they would be all right.

Wendy's lips thinned into a hard line. She would never admit that last thought to anyone. She didn't even like admitting it to *herself*. But it brought her some peace nonetheless as she rose back up into the air, heading out once again toward Hertfordshire.

CHAPTER
37

By the time Wendy saw the now-familiar outline of Hook's manor house looming in the distance, the first rays of the sun were just barely peeking over the edge of the world. Thankfully, the magic of the fairy dust did not begin to wear off until she had reached the outskirts of the closest hunting fields. It was only the last quarter mile or so that she had to trudge through on foot.

Nana and Poppy took off running as soon as they saw her descending from the sky. They were the first to reach her, whining in delight and relief, followed soon thereafter by John and Michael and Colin, who had waited for her in the garden all night, despite the cold. They sprinted toward her through the tall grass, arriving flushed and breathless and anxious.

"Wendy! Thank heaven you're all right!" John dispensed of all propriety and hugged her tightly, only stepping back after several long moments to hold her at arm's length, searching frantically for any sign of injury. "What happened? Are you hurt?"

"No, no. I'm quite well, I promise."

"Where did he take you?" Michael demanded, glaring at John until he finally let Wendy go so Michael could hug her himself. When Michael was done, Colin decided he deserved a hug as well, being a part of the team. Wendy was only too happy to oblige them all.

"He took me to his ship, of course," she told them, once she was free again. "Just as he said he would."

John's eyes lit up at that. "Could you locate it on a map?"

"Honestly, John," Michael snapped, "that can wait! She's been through something out there. Can't you see that?"

"What was the ship like?" Colin asked, bouncing up and down on his toes, hardly able to contain himself. It wasn't every day he saw people fly. He could only imagine what other wonders she had seen.

"At least let her get in out of the cold, the both of you," Michael growled. "She'll catch her death satisfying your curiosity."

"Oh yes, of course. You're quite right," John agreed, looking at Wendy with an apologetic blush. "We must get you inside."

"Sorry," Colin added.

"I'll admit, I could use a nice warm fire and a cup of hot tea. I'm sure we all could. But while we're still out here, just the six of us," Wendy said, making sure to include Nana and Poppy, "we all need to remember that everything we've seen tonight must remain in this company. We can tell no one else. Not for any reason. It is a matter of the utmost importance to king and country." Her words were addressed to everyone, but she finished by looking Colin straight in the eye.

"Never! I promise!" the boy protested. "I'll never tell a soul!"

"I know you won't," she assured him. "Now, let's all go in and get warm. And after that, we'll need the carriage. Colin, I do

apologize. I know you must be exhausted. But we're going to need you to drive us all the way to London. We must report to Captain Hook immediately."

"Yes, ma'am!"

As they walked the rest of the way through the field together, Wendy buried her hands in the pockets of her coat. She felt the slight warmth of the thimble as she rubbed it idly between her fingers, pondering what to do about it. But for now, she said nothing at all.

After a hot breakfast, prepared by Mrs. Medcalf, who was always up early, they packed their bags and gathered at the front entrance.

"Aren't you coming back?" Mrs. Medcalf exclaimed upon seeing that Wendy had all her luggage with her.

"I don't think so." Wendy hesitated. She couldn't tell Mrs. Medcalf they were going back to their secret platoon in Dover Castle. "I think the captain wants me near him in London," she said instead, wishing she had a better excuse.

Mrs. Medcalf, of course, was ecstatic.

"Oh, my dear!" she exclaimed, clasping her hands together against her heart in delight. "What wonderful news! You see? I told you everything would be all right!"

"You did," Wendy agreed with a smile. "You were quite right."

"But don't let him try to hold your wedding in the city!" Mrs. Medcalf continued, shaking a finger in the air for emphasis. "You make sure you put your foot down about that! It's loud and dirty— no place for a wedding. The two of you are to be married right here

in Hertfordshire. You tell him! On a beautiful summer day with the whole family in attendance!"

"Of course, Mrs. Medcalf. I'll tell him," Wendy promised, while John and Michael exchanged a dark look.

"And with lemon cake," Mrs. Medcalf finished, looking hopeful.

"I wouldn't have it any other way," Wendy assured her.

Wendy hugged the woman, holding back a sudden tear, and then left the Hook Estate behind her, but not before leaning out the window in a very unladylike manor—just for a moment, mind you—waving goodbye one last time.

She was oddly silent throughout the long ride to London, despite John and Michael's many questions. The two men sat across from her while the dogs lay curled up next to her, one on each side, blissfully content. Wendy had insisted on bringing Poppy along to protect Colin and the carriage on the way back to Hertfordshire, for which Mrs. Medcalf had been grateful.

"The ship is anchored off the coast of Dover?" John asked, after Wendy had given them just the briefest overview of her long night. She had left out most of the details—and any mention whatsoever of the thimble.

Wendy only nodded.

"And it really flies! That's incredible!" Michael exclaimed, to which Wendy said nothing.

"How does it work? The flying?" John asked, but Wendy shook her head.

"You don't know? Or you won't say?"

If John's voice held a hint of suspicion, Wendy raised a dangerous eyebrow and he dropped the subject. She had decided, after careful consideration, to hide the thimble in plain sight in her personal sewing kit, which was packed away in her luggage. She

trusted both John and Michael with her very life, but she knew she would be on the verge of treason not to turn the thimble over to Hook. She didn't want either of her closest friends to carry that burden with her.

So she had no intention of answering their questions until she had decided for herself what to do.

On the one hand, she had a clear obligation to inform her superior officers of anything she knew about the enemy. On the other hand, she had *stolen* the thing, and she wasn't entirely sure how she felt about that.

Besides, it wasn't as though Hook could use it. He was going to sink Peter's ship. Wendy was certain of it. And he didn't have any innisfay dust—let alone any innisfay—with which to build a new one. Not that Hook believed in magic in the first place. He probably wouldn't even believe in an innisfay if it flew right up to him and smacked him in the face.

Wendy sat up straighter, her eyes narrowing.

Of course. Hook didn't believe in magic. He was going to sink the ship while it was still floating in the ocean, looking as normal as you please! He was never going to believe that it had ever flown at all! If Wendy gave him the thimble without any proof, he would only laugh at her. He certainly wouldn't try to *use* it. He would never feel it come alive, hissing and spitting against the palm of his hand.

Come to think of it, she wasn't sure it would do that without the ship to control.

Well, Wendy had had just about enough of being laughed at. She saw no reason to risk going through it again. And she *certainly* didn't want to risk him throwing it away!

No. Just ... *no.*

Having come to her decision, Wendy settled back in her seat,

her eyes narrow with determination, her jaw set firmly, her fingers drumming the March of the Executioner on Nana's sleeping head.

John and Michael shot an alarmed glance at each other, silently demanding, "Say something; no, *you* say something." But even John's superior rank wasn't enough to make Michael utter a single word.

CHAPTER
38

Y our fiancée is here to see you." Sir William folded his hands behind his back and glanced around Hook's office, taking in the vast collection of maps the younger man had plastered across the walls. In recent weeks they had accumulated a new, sprawling cipher of lines and circles and enigmatic notations, all written in Hook's own hand. "I wouldn't let her see this, if I were you. She'll be convinced you're not well."

"Hmm?" It was more of a grunt than a question. Hook ran his good left hand through his dark locks and skewered the page before him with his hook, dragging it heavily across the desk until the paper fell off the edge into the empty air, fluttering down to join several dozen more, scattered below.

"Your fiancée? Surely that's clear enough. Unless you have more than the one?"

"William, by all that's holy, what are you talking about?" Hook removed his hand from his head and glanced up from the

desk in annoyance. When he did, his hair fell across his eyes, wild and unkempt.

"*Sir* William. Try to behave like a civilized Englishman long enough to get rid of her without scaring her to death. The Home Office doesn't need the sort of attention that would follow if a young woman were to run screaming from the building."

"You're saying she's here? Wendy Darling is *here*?"

"That's what I've been trying to tell you, yes. Who else would I be talking about?"

"But ... how did she even get here?"

"Your houseboy. Said his name was Colin. He drove her in the carriage all the way from Hertfordshire. *Your* carriage, I presume. He's wearing your family's livery."

"She brought Colin to London?" Hook's voice remained subdued, but the undertone of amusement had disappeared. Now it was ice cold, and he slammed his hook into the desk before him, burying its tip deep in the wood as he rose to his feet.

"Not just him. She brought her two guards too. And a couple of dogs. It's a veritable circus downstairs."

"The dogs?" Hook asked, blinking. "She brought the *dogs*?"

Sir William grunted his assent. "Come to think of it, she doesn't seem that well herself. You might be a good match for each other."

Hook scowled. "Well, why is she here? What does she want?"

"She wouldn't say. Says she'll only report to you. I explained that I outrank you, but she didn't seem to care. Said she had information you requested. *Sensitive* information. If you've gotten that girl in trouble—"

Hook waved the idea away. "Of course not. I told you, there's nothing between us. I gave her a task to complete. But I didn't think she'd actually *do* it." His voice trailed off as he considered

the possibility. "Just keep the carriage here. Find a place for them to stay tonight. All of them. I don't want that boy on the road after dark. But bring the girl to me."

From the moment Wendy entered Hook's office, she was accosted by the immediate and overwhelming impression of a mind on the verge of ... well, on the verge of something extraordinary. But whether that something was to be an epiphany or a collapse remained to be seen.

The maps lining the walls now bore the calculated ravings of a man obsessed. His coat lay draped over the back of his chair, his shirt fell unbuttoned at the neck, and his hair hung loosely about his face as though he had no care for his appearance whatsoever. But his eyes ... his forget-me-not eyes held the grim determination of gunpowder and steel.

"Miss Darling. Is something wrong?" He asked the question lightly, but it held a distinctly threatening undercurrent. He stood in front of the sturdy desk, leaning against it, his arms crossed over his chest. A multitude of papers lay scattered about the floor, but the desk itself was clear save for a single stack of pages. What she could see of its surface behind him was horribly disfigured, crisscrossed by deep scars, as though it had been locked in the room with a tiger.

"No. I'm perfectly fine, thank you." But her eyes flicked involuntarily to the hook that extended from his wrist before returning to meet his gaze.

"It was suggested to me that I should clean up before inviting

you in, but I was afraid it might encourage you in future unannounced visits."

Wendy ignored the taunt and moved toward one of the maps on her left. She reached out and ran one finger over the bold, erratic lines, smudged in several places and bleeding in others, where the ink had been over-applied and had dripped down the canvas before drying.

"You'll have to forgive my penmanship," he growled. "It isn't what it used to be."

"Oh! No ... that isn't—"

"Why did you bring Colin here?"

"Excuse me?"

"Why ... did ... you ... bring ... Colin ... *here*?" He stepped away from the desk, prowling toward her until Wendy felt compelled to back into the wall.

"He just drove the carriage."

"He's a *boy*! And you brought him *here*! To *London*! Where more boys are going missing every week! Their guardians killed in the streets! The public doesn't know, but *you* do! You know the risks! And you brought him anyway!"

"They wouldn't hurt him—"

"They wouldn't hurt *you*, you mean. Or so you *think*. But even if you're right, you have no idea what they would do to him!"

"I *do* know! Pan could have hurt him if he had wanted to. He could have taken him. But he didn't. He took me. Colin was perfectly safe."

"What are you talking about?"

"My report. The report I came to deliver in person, if you would stop trying to intimidate me for one second and *listen*. You told me to find an everlost ship, and then we could return to our platoon. Well I found one. Peter took me to it, and I know where it is."

Excitement flashed in his eyes, followed immediately by suspicion. "Oh, *Peter* took you to it, did he? This I have to hear. By all means, deliver your report."

"Are you going to stand this close to me the entire time? Have you truly lost all civility?"

"You're not the first today to suggest that I have. And yes, I will stand where I please. The men of my unit are trained to hold their ground under *gunfire*, Miss Darling. Surely you can deliver a report while confronted by the open skepticism of a superior officer."

Wendy squared her shoulders and stared him right in the eye. "Fine. Pan appeared again at the Hertfordshire estate." (She thought it best not to mention the tiny dragon-fairy she had used to summon him.) "I pretended to be your prisoner so he would trust me."

"I'm taking English ladies prisoner now, am I?"

"It's not entirely inaccurate," Wendy shot back.

"You are in the king's service, Miss Darling," Hook growled. "I *ordered* you to stay at the estate. I did not take you prisoner. There is a significant difference between the two. If you were my *prisoner*, you would not be standing here in my office, having traveled to London of your own accord. But please, continue."

"Yes, well ... in any event, the ruse worked. He 'rescued' me and took me to his ship—"

"How did you get there?"

"He was able to carry me in his arms while he flew." She thought it best not to mention fairy dust either, under the circumstances.

"All right. Continue."

"He took me all the way to Dover Castle and out over the straits until we were no longer within sight of land. His ship was in the sea to the northeast."

"That's an exceptionally vague location, Miss Darling, considering the size of one ship as measured against the size of the ocean."

"I'm not finished. He took me to his ship and demonstrated that it does, in fact, fly."

The muscles of his jaw flexed at this, just once, but whether in disbelief or surprise, Wendy didn't know.

"I asked him to take me to Dover, leaving the ship where you could find it." *And stranding it there without its magical flying thimble,* she thought. But she left that bit out too.

"And what guarantee do I have that the ship hasn't *flown* away?" Hook demanded.

"They're waiting for me to return," she said, raising her chin and holding his gaze. It was not entirely true, but it was close enough.

Hook just stood there, watching her.

"It's there, I tell you!" she insisted. "Just east of the castle, and just far enough away as to be out of sight of land. Send a ship. You'll find them."

He stared at her a moment longer, then strode to the door, finally giving her room to breathe.

"Runner!" he shouted into the hallway. "I need a runner!" In moments, Wendy heard racing footsteps and then a reply, barked out between excited breaths.

"Yessir!"

"Find me Sir William at once."

"Is there a message, sir?"

"No message. Just tell him I need him immediately. No matter what he's doing. I don't care if he's three bites into a partridge. Now. Understood?"

"Yessir!"

The boy raced off again, and Hook closed the door.

"Well then," Wendy said, "I've done as you asked. I'd prefer to return to Dover as soon as possible, but if transportation can't be arranged until morning, I'd certainly understand. Either way, we can be ready to leave as soon as needed."

"The only place you're going is back to Hertfordshire." He didn't even look at her when he said it, staring instead at a relatively unaltered map of the southeastern coast of England on the wall.

"What?"

"You heard me. If we find the ship where you say it is, I'll consider sending you back to your post once the everlost threat has been eliminated. I won't send a woman to a massacre."

"Massacre?" Wendy echoed.

"What did you think, Miss Darling? That I would invite them to a tea party? We ... are ... at ... *war.* We'll take one or two as our prisoners, if we can, for interrogation. The rest will die."

"But that's impossible," Wendy protested. "We don't even know how to kill them."

"*You* don't know how to kill them. That information is classified."

A memory flashed before her eyes: Peter's face, flushed and in pain, shouting at her in the darkness at the Hertfordshire estate. *Hook is my enemy! He is death to all my kind!*

But that didn't make any sense ...

"You're lying," she said. "If we knew how to kill them, you would have told our platoon."

"Outlying platoons, Miss Darling, are little more than sentries. They are not meant to engage the enemy and do not, therefore, need to know our most tightly held military secrets. Do you really think you are my *confidante*? Do you believe I would entrust the king's highest military secrets to you just because you came to me with some wild story about resurrection and flying ships?"

He paused and smiled at her cruelly. "Or is it perhaps on account of your *beauty* that you assume men will do anything to please you? You do *not* know everything I do, nor will I tell you my reasons for doing it. You will return to Hertfordshire and await further instructions. If all goes well, I will restore you to your post, as we agreed. But it will be at *my* discretion. Is that clear?"

Wendy felt a ball of cold, hard ice settle into the pit of her stomach, and her heart shivered in her chest. It was all too clear, in fact. She had just betrayed Peter and his entire crew to their mortal enemy. She had stolen their only means of escape, and then she had offered them up for slaughter.

CHAPTER
39

The Home Office kept several rooms on the top floor of its headquarters for official guests, and Hook insisted—citing Colin's safety—that they all remain there until morning. Wendy could see no way around it and was forced to spend a long, sleepless night in London, trying to decide what to do. She couldn't let Peter die. Not because of her. She just couldn't.

She knew it was a traitorous thought, but it didn't *feel* traitorous. She hadn't decided to give up her position with the Home Office. Or to abandon her platoon. Or anything nearly so dramatic. It was a simple matter of logic. If Peter remained alive, she would have time to investigate the reports of missing orphans and murdered guardians. She would have time to hear Peter's version of things. But if he *died* there would be no more time for anything.

Besides which, he had saved her life more than once, and he had saved poor Reginald on her behalf. Saving Peter's life in return was the right thing to do. It was a matter of honor.

She just didn't know how to keep him alive without putting good Englishmen in danger, and she wasn't about to do that either. Even if she could figure out how to warn Peter, she couldn't let the everlost ship ambush Hook's men. She didn't want to give Peter an *advantage* in the fight. She wanted to *stop* them from fighting at all. At least for now. At least under these circumstances.

But getting to Peter was a problem in and of itself. She couldn't fly anymore, and even though she had never in her life been able to fly until—goodness, was it only last night?—she was already finding the lack of it to be a considerable inconvenience. Still, no matter how hard she thought *up*, her feet remained firmly planted on the floor. (She even tried thinking happy thoughts, just in case, but that didn't work any better than it had the first time.)

Nor did she have the funds to sneak off and arrange transportation.

Colin had always been happy to take her anywhere she pleased, but she couldn't involve any of her friends in *this*. Treason was punishable by death. And even if she were willing to drag them into this mess, she wasn't entirely sure they would be sympathetic to a plan that involved saving the enemy.

Not to mention that if she left without telling them, they would alert Captain Hook as soon as they discovered her missing, thinking they were protecting her.

No, there wasn't anything for it. She was going to have to stay right where she was until morning and endure the long ride to Hertfordshire, knowing all the while that Hook was preparing to set sail for Dover and that she was traveling in the wrong direction. Moving farther away from Peter with every passing mile.

Wendy woke them all early enough that they were ready to leave by dawn, but the journey still lasted some five or six hours. To Wendy, they were longest hours of her life. She spent almost every minute drumming on Nana's head, her anxious fingers rolling out the cadence of a galloping horse—onetwothreefour, onetwothreefour, onetwothreefour—while the actual horses drawing the carriage never came close to that pace.

When they finally arrived, Mrs. Medcalf was delighted to welcome them all back. The explanation offered was that the captain had found himself called out upon another, rather unexpected sea voyage, and the sympathetic woman spent almost an hour reassuring Wendy that her fake engagement was still very much intact. Not that Wendy was really listening. Instead, she was imagining how Hook was going to kill Peter. Or how he might be killing him this very moment.

As soon as she could, Wendy broke away into the garden and tried to call for Tinker Bell, but there was no delicate jingling in reply. As she had feared, Tinker Bell was still angry with her and had stopped spying on her altogether.

But Wendy hadn't counted on Tinker Bell's help. She knew that had been a long shot, at best. Instead, a far more intricate plan had formed in Wendy's mind over the hours it had taken them to return. It was a good plan, and it left John and Michael and Colin and Nana and Poppy completely out of everything. But it required waiting until after dinner so as not to be discovered.

Wendy got through the afternoon by unpacking (which included placing the thimble back in her coat pocket), and then sitting

in the library pretending to read, her eyes restlessly scanning the pages without taking in anything at all. When dinner finally arrived, she wolfed down the meal in a very unladylike manner, blaming her behavior on the stress of travel, and then retired early to her room—making it very clear that she needed her rest.

Once she was sure no one would come looking for her before morning, she snuck back out to the stables, stole a lovely bay mare, and rode the horse at breakneck speed to the home of Monsieur Dumas. She would have loved to ride all the way to Dover, but that was a distance of ninety miles or so, roughly three times the trip from London to Hertfordshire. A gallop like that would kill a horse long before it arrived.

The only way she could ride ninety miles in one night would be to trade out horses as she went. She didn't know anyone along most of the route, but Monsieur Dumas had hinted that French-men in England tended to seek out each other's company, being something of an oddity and universally distrusted—and, of course, finding common familiarity in the French language and customs.

If Monsieur Dumas was surprised when Wendy arrived at his home at such a late hour on the back of a sweat-lathered horse, that was nothing compared to his shock when he learned what she needed him to do.

"So, you want me to tell you where to change horses some eight to ten times between here and Dover," he said, after she had explained her plan, "provide you with a letter of introduction for each stop along the way, and encourage my fellow countrymen to give an Englishwoman a fresh horse in exchange for a spent one in the middle of the night, no questions asked? And you can't tell me why."

When he put it like that, Wendy realized she was asking the impossible, and tears welled up in her eyes.

"You're right. I'm sorry," she said sniffling. "I didn't think it all out. It was desperate and stupid. I should not have asked you."

She turned away, embarrassed, but Monsieur Dumas placed a gentle hand on her arm. "Desperate?" he prompted.

"It's a matter of life and death, as I said."

"Whose death?" he wanted to know.

"I can't tell you that."

"Can you at least tell me why you can't tell me?"

"It would be treason to tell you," she replied.

Monsieur Dumas might not have known anything about magical creatures or flying men, but he was no fool.

"So," he said, "you intend to save the life of a man King George views as an enemy."

Wendy nodded, watching him carefully.

"And you can't ask your friends at the Hook Estate to help you because they, too, would see your efforts as treason."

Wendy nodded again.

There was only one sort of man that Monsieur Dumas would expect to be hated by all of England, and that, of course, was a Frenchman. If Wendy had, perhaps, expected Monsieur Dumas to leap to this very conclusion, well, that wasn't the same thing as lying, in her opinion. And she really *was* trying to save a man's life. The fact that it didn't happen to be a *French* life didn't make it any less worth saving.

"I see," Monsieur Dumas told her. "Unfortunately, I cannot do as you ask."

Wendy's heart sank, but then the man smiled.

"Instead," he told her, "I'm afraid I must insist on coming with you. No Frenchman will trust an Englishwoman dashing across the countryside in the dead of night. But they will trust me. Come. Your mare is already spent. We will retrieve two rested

animals from my stables. Like me, they still have some fight left in them."

He said this last with an even wider grin and a wink, and Wendy was so overcome with relief that she rushed into his arms and hugged him tightly.

"You're welcome," he said, chuckling. "We will save the life of your young man. But we must hurry, yes?"

"Yes," she agreed. "I pray we are not already too late."

They raced through the dead of night on horseback. Wendy gave up any attempt at propriety from the beginning, discarding her dress to reveal her fighting leggings and tunic so she could ride more easily. If Monsieur Dumas was surprised, he gave no sign of it, only nodding his approval. They had a long night ahead of them, and the stakes were high. It was not the time for parlor manners.

Changing out their horses went more smoothly than Wendy could have hoped. At each new farm, Monsieur Dumas exchanged a few clipped words in French with his fellow countryman, and they were on their way again. During the third exchange, they were met by a young couple, barely older than Wendy herself, and the woman smiled knowingly.

"I hope you save your love," she said to Wendy, gripping the arm of her own French husband tightly.

That's why they're all here, Wendy realized. *These are all Frenchmen who fell in love with Englishwomen. That's why they're helping us. They think I'm like them.*

It gave her a fresh pang of guilt, but she didn't have time to

worry over it. She was more worried about what she was going to do when they reached the shore. After all, Peter wasn't in Dover. Peter was on a ship out at sea.

She had vague thoughts of trying to use the thimble to communicate with him once she was close. Or maybe using it to raise the ship out of the water and fly it to her. But she didn't know whether either of those things would work. All she knew was that she had to try. She had figured out how to get to Dover. Once she was there, she would see what possibilities might reveal themselves. It was all she could do.

So when they reached the white cliffs of Dover, she shoved her hand into her pocket and gripped the thimble tightly. But aside from its slight warmth, she felt no power running through it. She could not hear Peter in her mind. She could not feel the ship responding to her thoughts. She could only stare out into the distance at the rising sun, the clear skies, and the vast expanse of the water, without even a hint of Pan's ship anywhere to be seen.

There was just one sailing ship in sight, and it proudly flew the English flag.

Wendy's heart sank into the pit of her stomach.

Hook.

He had arrived ahead of her after all.

Was he about to discover Peter's ship? Or had he already sunk it? For all Wendy knew, Peter could already be dead, his lifeless, winged body sinking slowly to the bottom of the straits. She imagined his beautiful face submerged in the water, his blue eyes unseeing, staring up at the morning sun filtering down from the sky above, as his hair fanned out around his temples. There was nothing she could do to save him. Nothing. She had come all this way for nothing.

And it was all her fault.

CHAPTER

40

fter staying up all night galloping across the English countryside—to get this close and still be too far away, well, it
was all a bit more than Wendy could take. She sat upon the back
of her tired horse near the edge of the cliff, wiping furiously at the
tears that blurred her vision of the sea.

Monsieur Dumas brought his own horse next to hers and
spoke to her gently.

"He was supposed to meet you here?" he asked.

"No," she admitted. "I didn't ... that is, we didn't ..." Her
voice trailed off into silence.

"Ah. He doesn't know you are coming. But then, it means
nothing that he is not here, yes? There could still be time?" His
crestfallen expression took on the barest glimmer of hope.

"I suppose that's true," Wendy said, sniffling. "But even if we
aren't too late, I don't know how to get to him from here. And
after we've come all this way ..."

Monsieur Dumas smiled just a little and cocked his head to one side, watching her. "Well, I have not known such a small thing to stop you before."

In that moment, Wendy paused to think about what a true friend she had in Antoine Dumas. He had galloped through the entire night by her side, believing that if they were caught they would both be jailed or killed. Especially him, a Frenchman on English soil. By that logic, he had risked the safety of all his friends along the way as well, just to do this one thing for her, and without knowing anything more about it than that she was trying to save a life.

She couldn't bear to let him down after all that. She couldn't let him believe it had all been for nothing. Whether she could save Peter or not, at least she could send Monsieur Dumas home with a heroic memory to keep him company in his quiet little cottage in Hertfordshire.

So she smiled for him and sat up straighter, trying to appear confident. She looked around for inspiration, intending to come up with some story to tell him about what she was going to do next, and why he could leave her here. Why he could believe that everything was going to be all right.

But what she found was even better.

When she looked down, she saw the same leggings she had been wearing the first time she had ever laid eyes on Peter. When she had fought him on the lawn of Dover Castle with her platoon. And when she looked up, she saw that very same lawn. And that very same castle.

Of course! she thought wildly. *The Fourteenth Platoon!*

They were all still stationed in the castle—a castle that had boats. John and Michael and Nana might be in Hertfordshire, but the others would still be there, including poor Reginald. They

would help her. Even if she had to be a bit vague about the details. It might not be too late to reach Peter first.

Or at least find a way to warn him!

"Oh!" she exclaimed. "Monsieur Dumas! I know what I have to do! Thank you so much for everything you've done for me! I have friends in the castle. They can help me from here. I know they can!"

"Good!" he exclaimed, clearly relieved. "Excellent! Do you need me to wait for you?"

It was understood that he would not go with her to the castle. The appearance of a Frenchman here in Dover would only raise suspicions.

"No," she assured him. "I'll be quite all right from here. You've done more than enough. Thank you. You have saved more than one life this night."

"Whatever good we have done, we have done together," he replied, smiling at her fondly. "But there is no time to waste, yes? Go. Do what you must. I will take the horses back to their owners, as promised."

"You'll be all right?" Wendy asked.

"Of course!" He dismounted at once and reached for her reins. "Although after so many hours in the saddle, I think I'll walk for a bit."

He said this last with a small chuckle, and Wendy all but leaped out of her own saddle to hug him.

"Go on!" he said to her, laughing more fully now. "Just promise you will come tell me the rest of the story, yes?"

"I promise!" And with one final grin at her friend, she took off running for Dover Castle.

But as the castle grew closer, what began as a run turned into a jog ... and then eventually into a brisk walk. It wasn't that she was tired. (Or rather, she was, but she could have run the whole way if she had felt like she should.) It was just that she needed to think about what she was about to do.

She needed a *plan.*

She wouldn't know the new lieutenant in charge, whoever he was. The rest of the platoon would vouch for her, but she needed a plausible story to secure their help. And then there was the bit about arriving at the everlost ship with a small boat of British soldiers and convincing them all not to kill each other.

Obviously, she had a few things to work out yet. But still, it was *hope,* and even the tiniest bit of hope is infinitely better than having no hope at all. She just had to figure out how to grow that seed of possibility in the direction she wanted it to go, and away from any future in which Peter's dead body lay sinking through the water.

She could see it so vividly that it made her shudder. His unseeing eyes. His hair fanning out around his noble features. She tried not to think about it. She remembered instead how strong and safe his arms felt, catching her out of the air as she fell. She remembered the green scent of him, almost as though he were right there with her. But her mind kept returning to the same image. His body sinking through the water. His hair fanning out against the sky—no, the sea ...

Wait ... what?

Catching a hint of movement out of the corner of her eye, she turned—to discover Peter hovering in the air beside her, his body

almost horizontal, his head tilted to one side, watching her, his hair falling below, rippling in the air, very much like it had in her imagination.

"Hullo," he said.

"Peter!" she cried. "You're all right!" Her first instinct was to try to hug him but immediately she thought of his ship and his crew. They weren't out of danger yet. "Oh! But your ship! Hook's coming for you! You have to leave!" The words poured out in a jumble as she fished in her pocket for the thimble.

"Don't worry," he said before she could finish. "The ship isn't here." He grinned when he said it, with his usual fair measure of smugness, but somehow that didn't bother her so much right this second.

"It isn't? Oh, thank goodness! But how? I thought ... that is, I was afraid ..."

"The ship doesn't need magic to *sail*, of course. Curly and Tink and the rest are safely out to sea. I only came back for my kiss."

"I ... what?"

"My kiss." He set both feet on the ground and held out his hand expectantly. "Why did you take it? Tink said you stole it and sent Hook to kill us, but I knew you would never do that. The boys and I all stood up for you. I said it was so we wouldn't leave without you. But all you had to do was ask, you know. I can't *wait* to tell Tink you came back to warn us. That'll show her!"

"Well, of course I came back to warn you," Wendy said. "As soon as I heard what Hook was planning to do, I came as quickly as I could!" It was the truth, even if it wasn't the *entire* truth. She pulled the thimble from her pocket and handed it over.

"I know." Peter smiled at her fondly. "I've been watching you since Canterbury. That was quite the galloping adventure! Not as good as flying, mind you, but still."

"You let me ride all that way, not knowing whether you were dead or alive? That's awful!"

"I wasn't sure you cared," he said, his voice turning dark. "For all I knew, you were racing to join Hook's ship. You just missed him, by the way."

"Well, I wasn't," she said, tilting her chin up and gazing defiantly into his eyes.

"I know," he said, his voice softening again. "I heard you talking to the other man. 'You have saved more than one life this night.' You were riding to warn me, to protect my crew."

"Yes," she said. And then, more to herself as she realized the truth of it, "In fact, I'm going to be in a good bit of trouble when he doesn't find you."

"Really? Why?"

Because I swore to him that you would be there for his massacre, she thought, cringing at the way it sounded, even in her own mind.

"Because he wants to find your ship," she blurted out instead. It was probably too much of the truth, and she knew it as soon as she had said it. But still, it seemed better than telling him the *whole* truth. This web of lies was getting far too complicated. "He said the only way he would release us is if we found either your ship or your island for him."

"But you're free already," Peter pointed out, frowning in confusion.

"He's holding some friends of mine at his estate," she explained. "I have to go back."

"To rescue them!" Peter exclaimed. "That would be a grand adventure! I'll help you!"

"No!" Wendy protested, perhaps a bit too quickly. "I mean, it doesn't work that way."

"But that's exactly how prisons work," Peter objected, cocking

his head at her quizzically. "One person holds another person in prison. Then the prisoner and his or her friends try to break them out. That's the whole point of the game."

"It isn't a game," Wendy said.

"It is on *my* island."

"Well, it isn't in England."

Peter regarded her quietly for a long moment.

"Then perhaps this will help you," he said finally. He reached into a small pouch that hung from his belt and withdrew a flat, round metal object, holding it out to her on the palm of his hand.

"A pocket watch?" she asked.

"Open it," he told her.

She took it carefully and did so, revealing a compass needle under glass, suspended above a faintly glowing outline of an irregular shape—a shape that looked very much like it could be the outline of an island. But because she was standing by the cliffs of Dover, she had a perfectly clear understanding of where north was, and it was equally clear that the compass was not pointing toward the north at all.

"It's magnificent!" she exclaimed, her voice reflecting her amazement. "Is that your island?"

"We call it Neverland," he confirmed. "And this will take you there. Whenever you want to go."

"Neverland," Wendy whispered. Even its *name* sounded magical. She looked up from the compass into his eyes. "But ... but I just told you I'd have to give this to Hook. So he'll let my friends go. Why would you give it to *me*?"

Peter grinned wickedly. "Ha! I'd love to see the look on his face! You can give it to him if you like, but it won't work. It's a trick. See? Open it and hold it just like that. Show it to him. Then

close it and give it to him. You and your friends will go free. But when he opens it again, it won't work. It will never work for him.

"*Or*," he continued, "you can keep it for yourself and use it to find me. It will work for *you*, obviously. I would very much like it if you came to find me." He smiled at her again, but it was a very different sort of smile this time. Wendy thought he might be about to thimble her, and she took a quick step back before she could find out.

"Thank you," was all she could think to say.

"Keep it and come find me," he said, shrugging a little. "Or give it to Hook for your freedom, and then *I'll* find *you*. Either way, we'll see each other again soon, the Wendy." And with that, he snapped his wings wide and flew away.

CHAPTER

41

Hook stood on the deck of his ship, a spyglass clutched in his good left hand as he stared out to sea. Normally he would have enjoyed the feel of the ship swaying gently beneath his feet after so many long weeks ashore, but even the spring breeze that filled the sails was doing nothing for his disposition. The ship had just passed Dover Castle, and there was no sign of Pan. He had the sinking feeling that the Darling woman was toying with him. Again. If there was one thing he hated, it was being played for a fool.

What was her game? Had she told him the truth? Was Pan almost within his grasp—his elusive ship about to appear on the horizon if Hook sailed just a little bit farther? Or was that what she *wanted* him to think, sending him off on a wild goose chase so she could put some devious scheme into play back at his estate?

But that didn't make any sense. She hadn't wanted to go back to the estate at all. That much had been clear enough. She had

honestly expected him to send her back here, to Dover Castle, on the strength of her word alone.

Ha! At least he hadn't fallen for *that*!

Hook was just lowering the glass when he heard the strangest sound. It wasn't that the noise *itself* was strange, but the *context* of it was certainly peculiar. He could not for the life of him think of anything that would make a sound like jingling bells here, in the open air over the middle of the straits.

He turned toward the delicate chimes and saw a flash of gold in the sky. A bird, was it? But it was far too bright to be a gold-finch. It was more the sort of color one would find in the tropics, he thought.

Curious, he lifted the glass to his eye once more, but the tiny creature kept flitting just out of view. Was it a hummingbird? It certainly flew like a hummingbird. He followed it as best he could until the scene in the glass suddenly brought him up short, all thoughts of the hummingbird forgotten.

Wendy! Here, at Dover Castle!

How on earth had she gotten here? He had no idea how she could have managed it, but there she was nonetheless, the sunrise dancing over her hair like a fiery halo as she took a delicate step back from ...

In that very moment, the man she had been speaking with turned his full profile to the sea, sprouted a pair of wings, and leaped into the air.

The growl that burst from Hook's chest turned into a full-throated battle cry by the time he got to the end of it: "*Peter PAN!*"

His well-trained crew had their weapons raised and ready to fire before he had even finished yelling, but they saw no sign of an enemy ship.

"Where, Captain?"

"*Where is the Fourteenth?*" Hook howled, watching helplessly as Pan flew away. "*What is their useless diviner doing? WHY AREN'T THEY AFTER HIM?*"

"Shall we follow him, Captain?"

But it was clear that the ship held no hope of chasing the flying man across the skies.

"No!" Hook barked. He took a moment to compose himself, continuing in calmer tones, but the fierce light in his eyes never dimmed. "No. Take me to the castle. They will answer for their failure."

His eyes narrowed further still.

"And she will answer for her treachery."

Wendy, on the other hand, was having a perfectly lovely morning.

After ensuring that Pan and his crew were safe, she had enjoyed a boisterous reunion with her platoon—and especially with poor Reginald, who had come to understand that he owed Wendy his life, even if he was a bit fuzzy on the details. She had dined in the castle mess with the others and then retired to John's office, which remained largely unchanged despite its temporary substitution of occupants.

The new lieutenant in charge of the platoon, a man named Stratton, was out in Dover with his wife, who was also the platoon's diviner. Mrs. Stratton had a tremendous fondness for pear-and-apricot tarts, and she encouraged her husband to escort

her to market at dawn every morning for the very first batch from her favorite bakery.

They always left the platoon's dog behind when they went on these excursions, but old Jollyboy hadn't been able to smell a thing in over three years. He was mostly blind now and could hardly walk, and he should have been retired years ago, only no one had ever thought to do it since he wasn't on the payroll. Even now, on this crisp spring morning, he was sound asleep, draped across Wendy's feet as she sat at his master's desk trying to decide exactly how to word her report.

It is a well-known fact that one should never lie. Especially not to a superior officer. And very especially never *ever* to a superior officer in a written document. But Wendy was going to have to do exactly that. For one thing, she wasn't about to betray Monsieur Dumas—not under any circumstances. And she didn't want to get herself into trouble either. At least not if she could help it. So she couldn't admit she had tried to save Peter's life.

But Peter hadn't needed any help on that account, so she hadn't really done anything wrong, had she? She had only been *willing* to do something wrong, which was not the same thing. She wished she could have talked the entire matter over with one of the dogs, but Jollyboy was the only one present and he couldn't stay awake for it. (She wasn't even sure he could hear her anyway.)

Which is why she still hadn't written a single word when Hook himself burst through the office door.

"Miss Darling." His voice was controlled, but there was a spark in his eyes that threatened to light a wildfire beneath her feet.

"Captain," was all she said. She was glad to be sitting behind the desk. It suddenly felt safer than the alternative.

Hook paced back and forth across the center of the room, eyeing her all the while. A panther sizing up his prey. His glorious hair was tied back at the nape of his neck, but the wind and the movement of the ship had worked it loose so that various tendrils had escaped to float about his face, further enhancing the look of a man living outside of civilization—in a dark and wild place.

He wanted to make her nervous. He wanted her to blurt out the truth under the pressure of his gaze, his strength, his obvious agitation. But she said nothing. She only watched him. Was he the panther stalking his prey? Or was she the hunter lying in wait for him?

"I ordered you to return to my estate," he said finally.

"Yes, Captain. And I did."

"The implication, Miss Darling," he said immediately, "was that you were to *stay* there."

"It ... it couldn't be helped," she replied.

"I see." Hook stopped pacing to glare at her more directly. "And I suppose you're going to tell me you were kidnapped. *Again.*"

He said it in a tone that implied very clearly he did not believe this at all, but it occurred to Wendy, upon hearing it, that this explanation would solve both of her problems at once. It would explain how she got to Dover Castle so quickly without involving Monsieur Dumas in the slightest, and it would explain what she was doing here in the first place.

"Well yes, Captain," she replied. "Despite your obvious skepticism, that is precisely what happened. Peter came to find me and carried me here."

"Entirely against your will," Hook said, taunting her.

"Of course not," she told him, thinking quickly. "You wanted me to get information, did you not? Specifically, the location of his island. That is what you had originally asked for, and I assumed

236

that information would still interest you. I don't know of any way to do that without interacting with him. If he has to carry me about for me to accomplish my mission, then so be it."

"And I suppose he forced you to dress like a man while he was at it."

Wendy was so comfortable wearing her pants and boots after riding through the night that she had forgotten about them entirely.

"What, this?" she replied, trying to sound as innocent as possible. "Did you suppose I trained in swordsmanship while wearing a dress? I was out on the lawn completing my exercises when he dove in from the sky and snatched me away. I can't help what I was wearing at the time."

"And he flew you to Dover Castle."

"Yes."

"At a time when there was no diviner present to notice his arrival."

This one was easier to answer. "Well for heaven's sake, that certainly had nothing to do with *me*. It isn't *my* fault if the new diviner likes fresh-baked pastries. *I* didn't tell her to leave her post."

"Then how did Pan know she was away?"

"I'm sure I have no idea. He's probably watching the castle. Learning the habits of the platoon. When *I* was here, I did my job."

In two long strides, Hook was at the desk. He slammed his good left hand down in its center, fingers splayed wide, and leaned forward across the wood. "If Pan wants you here," he shouted, "then it is the *last* place *I* want you. You will *never* come back to this platoon! *Never!*"

It took every ounce of Wendy's self-discipline not to shove her chair back away from him and leap to her feet, but she didn't

budge. Instead, she held his gaze steadily while she reached behind her, fishing Peter's strange device out of the pocket of her riding coat, which was hanging across the back of her chair.

"There is a better use for me now anyway, I think," she said calmly, and she slid the strange compass toward him across the surface of the desk.

"What's this?" he demanded.

He would have had to take it in his left hand, which he was still leaning on in a highly intimidating way, so he left the item where it was, leaving her to demonstrate. She opened the device and pulled her hands back from it.

"A compass? It's small, to be sure," he admitted. "The smallest I've ever seen. But what does it have to do with anything?"

"It isn't a normal compass," Wendy replied. She picked it up in her hands, and the needle swung away from north as a glow began to emanate from the island-shaped outline behind it. "It doesn't point toward north when I hold it. It points toward the everlost island."

When it first started glowing, Hook jerked away from it in surprise, but then he leaned in to try to see it more closely. He finally stood upright and plucked it out of her hands with a grunt to study it. It went dark immediately, and the needle spun back to the north.

"It only works for me," Wendy said quietly.

"What trickery is this?" Hook demanded, but she leaned forward gently, reaching across the desk for it. When he handed it to her, reluctantly, it lit up again, and the needle swung away from north once more.

"It isn't trickery," she replied. "It's magic."

CHAPTER
42

How did you say it worked?"

Sir William paced back and forth in Hook's office while Hook remained seated at his desk, unusually subdued.

"It didn't *work*. I'm telling you, it was a trick." Hook leaned back in his chair, waving his steel appendage in dismissal. "The investigator's report will say the same thing, and we're all going to look foolish for cloistering the man away over nothing."

"It wasn't nothing," Sir William protested. "Even if it's just a compass, it's the most unusual one I've ever seen. We can't admit where it came from, and I don't want the entire Royal Society asking questions. Better to have him look into it here."

"Hmph," Hook grunted. "I suppose you're right. Besides, we can keep a better eye on the Darling girl here too. I can't even imagine unleashing her on Somerset House."

Sir William snorted. "'The darling girl,'" he repeated. "If

you're not careful, I might start thinking that engagement of yours is more than just a ruse."

"It's her *name*," Hook growled, but Sir William was still grinning when a knock sounded at the door. He stopped pacing and opened it for a tall, lean young man, who bowed at once.

"Thomas Pettigrew, at your service," he announced. He was dressed in a poor man's wools rather than a rich man's silks, and his cutaway coat hung somewhat loosely. A hand-me-down from a brother, or perhaps even from his father, Hook supposed. The cuffs of his white linen shirt were so plain that Hook wouldn't have been caught dead in them. But by God, his *hair*. Hook almost grimaced. His medium-brown hair flew every which way, as though he had only just now rolled out of bed at three o'clock in the afternoon.

"Where's our Royal Society fellow?" Sir William demanded. "You were supposed to bring him with you."

Sir William assumed from looking at him that Thomas Pettigrew was an errand boy. In fact, at only eighteen years of age, he was one of the youngest members ever to be admitted to the Royal Society. He was already well on his way to a brilliant career in mathematics and the natural sciences, and you surely would have read of him in one of your history books were it not for the events which were about to transpire over these next few minutes.

"Right here," Thomas replied. "He is I. Or I am he. As you prefer."

Suddenly he fell silent, and his eyes opened wide. They darted to the left, and to the right, and to the left again, his chin following slightly with each change in direction. Then he began chattering in a distracted sort of way that was clearly intended only for himself.

"Ha!" he exclaimed. "It's commutative, isn't it! He is I, or I am he! It doesn't matter which! Grammatically or mathematically! I must write that down!" He patted at the pockets of his waistcoat,

eventually producing a pencil and a scrap of paper and marching them straight to Hook's desk, leaning over the wooden surface and scribbling furiously.

"But you're not Banks," Sir William protested. "I was told the president of the Society would see to it himself."

"Not Banks! Quite correct!" he agreed, writing even as he spoke. "No, no. Sir Joseph intended to assist you. He did. At least, that is, until it was explained to him that he would not be permitted to leave the premises once he entered. So he left *before* he entered, and you got me instead."

Thomas Pettigrew finished his note with a flourish and stood up straight, stuffing the paper and pencil into his pocket and grinning from ear to ear. He looked back and forth between Sir William and Hook, both of whom stared back at him in expectation, but he said nothing more.

"Well?" Sir William finally prompted.

"Well what?" Thomas asked.

"What is your report regarding the compass, man? Out with it!"

"Oh! Why, it's extraordinary! *Quite* extraordinary! Even as a compass! I've never seen a liquid variety so small and portable! A man can carry it in his hand! Or a woman, of course. *Especially* a woman, as it turns out. Very unexpected!"

"*What* is unexpected?" Hook demanded.

"Well, the mechanism by which it changes direction for Miss Darling, for one thing. Clearly it's responding to some invisible force, but it isn't magnetic. That much is certain. As a *compass*, it's magnetic, but as ... well, as whatever else it is ... it's responding to something else entirely."

"So what *is* it responding to?" Sir William asked.

"I have no idea!" Thomas declared. "Isn't that wonderful? It's

a complete mystery! A whole new area of science on the brink of discovery! When the Royal Society reads my paper—"

"No!" both men exclaimed, and Thomas took half a step back, blinking in surprise.

"You can't write a paper about this," Sir William told him. "Not about any of it. Not about a handheld liquid compass, not about any unknown force, nothing."

"But I *must!*" Thomas protested. "In the name of science! It will be the greatest discovery since the lightning conductor!"

"Now look—" Hook started, but Sir William cleared his throat loudly enough to catch his attention.

"We understand your position, Thomas," Sir William said with a smile. "Give us some time to discuss it. Wait for us in the laboratory, won't you?"

"Of course!" Thomas said, bouncing up and down a little on the balls of his feet. "Would you be willing to send Miss Darling back, too? I'd like to investigate that glow a bit further."

Sir William nodded and waved his hand through the air in an annoyed sort of way, dismissing Thomas Pettigrew from the room.

Once the young man had left, Sir William turned to Hook, looking for all the world as though he'd just eaten a bad fish.

"You're going to have to take them both with you," he said.

"Take both of *whom* with me *where?*" Hook stared at Sir William with tight lips and a dark glare.

"You know precisely whom, and you know where as well. If he says there's something to it, then there's something to it."

"You can't be serious."

"I'm deadly serious. We have to be sure. You have to take the girl to make the thing work, and you have to take that Pettigrew fellow to keep him from talking."

"A scientist. And a *woman.* On a fighting ship. It could very well be a trap, you know."

"I know the risks." Sir William's tone was sharp, intended to remind Hook of both his rank and his experience. "That's why I'm sending two extra ships with you, but no more. If this whole thing is just an elaborate trap, at least you'll have enough firepower to stand a chance. If it's some kind of decoy, designed to lure you away from our shores, the bulk of our forces will still be here to defend England.

"But if it is neither of those things," Sir William continued, "if that compass really is a magical device that will lead you to the everlost, then your orders are to scout and survey. Chart the island's position. Get Pettigrew to map what you can of their territory without being discovered, and then you *must* return that map to England. At any cost."

Hook sat in his office, finally alone, staring at the deep scars on his desk and slowly working his jaw from side to side. Left, front, right, front, left, front, right.

Magic. The very word made his skin crawl. What had become of the Royal Society that *any* of its fellows, no matter how untested, would throw up his hands so easily? An unknown force, indeed. Even Hook's magnificent hair would have stiffened in protest, had it been able.

And that *woman.* On his *ship*!

At least he had discovered her in Dover and forced her to return

to London. *That* hadn't been part of her plan. He allowed himself a small smile, but it was short-lived. What *was* her plan? He couldn't help but feel that somehow this was part of it all along. To get him away from England. To get aboard his ship.

His jaw stopped moving and fell open. Had Sir William been right from the beginning? Was this entire convoluted enterprise just an elaborate ploy to get him alone at sea and beguile him into marriage?

His jaw snapped shut. No. His instincts couldn't be *that* wrong. She was up to something far more devious than that. But why else would she want to get him alone?

Or to get him away from England, as Sir William had suggested. With her lieutenant and his sergeant left behind.

Hook sat up straighter.

Did she expect him to return them to Dover? That would certainly make sense. A cold pit of dread formed low in his belly. If they were in Dover, and they failed to sound the alarm, the everlost could reach London in force before anyone even suspected. Were they really everlost collaborators? It didn't seem likely, but he couldn't take that chance.

But then he thought about leaving them at his estate. What if *that* was what she wanted …?

By God, this was getting him nowhere.

He had to relocate them somewhere entirely different. Somewhere she would never expect. But where?

What he *really* wanted to do was lock them all in irons. If only they had broken the law. Any law.

A cold, hard smile finally danced across his lips.

There was one place, and only one, where his word was *absolute* law. And it was exactly where he had just been ordered to take Wendy Darling.

As Hook imagined the possibilities, a veritable flood tide of glee welled up within him. He couldn't punish them for no reason, not even aboard his own ship. He would lose the trust and faith of his men. But a man without training would make a mistake soon enough. He would fail at his assigned task. Or he would fall asleep at his post. And then ...

Yes, perhaps Wendy Darling should be reunited with her friends after all.

There is a particular feeling that results when a child hears his or her *entire* name spoken sharply by an adult. It ignites with a sudden intake of the lungs. A tightening of the chest. And then it plummets down the gullet, settling into a cold, hard lump of dread in the pit of one's stomach. It is the feeling of being in trouble. It is a universal human experience, binding us all together indisputably as a single species, like love or familial fondness, only far less pleasant than those, and unfortunately the feeling does not belong exclusively to children.

In fact, this is the exact feeling Wendy experienced as she stood outside Hook's office, nervously smoothing down her favorite blue dress even though there was nothing wrinkled about it to begin with, and preparing to face the captain's wrath. Her wardrobe had been fetched from Hook's estate, but she would have preferred to appear before the man in her fighting breeches. She wanted to make the best case she could for being allowed to join the everlost

expedition, and a blue chemise dress, no matter how fetching, did not look very adventure-like.

Unfortunately, it would have to do. It was a matter of propriety. She took a deep breath, steeled herself as best she could, and opened the door.

She had last seen Hook at Dover Castle, fresh from his ship, wild and free. He had returned to London on the same vessel, and she had returned by carriage. She had not seen him since. So although she was prepared for the tiger—the disheveled hair, the predator's stance, the piercing gaze—she was not prepared for the young, civilized lord who sat before her, looking almost exactly as he had the first time they had met. His glorious hair lay impeccably subdued. His forget-me-not eyes smoldered with a quiet confidence. He even smiled.

Only the sprawling fury of maps and the scars across the desk remained to whisper of a different Hook. An unpredictable and dangerous Hook.

Something was terribly wrong.

"Miss Darling." His voice was warm and pleasant, and he stood politely, acknowledging her feminine presence.

Wendy's eyebrow shot high into the air, trying to warn her, but she forged ahead nonetheless.

"Captain Hook," she began. "Firstly, I have completed the mission you set before me. I have discovered, if not the location of the everlost island itself, at least a clear path toward it. Which is even better than finding a mere ship—which is all you asked me to do.

"Secondly, the compass I procured from Pan only works for me, as I'm sure Thomas has already informed you. His scientific examination has uncovered no other way to operate it, meaning you cannot reach the island without me.

"Thirdly, although yes, I am a woman, I am nonetheless a member of the Nineteenth Light Dragoons, sworn to protect the shores of England from the magical threat you intend to pursue. I have been fully trained in both marksmanship and swordsmanship, and you'll find I am as competent in a fight as any man. Especially when armed with a musket—a weapon which depends on neither the strength nor the size of the one who holds it for its efficacy—"

"Miss Darling," Hook repeated, finally interrupting her. She had delivered the entire spiel without seeming to draw breath, pacing back and forth at a steady clip, her heels clicking sharply against the floor as she ticked each item off on her fingers. "I agree."

Wendy stopped short and blinked twice, trying to catch up.

"What?"

She had prepared ahead for several possible responses. Winning right off the bat wasn't one of them.

"I said, 'I agree.' Those are all excellent points. Welcome aboard."

"Oh! Yes, well ... thank you." She drew herself up to her full height and squared her shoulders, watching him with suspicion.

"Gather your men and then report to the armory. You'll find them in the officers' quarters. I had them returned to London along with your things."

"You ... what? But then, you must have already planned—"

"Yes, Miss Darling, I was already going to bring you along. All of you. But still, it was an excellent presentation. Very convincing. I'm sure I would have been persuaded, had I needed to be."

Wendy tilted her head just the tiniest bit to the right and narrowed her eyes, continuing to stare.

"Oh," he continued, "and don't forget Mr. Pettigrew. I'm assigning him to your little lost complement of the Fourteenth."

"All right," Wendy finally replied. "Thank you."

Hook said nothing more, waving her away with his good left hand and returning his attention to a small stack of journals on his desk. If he muttered something as she left about keeping all the useless people in one place, she pretended not to hear it.

"Flogged, I tell you. Publicly flogged."

John sat wedged behind the tiny desk in their assigned room—his chin propped forlornly against the heel of his left hand—doing nothing.

He hated doing nothing, but there it was. He had no accounts to keep, no reports to write, no scheduled duties to post. He had nothing but time to sit and reflect on the fact that they had lost Wendy. Again. Nothing Hook could do to him could possibly make him feel worse, so contemplating the form of his punishment made for a welcome distraction.

Michael, however, was not so dour. He stood against the doorframe, leaning against it with his right shoulder, his arms crossed over his chest, grinning easily.

"Daily bootlicking at dawn. Literally," he countered. "Followed by mornings of barnacle scraping, lunches of rock soup, afternoons of button polishing, and sea ration suppers."

"For how long?" John asked.

Michael thought for a moment, then freed his right hand just long enough to point in John's general direction. "Three years," he announced.

"I'd rather be flogged," John muttered.

"Latrine duty for six months?" Michael suggested.

"I'd rather be drawn and quartered."

It was an exaggeration, of course, being drawn and quartered, but both men paused to look at Nana, who was hiding under the far bed. All punishments aside, at least their lives—not to mention John's commission—were probably not under threat. Nana, however, could easily be dismissed from the king's service, if not worse. Working animals that didn't earn their keep were not considered worth the meat to feed them, and both men knew it.

Just as they looked back at each other to share a worried glance, Nana burst out from under the bed, tossing the near edge of the frame violently into the air and toppling the straw mattress off the far side.

"What in the world—" John began, and then a light knock came at the door as Nana whined desperately, struggling all the while to shove her monstrous nose into the tiny gap beneath it.

"Wendy!" both men exclaimed.

Michael turned and threw open the door, grabbing her into his arms right there in the doorway while John struggled to extricate himself from the desk.

"Wendy!" John exclaimed again, this time addressing her directly. "Are you hurt? Where in the world have you been?"

"Dover!" she cried. "Dover and back again! And I have wonderful news!"

"No flogging?" Michael asked, smirking at John over Wendy's head.

"What? No, of course not. Flogging. Honestly. What would make you say such a thing?"

"Let her go already." John scowled at both of them until Michael finally took a step backward, allowing John to rush in and hold her at arm's length, inspecting her for signs of damage.

"So what's the good news?" Michael asked.

"We're sailing with Hook to seek the home of the everlost! All of us! Even you, Nana!" Wendy knelt by the dog as she said this, and Nana nuzzled gratefully under her chin, relieved that her mistress had not come to any harm.

"What?" John just stared down at her, trying to take in this sudden turn of events.

"Who's this?" Michael demanded.

When Wendy had knelt beside Nana, Thomas Pettigrew had become far more conspicuous. He stood a few steps behind her down the hall, watching the entire scene with a look of detached interest, his dark brown eyes glancing innocently back and forth among the four of them.

"Oh! This is Thomas Pettigrew," Wendy said. "He's the youngest fellow of the Royal Society. He's coming with us."

"Mister Pettigrew," John said, bowing slightly.

"Just Thomas, please," he replied, bouncing slightly on the balls of his feet, which made his hair look even more disheveled than it already had. He did not, however, return the bow.

"I'm *Lieutenant* John Abbot." John stressed the lieutenant bit, just for good measure. He knew Wendy had a predilection for science, and he found himself hoping that particular fondness did not extend equally to scientists.

"Oh, hey! I'm a lieutenant, too!" Thomas exclaimed. "Fancy that, what?"

"I ... what?" John asked.

"They said I had to be," Thomas said, shrugging. "King's vessel and secrets of the realm and all that. They swore me in this morning. Didn't matter to me, of course. Happy to do it."

Now John and Michael exchanged a new glance—a very *particular* glance—and the glance said this: "A genius scientist *and* an

officer, with a puppy dog demeanor. On a ship. With Wendy. I think I would have preferred the flogging."

CHAPTER
44

As they made their way toward the armory, Wendy had a definite bounce in her step, unconsciously matching Thomas in a way John did not like at all.

"I'll need a sword, of course," she was saying, mostly to herself. "Something light. And a musket. Or perhaps a pistol. Which would be better, I wonder, for a sea battle? Do you think they'll allow us both?"

This last was addressed to John. "I'm sure it depends on the size of the armory on board," he replied. "On a ship, it's all a matter of space."

"Oh, yes. Yes, of course," Wendy agreed. "I understand perfectly. But it is a rather *large* ship, isn't it?"

Unfortunately, John was certain she didn't understand the most important bit at all. He and Michael might recognize Wendy's true potential, after having served with her and having seen what she was capable of, but the same could not be said for the rest

of the men in the Home Office. The quartermaster was only going to see a woman. And he was not going to allow a woman to draw any weapons whatsoever, let alone two of them.

"It's a fighting ship, John!" Michael protested. "I wouldn't be surprised if we each get *two* swords! And *two* pistols!"

John shot him a warning glance, but Michael didn't notice.

"I don't see what the fuss is about," Thomas offered, looking a bit worried. "Are we really expecting to need swords? And firearms? It seems a bit extreme."

"Yes, Thomas," Wendy said firmly. She placed her right hand within the crook of his arm and patted his elbow with her left. "The everlost are not the only threat we will face at sea. There are pirates. And French gunships. And who knows what sort of creatures we might encounter living among the everlost? Every hand must be ready to defend the ship by force, if need be. We must all be prepared."

"Well, if you say so, Miss Darling. But my expertise lies in science, I'm afraid, not armaments." He shrugged and grinned down at her, apparently unconcerned by the admission.

"Just ask for a sword and a musket," Wendy advised him. "I can show you how to use them. You'll need to be armed for any landing party."

"Oh! Of course I want to be in the landing party!" Thomas came to a sudden halt, dropping his arm from hers and turning to face her in earnest. "The scientists among the everlost are clearly aware of forces that are beyond our grasp! I must be allowed to meet them! To learn from them!"

"Scientists?" Wendy started, but then she trailed off. She didn't see the need to start a debate over science and magic when Thomas would learn the truth about *that* soon enough.

"Yes, well, you'll need to be armed to leave the ship," she said instead. "So if you want to meet ... any of the everlost, allow the quartermaster to assign you a sword at least. Preferably a musket as well."

"As you say," Thomas agreed, already grinning again.

Meet them? John and Michael both wondered. *I thought we were trying to kill them.* But they kept this thought to themselves.

They arrived at the armory to find the quartermaster already scowling. He was a portly man with jet black hair, beady eyes, and habitually angry jowls that had taken an instant dislike to the entire party—and that seemed perfectly willing to make their opinion known. Whether they were more offended by the woman or by the dog was hard to say, but Wendy had her suspicions.

Nevertheless, she smoothed her dress and forged ahead, ignoring the nervous glances that both John and Michael were now aiming at each other.

"We were told to report for the crew of *The Dragon*," Wendy began. "To draw arms for the journey."

"*They* might be drawing arms," he said, whipping his jowls toward the men behind her, "but *you* won't."

"I assure you—" Wendy insisted, speaking calmly but firmly.

"And *I* assure *you*," he snapped, interrupting her, "that I won't be issuing any arms to a woman! If you don't need 'em, you don't get 'em. And *you* don't need 'em."

Wendy's eyes narrowed immediately, and you can imagine

how her eyebrow felt about the subject. *Girls can't be in the navy! Girls take care of babies!* The taunts of her childhood echoed across the years.

Well, not today, she thought to herself. *Not anymore.*

"I am as much a part of this crew as anyone else!" she proclaimed, standing straighter and raising her voice.

"You can have my sword," Thomas offered, shifting from foot to foot even more awkwardly than usual. "I didn't want one anyway."

"You can have *my* sword," Michael chimed in, not to be outdone by Thomas. "In fact, I'll draw any weapon you like."

"You'll do no such thing!" Wendy and the quartermaster both declared at once, causing them to glare at each other with even more venom than before.

Nana started to growl low in her throat, and John was about to step between Wendy and the quartermaster to prevent any possible fisticuffs when Hook's menacing baritone bellowed out behind them all.

"What is the meaning of this?"

"Captain!" the quartermaster answered, and he snapped out a smart salute. "This woman was trying to draw arms for *The Dragon,* sir. As if you would allow such a thing!"

"Was she?" Hook regarded Wendy with only the smallest hint of a smile. He had arrived with another man in tow, one whom Wendy had never seen before. She would not usually ignore introductions—Wendy hated rudeness of any kind—but at the moment she was rather worked up.

"I was," she affirmed, her chin thrust defiantly before her. "It would be foolish to leave any able-bodied sailor unarmed in the event of a sea battle, and I was about to assure this man that you are no fool."

At this Hook laughed out loud. "Well said, Miss Darling! That would be foolish indeed! But how am I to know whether you are able-bodied? For all I know, you would be no more help than a monkey. A clever pet, to be sure, but hardly worthy of the king's steel in battle."

Wendy thought of at least a hundred things she wanted to say in the space of a single blink, but to her credit she discarded them all. He was baiting her, and she would not lose her temper. Not in front of her men. For that was how she thought of John and Michael and Nana—and now Thomas, as well.

Instead, she said only this: "Then let us prove it. But if I succeed, you will allow me to draw my own weapons, like any other man on the crew."

"And how will you prove it, little monkey?" Hook asked, drawing a smirk from his man behind. The newcomer looked no older than John, standing about average height, with dark hair and dark eyes, a barrel chest and a small button nose, and an unusually wide mouth.

"I shall fight *him*," Wendy announced, indicating whom she meant with a nod of her head. This was a bit impetuous, to say the least, as she had no idea who the man was. But his smirk reminded her of Mortimer Black, the boy from the orphanage all those years ago, so she disliked him immediately.

"Smee?" Hook asked, laughing even harder.

"Do you agree to my terms?" Wendy demanded.

"Oh, I most certainly do," Hook affirmed, and he waved the man forward.

They were each permitted their blade of choice. Smee chose a dull, training version of a British spadroon with a basket hilt, while Wendy selected a French smallsword that had obviously

been liberated from the enemy. Because it was not a training sword, she requested John's neck scarf to wrap around the end, to which John readily agreed.

As they squared off in the hallway, Hook addressed his man.

"Use the left," he said, by which he meant the left hand. "Let's at least give her a chance, shall we?" But of course Hook didn't intend to give Wendy a chance at all. He only meant to humiliate her, and he grinned at her wickedly to prove it.

"Prepare yourself!" she declared, and Smee barely had time to raise his weapon before she aimed her silk-tipped sword at his heart.

He fended off the blow just in time, raising his own sword to catch her blade so that it slid away harmlessly along the steel. He moved immediately into a thrust, but Wendy anticipated it, flipping her weapon upside-down over his, pushing his spadroon harmlessly beyond her side while aiming at his gut.

She had him already, and she knew she had him, but she disengaged before she connected, taking three quick steps backward in the classic fencing style that Monsieur Dumas had helped her to perfect.

"'Twas luck, girl, and nothing more," Smee growled, his accent marking him as an Irishman, but Wendy made no reply other than to raise a contrary eyebrow. Smee narrowed his eyes, thrust out his chin, and charged, swinging his blade fast and hard, chopping in a backhanded sweep toward her left side.

Wendy knew she didn't have the strength to block such a wide blow directly, but she had trained for this. She dropped to her knees to duck his swing and raised her smallsword over her head, guiding his steel away rather than fighting against it. Suddenly, his longer weapon was not a blessing but a curse. She sprang back to her feet, flicked the tip of her thin blade inside his ornamental hilt,

slid the smallsword as far as it would go, and used the leverage of her position to wrench the spadroon from his grasp.

Again she quick-stepped backward, this time removing his sword from her own and lobbing it back to him in a gentle arc. His eyes flicked toward Hook, who offered a small, grim nod. Smee tossed the sword lightly from his left hand to his right, and Wendy smiled.

He came at her with four fast jabs, but the smallsword was by far the more agile weapon, which was why Wendy had chosen it. Again she used Smee's momentum against him, guiding his blade harmlessly away, first to one side and then the other. Left. Right. Left. Right. With each failed thrust he became more enraged, extending his reach that much farther, until finally he stepped too close.

Before his foot could plant, Wendy snapped her own foot up and out, blocking him at the ankle. He stumbled, falling hard to the right, and he dropped his sword to catch himself.

With a triumphant smile, Wendy touched the tip of her silk-wrapped blade lightly to his side.

"Now then," she said, "I believe we had a deal."

CHAPTER
45

The deal, you might remember, was only for weapons. But Hook had tried to humiliate Wendy, and now he looked like a fool. He took a deep breath, containing his fury. Only a subtle twitch of his left eye gave any hint of the storm that raged within. But rage, it did. And sometimes when people are angry, they say things they don't mean. Things they might even come to regret.

What Hook said was this: "Let her draw whatever she wants."

Then he stalked away, ordering Smee to follow.

Wendy smiled.

She kept the smallsword and drew a musket and two pistols besides. She also drew a belt and a new pair of tall boots. It was not unusual for boys to enlist at a fairly young age, and the quarter-master stocked all manner of gear in smaller sizes to accommodate the practice.

He balked when she asked for several pairs of breeches along

with a small stack of shirts and vests, but Wendy narrowed her eyes and said firmly, "His order was to let me draw what I wish. Shall we call him back to clarify?"

The man grumbled and glared, his jowls quiveringly indignant, but he stepped aside nonetheless, allowing her to peruse the aisles at will.

In the end, she emerged with a towering stack of items, including several fresh, leather-bound journals; as many ink bottles as she could reasonably carry; and an exquisite pocket watch, its casing forged in silver so it wouldn't rust in the sea air. She had also claimed any equipment she thought might be useful to Thomas for his experiments; an extra sword and pistol each for John and Michael; and even a new, leather collar for Nana, who donned it with pride.

Finally, she requisitioned four large sea chests—humble but strong—to house their stockpile of treasure.

They filled the chests and lumbered off together, straining under the burden of their loot. Michael glanced back, just once, to aim a final, smug grin at the scowling quartermaster before launching into a sea shanty at the top of his lungs.

Her sails raised by sailors' hands,
Her sturdy deck beneath our feet,
She'll carry us to distant lands,
Our sailing ship, fine and fleet!

A sailing ship! A life at sea!
A sailing ship for me!

John and Wendy responded with the answering chorus, singing just as loudly:

A sailing ship! A life at sea!
A sailing ship for me!

Thomas joined in, too, providing harmony in a smooth baritone that raised Wendy's eyebrow in approval. Even Nana howled along with the rest—entirely off key, but with obvious feeling.

When they reached their quarters, the men left Wendy alone with Nana to change. They remained in the hallway for what seemed an eternity, so that by the time Wendy opened the door again, John was sitting on the floor, and Thomas was lying flat on his back, arms folded behind his head, staring at the ceiling. Only Michael was still on his feet, leaning jauntily against the wall across from the doorway, but even he was not prepared for the sight they beheld.

Wendy was radiant.

Her charcoal-gray breeches were tucked into tall, black leather boots. The sleeves of a man's white linen shirt peeked out from beneath a cream silk vest, which was embroidered lightly in the same color. A black leather belt held her bare sword in a metal ring at her left hip, with a pistol cinched high on each outer thigh.

She had fashioned a sort of sheath for her musket out of black leather, with a strap that hung over her left shoulder, crossing her chest and fastening to her belt on her right. The gun was secured in the sheath upon her back, its stock protruding above her left shoulder.

She was dressed entirely in a man's clothing, but not one of the men in the hallway thought he had ever seen a woman more beautiful in all his life.

John and Thomas rose to their feet, and then all three stood transfixed, without saying a word, until Thomas lowered himself to one knee before her.

John and Michael sprang into action, grabbing him by the shoulders and shouting, "What?" and "No!" respectively, to which Thomas looked up in confusion.

"I'm sorry," he said. "Should I leave it there?"

"Leave what where?" John demanded.

"Your neck scarf," Thomas replied, pointing to the delicate silk that was still wrapped securely over the tip of Wendy's sword.

John and Michael both sighed in relief.

"Just leave it there," John muttered. "It's fine where it is."

"All right, then." Thomas shrugged and stood back up, while Wendy hid a delicate smile, her secret kiss dancing softly in the far corner.

Tomorrow! We sail tomorrow!

Every time she thought it, a thrill raced from the top of Wendy's skull down her spine, only to settle, fluttering, in the pit of her belly. She wanted more than anything to stay with the others through the evening. To marvel with them over the possibilities. Where would Pan's strange device lead them? And what would they find when they arrived?

But she had made a promise to a friend, and Wendy intended to keep it. So instead of staying and wondering aloud over the likelihood of discovering giants or ogres or witches or trolls, Wendy retired to the quarters she had been assigned alone, as the only woman in a crew of men. And she began to write a letter.

My Dear M. Dumas,

I am writing, as promised, to assure you that all is well. We succeeded, and I am safe among friends. I wish I could tell you that I will be visiting soon, to thank you in person for your unparalleled kindness, but I shall not be returning to Hertfordshire within the foreseeable future.

I find myself on the brink of a tremendous journey, one which will take me far from England's shores. Perhaps only you, of all the people I have ever known, will truly understand what I am feeling in this moment. The excitement of it. And the uncertainty. To leave all that is home—perhaps forever— but also to embrace the unfamiliar with joy and wonder. I am nervous, certainly. But I am unafraid.

No matter what happens, I would make no other choice. I must follow my heart. I know that you will understand this too. But I do hope that we will see each other again. Truly.

I owe you a far greater debt than I fear I can ever repay.

> *Your friend,*
> *Wendy Darling*

If the details were a bit scarce, M. Dumas would assume it was because she did not want to write openly of her beloved Frenchman and their plans to escape. And if anyone intercepted the missive, it was innocent enough—a final letter to a friend, to ensure he did not come looking for her. Even the Home Office would approve of that intent.

Satisfied, she folded the page and sealed it in wax. But there was one more letter she needed to write—one that held even more meaning for her, but which needed to be even more discreet. She thought for a long time before finally placing her pen to a second sheet of paper. On it, she wrote only this:

You were right. I found a way.

Thank you,
W.

She addressed the envelope to "Mr. Gustavus Vassa," to be sure it reached him, and added "Mr. Olaudah Equiano" in parentheses beneath. Then she stretched her legs beneath the writing desk and felt the heels of her new boots scrape along the floor, making her grin all over again. She had disarmed herself for the evening but had refused to change out of her new outfit.

These were the clothes of a journey. They were clothes of strength and adventure. Clothes she had spent a lifetime fighting for. She snuffed out the candle and lay down on the bed without taking off her boots. They were brand new, after all. They had never even touched a street.

But that would change soon enough.

Tomorrow, she would wear them in the streets of London.

And at the docks. She would wear them as she set foot upon the deck of *The Dragon* for the very first time. She lay in bed imagining it, watching a small sliver of moonlight creep along the wall until she finally fell asleep.

But in all of her imagining, not once did she imagine the surprise that lay in store for her in the morning.

CHAPTER
46

I t was time.

Even after Wendy awoke to a warm, cloudless dawn, she still felt as though she were wandering through a dream. Her boots seemed barely to touch the ground as she and Nana collected their crew and made their way toward the carriage that would take them to the docks.

She was met by silent glances throughout the hallways of the Nineteenth Light Dragoon headquarters. A few were glances of wide-eyed wonder; a few others, of surprised respect; but most were scathing glances of contempt and loathing, barely contained.

She thought at first that word of her fight with Smee must have spread already. That they were angry at her, a woman, for besting one of their own. But who would have done the telling? Not Hook, surely. And not the quartermaster. Not in a clandestine operation.

Certainly not Smee.

But then she realized the truth: No one knew about the fight. It was her *clothing.* She was dressed as a man. And not just any man, but a sailor, prepared for battle. In her excitement, she had not even considered how her transformation might be taken by those who did not know her.

"They will get used to it," Michael murmured in her ear. "Keep your head up. They will come to see you as we do."

Wendy nodded, once. And she forced herself to walk with a confident gait. Strong and proud. But she had first introduced herself to John and Michael as a demure woman, dressed in a woman's clothing. With a woman's poise and a woman's manners.

She had hidden her intelligence and her vast repertoire of skills, allowing these to shine through only in small, subtle ways. She had allowed the Fourteenth Platoon to get to know her slowly, over their long months together, careful never to threaten. Never to intimidate.

Never to challenge.

This was different, and she knew it.

She navigated the hallways and finally descended the stairs, making her way toward the outside world, all the while staring straight ahead. Forcing steel into her eyes and into her step. Forcing herself to bear the sudden, devastating weight of it. Refusing to be crushed beneath their hatred.

But even the exit would provide no escape. She would set foot in the street for the very first time dressed as her true self, as the woman she had always dreamed of becoming, and the people of London would stare and point and laugh. Their faces would whirl around her, and every face would be the pale, merciless face of Mortimer Black, mocking and taunting her across the years.

She braced herself, and she stepped through the door.

It was early yet, but already there were people in the street. Not the ladies and gentlemen who would appear later to shop at the establishments of the boot maker or the tailor next door. Instead, they were beggars, cart merchants, flower girls. Those who had spent the night huddled in a doorway, or those who had risen early to claim a popular street corner for the business of the day.

No one laughed. She needn't have worried about *that*. Not with an escort of armed men surrounding her. But they stopped and stared and pointed, whispering to each other. Smiling cruelly behind coal-smudged hands, as though they were better than she. Because at least *they* knew how to dress. At least *they* knew their place—and who they were supposed to be.

Wendy's hands trembled slightly at her sides, but she gave no other sign that she saw them. That she heard them. She just walked toward the waiting carriage, carefully maintaining the appearance of stoic dignity and pride that now felt like an illusion, even to her.

And then—a horde of racing footsteps, scudding across the cobblestones.

She started and paused, turning her head, a deer sensing the presence of hunters, and a pack of yelling boys flew around the corner, chasing a long-legged terrier that raced merrily ahead with a cricket ball in its mouth.

They were too intent on their pursuit to notice the spectacle. The hunt split in two and passed around them. All but one small girl, who stopped dead in her tracks and stared. She was a street urchin, no older than ten, with skinny arms and skinny ankles and a tangled mess of dark brown hair.

But her eyes were crystal clear.

They darted to the sword upon Wendy's hip. To the pistols strapped against her thighs. To the musket that peeked over the

edge of her left shoulder. The girl stared at Wendy, and Wendy stared back at the girl, and for a moment, time stood still, which is what always happens when two souls truly *see* one another.

And then the girl drew herself up to her full height, sucked in her breath sharply, and saluted, her eyes wide and proud.

It was the first salute Wendy had ever received, and it would remain in her heart for the rest of her life. She stood straight and tall, nodded in recognition, and saluted back, her spirit reaching all the way to the sky.

There was an *immediacy* to the encounter with the young girl that stayed with her, restoring Wendy's strength and bolstering her pride, so that even when the sailors along the pier *did* point and laugh, she paid them no mind. She stepped out of the carriage to see the elegant masts of *The Dragon* soaring above her, and from that moment on she had eyes for nothing else.

Her ship.

Her sailing ship.

It didn't matter that she was not its captain. She was a member of its crew, so she thought of it as her own. It was thirty years old but it had been well kept, and Wendy's eyes threatened to well with tears when she first set foot upon it.

The deck all but gleamed beneath her boot heels in the morning light, and the smell of the salt air filled her memory with stories of adventure.

John scowled at the men who paused to gawk at the spectacle of a fully armed woman standing on deck in a man's clothing. He

barked a command, echoed by Michael, and the well-disciplined crew scattered, returning to the tasks at hand. The ship wouldn't leave until nightfall, but there were preparations to be made and fresh provisions to store away. The mystery of the girl could wait.

A cabin boy appeared to escort them to their quarters, introducing himself as Nicholas. He was about twelve years old, lean and agile, with a hawklike beak for a nose and a quick air about him, as though he were always taking in at least five different things at once. His eyes darted over Wendy's gear, over her dog, over her companions, and that was that.

"Well, come along then," he said. "Captain told me to watch for you. Make sure there wasn't any trouble. Get your things stowed right and proper. Follow me." With that, he turned smartly on his heel, clearly expecting them to follow.

He led them down a ladder into a narrow hallway below deck. They passed a sailor here and there, but far fewer than Wendy had expected.

"Nicholas," she asked, "doesn't *The Dragon* have a crew of five hundred? Where *is* everyone?"

"She does, ma'am," he affirmed. "Captain Hook plus five hundred and twenty, as of this morning." He glanced over his shoulder at Wendy, John, Michael, and Thomas.

"Make that five hundred and twenty-four," he said, correcting himself.

Nana narrowed her eyes at him and cocked her head meaningfully to the right, barking just once.

"Yes, ma'am. Five hundred and twenty-five," he added with a laugh. "My apologies."

Wendy liked him already.

"Some are still on leave," he continued. "Under orders to return by sunset. But most are either down in the hold storing

cargo, or on the gun decks seeing to the cannons. Just wait 'til tonight when we set sail. Everyone who doesn't have another job to do will be on deck for *that*."

Wendy smiled. *Tonight, when we set sail.* His words echoed over and over in her mind. *Tonight, when we set sail!* She was so caught up in the thought that she almost missed what he said next.

"Your own cabin, ma'am, is down this hallway. Your lieutenant's cabin is just beyond that, and his sergeant and the scientist will share a double. But first …"

He trailed off and rapped sharply on the door before him.

Wendy steeled herself, expecting to face Hook, but the man who opened the door wasn't Hook at all.

It was poor Reginald, grinning from ear to ear, with the rest of the Fourteenth Platoon leaping off their bunks and snapping to attention behind him.

CHAPTER
47

Lieutenant! Sergeant!" The joyful cries of the platoon met them as the men pressed forward, laughing and jostling each other, followed by a new round of shouts (and a few reverent whispers) when they saw who else had finally returned.

"Wendy!"

If John and Michael were their compass, Wendy was the wind itself, filling their sails with hopes and dreams and purpose. Without her, they had felt cast adrift. But now she flitted among them once again, clasping a shoulder here, touching a cheek there, her honey-brown smiles—and one mischievously arched eyebrow—promising extraordinary adventures that had only just begun.

And here, her new clothing served her well. She was every bit a guardian of England, just as they were, and they had always known it. But they were born of eighteenth-century England.

They could only expand their minds so far—at least until Wendy herself extended that horizon.

Young women were supposed to be sweet and innocent, and Wendy was both of those things. But standing before them today, she no longer appeared the sweet memory of innocence you left behind when you marched off to war. Today she was the beacon of courage you followed into battle.

No. More than that. Through her long months with the men, and now her final outward transformation, she had made herself into the very benchmark of their valor—the fury and the Valkyrie wrapped up into one. She was Joan of Arc. She was Athena.

She was the Wendy.

Their response to her presence was almost overwhelming. (And in any event, she was far too excited to remain in one place for long.) So she excused herself as soon as she could—without hurting their feelings, of course—offering reassurances as she left. Yes, she was sailing with them. Yes, she would see them again this evening. Yes, she would be on deck when they left harbor.

When they left harbor.

She could still hardly believe it.

She followed Nicholas to her cabin, where he took his leave of her, rattling off directions back to the deck so she could return at sunset. She had intended to unpack, but she discovered that the boy had secured her sea chest to a line of heavy iron rings, set low against the wall for that very purpose. The ropes would prevent the chest from sliding back and forth, or even tumbling across the floor during rough seas, keeping it safe—and making the very idea of unpacking seem foolish.

Settling in, as it turned out, did not amount to much.

There was a small, sturdy writing desk bolted to the front

wall of the cabin. It had a latching drawer, but her journals, ink, and quills would be safer in the chest, held firmly in place and protected by her clothing. There was an equally small and sturdy bunk secured to the rear wall. A humble lamp hung from an iron ring set into the low ceiling.

That was it. That was everything.

And it was the most beautiful room she had ever seen.

She paused for a moment to admire it. The desk, the lamp, the bunk, the chest. The smell of salt and the subtle creak of oiled wood.

But she hadn't come this far to sit in a cabin.

The sea was whispering her name.

So she opened the door for Nana and then shut it firmly behind them both, striding through the labyrinth toward the deck. Toward the sea. Toward the horizon that, by tomorrow, would be as endless as the sky.

When she reached the deck, at least a dozen members of the crew were scattered across its breadth and up into the rigging, checking ropes and masts and sails for anything that might need to be repaired or replaced. Having no assigned tasks herself, she strode to the railing to look out over the water, enjoying the way the heels of her heavy new boots hit the wooden planks beneath her feet.

But when she reached the railing itself, her footsteps fell still, and all was quiet. Much *too* quiet. She turned to find the men staring at her, and she was instantly reminded of the first time

she had boarded Pan's ship, when Peter had ordered the everlost to treat her as their own mother.

Somehow, she didn't think that would help her here.

They converged upon her, looking more like a band of pirates than a naval crew. Tattoos and earrings and bare skin and sweat and the odor of working men. If she had expected the gentlemen of the Fourteenth Platoon, she realized her mistake in an instant. These were Hook's men—the men of *The Dragon*, where his feral inner nature was unleashed.

"Thinks she's as good as a man, she does," snarled a barrel-chested man with tattoos plastered up and down his arms.

"Aye. Someone oughta show her the difference." This came from a thin man with an oiled mustache and a crooked nose. He leered at her suggestively while the others laughed. It was a cruel sort of laughter, and it made Wendy nervous coming from all of them at once.

Nana felt the shift in their mood by instinct, and she growled low in her throat, her hackles rising all along her spine. The closest among them took a step back, but then a new man pushed his way to the front.

Smee. The man Wendy had bested at the armory.

"I'll show her," he said, and his voice was perfectly calm, which made him even more terrifying than the others. "But first … Jukes, kill that dog."

The tattooed man drew his sword.

"No!" Wendy shouted, drawing her own.

The men laughed, but Smee knew better.

"Watch her," he warned them. "She knows how to use it."

The men shifted from foot to foot and glanced at each other, not sure whether they were supposed to laugh again or not. She

was just a woman in a man's clothing, wasn't she? What could be dangerous about that? But still, a sword was a sword, and Smee sounded like he meant it.

"Cecco," Smee barked. "Skylights. Keep her away from that dog. Back 'er up to the rail."

"Gladly." The man who answered was stunningly handsome— chiseled features beneath a mane of dark hair; his bare chest perfectly sculpted; his leg muscles rippling beneath blue leggings tucked into tall, black boots. But Wendy didn't like the smile on his face at all.

"Skylights," he said, and his voice was smooth as silk. "Get the left. I'll get the right."

"Nana! Heel!" Wendy ordered. But Nana was too angry to listen. These men were threatening *her* Wendy, and Nana wasn't about to stand for that. She took a slow step toward the man with the tattoos, her teeth bared viciously.

"Nana! No!" Wendy lunged toward the dog, ignoring Cecco and Skylights in her desperation, but the two men seized the opportunity to grab her, Cecco twisting her wrist cruelly until she dropped her sword.

Wendy could only watch as Jukes grinned. He pulled back his arm, ready to plunge his sword into Nana's chest.

"No!" Wendy screamed again, but this time another voice—a man's voice—answered her own.

"Stand down!"

For a long moment, not one of them moved. And then, as though by magic, Jukes dropped his arm to his side. Cecco and Skylights released their grip, and Wendy flew to Nana's side, reassuring herself that the dog had not come to any harm.

She looked up to find her rescuer, but she couldn't see him

through the pressing ranks of the crew. And then, reluctantly, the crowd parted for a young man wearing a blue long-tailed coat with bright gold buttons.

"Honestly, Wendy," the officer said, smiling down at her fondly. "You're finally on a ship, for less than an hour, and look at the trouble you've gotten yourself into."

"Charlie?" she breathed, hardly believing her eyes.

"Am I truly so hard to recognize?" he replied, grinning even more broadly. "It hasn't been *that* long."

"Charlie!" she shouted, and she threw herself into his arms.

They spent the rest of the day catching up, regaling each other with stories of their time apart. Mr. Equiano's extensive training in science and mathematics had served Charlie well. He had already been appointed first mate of *The Dragon*, second only to Hook himself, and he acted as the ship's navigator besides.

Wendy had a hard time reconciling this tall, confident young man with the boy she had said goodbye to more than a year ago, but he had the same smile, the same quick mind, and the same respect for her abilities that he had shown ever since they were children. It wasn't long before they were speaking together as easily as they had in Mr. Equiano's home, which felt like a lifetime ago.

And Wendy, of course, had some amazing stories to share.

In telling him about Pan and Tinker Bell and the everlost (well, telling him *most* of it anyway), she began to realize that these were the kinds of stories she had always longed to collect. She had wait-

ed so long and worked so hard to reach this place, to stand on the deck of this ship, that she hadn't noticed how incredible her life had already become. Magic and the innisfay and fairy dust and flying. She could hardly believe it herself, when she thought about it all at once.

But Charlie believed it, and it meant more to her than she could say to have her childhood friend back in her life, to share all the adventures to come.

And then it was time.

The sun continued its journey to the other side of the world, and Wendy was ready to follow—Pan's magic compass held tightly in her hand—as evening blossomed and the stars winked into view, one after another. The men assembled on deck and fell to a hush as Hook himself finally appeared, standing tall and proud against the backdrop of the night.

"Mr. Hawke!" he shouted, so that all on deck could hear.

"Aye, sir!" Charlie hollered back.

"Take the helm!"

"Aye, sir!" Charlie placed his hands on the ship's wheel and then shouted again, taking Wendy by surprise.

"Navigator Darling!" he yelled.

"Aye, sir!" she shouted back, for she was a member of the crew now, and he outranked her. But by addressing her as the navigator, he had just transferred a significant portion of his own duties to her, and at the same time conferred upon her a rank second only to his own. And in front of the entire crew. Wendy maintained a serious countenance, but her heart soared with pride and gratitude.

Hook scowled and flashed a dark look toward Charlie, but he said nothing.

"Set the course!" Charlie shouted.

Wendy opened Pan's compass, and the outline of an island glowed in the palm of her hand. The needle spun, and then settled. She looked up into the sky for her bearings.

"Once we clear England's shores, and counting, sir, from Stella Polaris, mark heading degree second to the right, and then straight on 'til morning!"

"Second to the right, and straight on 'til morning!" Charlie echoed.

And Wendy turned her gaze to the sea.

COMING SOON
MORE TALES OF THE WENDY!

We hope you enjoyed *The Wendy*! The second volume in the series is expected in 2019. If you can't wait to see what Wendy's up to, or if you'd like to learn more about the series and the authors, you can follow the development of the next book at *patreon.com/DragonAuthors*.

ACKNOWLEDGMENTS

The Wendy began as an experiment. Could an unknown writing duo attract enough of a following on Patreon.com to defray the cost of publishing a book? We were as surprised as anyone when the answer turned out to be "yes."

We posted the first chapter in February of 2016, and by September our extraordinary patrons had bought us a cover. For a book that wasn't even finished. Such was their faith in us. They went on to fund the book's editing, cover layout, and interior design—an entire book paid for in advance, one chapter at a time.

We will forever be humbled by the experience.

So first and foremost, to all of our patrons, who spent the last year and a half believing in us, thank you! You are the greatest friends any authors—or book—could ever have. *The Wendy* would not exist without you.

To Dwayne "@thatdwayne" Melancon and Rae McManus, for going above and beyond, and for your unwavering conviction that this story would one day end up in print. We wish you as many

Twitter followers and as much ice cream as any human being could ever want.

To Ken Howell, for reading all our drafts and waiting eagerly nonetheless for the next chapter of every single thing we write. You have no idea how much your enthusiasm does to keep us going.

To Donna Alvis, at the Ephesus Public Library, thank you for being excited about every little step along the way. You have provided us with countless morale boosts. We consider ourselves tremendously lucky to have such a wonderful librarian in our corner.

To our families (Molyna Richards, get in here for that photo), for supporting our dreams, for believing in our potential, for championing our books, and for loving us through the insanity of the creative process. We could not do it without you.

The Wendy was our first novel to take place in an historical setting, and that involves a whole slew of thanks beyond anything we could reasonably include here. We had no idea going into it how much research the book would require. We'll tell you—it's a lot. (Our Patreon commentary for each chapter is almost as long as the chapter itself!)

We have tried to make Wendy's world as historically accurate as possible. Where we have failed, those failures are our own. But where we have succeeded, we have to thank all the dedicated souls who spend untold hours chronicling the past and making it available to twenty-first century authors on the Internet. The following are a few of the websites to which we are most indebted. It is by no means a comprehensive list.

• **BBC**—British History in depth: Life at Sea in the Royal Navy of the 18th Century (*http://www.bbc.co.uk/history/british/empire_seapower/life_at_sea_01.shtml*).

- **The British Library**—Georgian entertainment: from pleasure gardens to blood sports (*https://www.bl.uk/georgian-britain/articles/georgian-entertainment-from-pleasure-gardens-to-blood-sports*).
- **The David Rumsey Historical Map Collection** (*http://www.davidrumsey.com/luna/servlet/detail/RUMSEY~8~1~3635~420010:-Composite-of--England-and-Wales,-d*).
- **London Lives 1690 to 1800**—Crime, Poverty & Social Policy in the Metropolis (*https://www.londonlives.org/*).
- **University of Michigan**—Money and Denominations in 18th c England (*http://www.umich.edu/~ece/student_projects/money/denom.html*). (Sorry, Dad. Go, Ohio State!)

And speaking of history, we also have to thank the many librarians who work tirelessly to preserve the texts of previous centuries, scanning the originals and placing them online for the benefit of the entire world. For example, Mary Wollstonecraft's *Thoughts on the Education of Daughters*, published in 1787, can be read online thanks to the LSE Digital Library: (https://digital.library.lse.ac.uk/objects/lse:ruf494jak).

Finally, we find ourselves indebted to a man who died more than two hundred years ago. We realized early on that Wendy needed a mentor. Someone to see past her gender and prepare her for a life at sea. But who in 18th-century England would have had both the knowledge and willingness to teach a ten-year-old girl how to be a sailor?

We reached out to our network with the problem, and cosplayer Ember Tay, who happens to be a history student, suggested we read *The Interesting Narrative of the Life of Olaudah Equiano*, written by Olaudah Equiano himself and published in 1789. Everything that character says to Wendy in chapter two about his life is chronicled in the actual autobiography, up to and including his story about watching his mother charge into battle with a broadsword.

A broadsword! Wendy would have been mesmerized.

His autobiography has long been a part of the public domain. It is available through most library systems and can be download-ed for free on most e-readers.

ABOUT THE AUTHORS

As a child, Erin fell in love with llamas and with the books of Anne McCaffrey, whose *Dragonriders of Pern* series inspired her to become a writer. When she finally met Anne McCaffrey at a fantasy convention some two decades later, she wept uncontrollably throughout the entire affair. She does significantly better with llamas.

Steven spent his childhood reading anything he could get his hands on, sharing his favorite stories with his younger brothers and then acting them out, especially if this required sword fighting on horseback. When they ran out of books, he wrote his own, including his brothers as the main characters by sketching original illustrations on magazine clippings.

Together, they are the team known as Dragon Authors, writing science fiction and fantasy for teens and adults. Their first novel, *The Intuitives*, was published in July of 2017.

You can find them online at DragonAuthors.com.

CPSIA information can be obtained
at www.ICGtesting.com
Printed in the USA
LVHW09*1306140818
586949LV00003B/11/P

9 781946 137050